TOMBOY OF THE TON

Misfits of the Ton
Book One

by

Emily Royal

ARE YOU SIGNED UP FOR DRAGONBLADE'S BLOG?

You'll get the latest news and information on exclusive giveaways, exclusive excerpts, coming releases, sales, free books, cover reveals and more.

Check out our complete list of authors, too!

No spam, no junk. That's a promise!

Sign Up Here

www.dragonbladepublishing.com

Dearest Reader;

Thank you for your support of a small press. At Dragonblade Publishing, we strive to bring you the highest quality Historical Romance from some of the best authors in the business. Without your support, there is no 'us', so we sincerely hope you adore these stories and find some new favorite authors along the way.

Happy Reading!

CEO, Dragonblade Publishing

Additional Dragonblade books by Author Emily Royal

Misfits of the Ton
Tomboy of the Ton, Book 1

Headstrong Harts
What the Hart Wants, Book 1
Queen of my Hart, Book 2
Hidden Hart, Book 3
The Prizefighter's Hart, Book 4
All I Want for Christmas is My Hart, Novella
Haunted Hart, Novella

London Libertines
Henry's Bride, Book 1
Hawthorne's Wife, Book 2
Roderick's Widow, Book 3
A Libertine's Christmas Miracle, Novella

The Lyon's Den Connected World
A Lyon's Pride

Dedication

*To my Dad who took me rock climbing
and encouraged my tomboy traits*

PROLOGUE

London, July 1814

"NOW, *THERE'S A* rake if ever I saw one!"

Henrietta turned her attention from the drink in her hand to her two companions. Lavinia—the one who'd spoken—sat, spine erect, gazing across the dance floor. The three of them occupied an overlooked corner of the ballroom—overlooked by virtue of the poor lighting that rendered its occupants invisible.

In Henrietta's experience, most guests at a ball attended for the purpose of being seen—and the Houghton Hall ball was no different. Thank heavens she'd found two acquaintances who shared her opinion that there was nothing worse than being *seen*. Each had different reasons for desiring invisibility. Lavinia, for example, was on some kind of clandestine mission that involved her slipping off unnoticed to indulge in goodness-knows-what, at all manner of social occasions. For many of them, she asked Henrietta to provide either sufficient diversion to enable her to slip away, or sworn testimony, if required, that she'd been by her side all the time.

Henrietta had no idea where Lavinia went when she disappeared—nor did she want to.

"How can you be sure that a man is a rake, merely by looking?" Henrietta asked.

"That's easy," Lavinia replied. "Beauty—at least that which

exists on the surface—generally comes hand in hand with a poor character. The fewer flaws in one's face, the more flaws in one's soul."

"Nonsense!" Henrietta laughed.

A quiet voice spoke up. "I agree with Lavinia."

Eleanor, who spoke only when she deemed it necessary, colored, and looked away when Henrietta turned her attention to her.

Eleanor desired invisibility because she disliked being looked at. Most of the time she kept her gaze focused on her lap, while she twirled her fingers round a scrap of lace, or the small pebble she carried around in her reticule. But, occasionally, when under observation, as if she possessed a sixth sense, Eleanor would stiffen and look up, panic in her eyes, like a rabbit caught in a snare. She'd flinch as if the gaze of others burned her skin.

But, in the weeks since Henrietta had first introduced herself to the quiet young woman—who was all the more intriguing for not pushing herself forward like other debutantes—Eleanor had begun to meet her gaze more directly, even if it occasionally shifted sideways to avoid direct eye contact.

"How can you dislike beauty, Ellie, when you draw such exquisite likenesses?" Lavinia asked.

"I appreciate beauty," Eleanor replied, "but, in a man—and often a woman—beauty is inversely proportional to honor. I find there's nothing more untrustworthy than a handsome man. A ballroom full of them is, frankly—*terrifying*." She sipped the remains of her punch, her hand trembling.

Sensing her friend's discomfort at having made such a long speech, Henrietta took Eleanor's hand. "I quite agree." She gestured round the ballroom. "Look at them! A den of wolves."

"Or a sea full of sharks," Lavinia added. "Better to view them *all* as the enemy than succumb to their charms."

"So you don't intend to dance?" Henrietta asked.

"Heavens, no!" Lavinia cried. "I intend to slip away and explore the house. How about you, Ellie?"

Eleanor shook her head. "I sometimes think I'd like to dance, but I'm unlikely to be asked."

Henrietta squeezed her friend's hand. Eleanor couldn't help being a little—eccentric—in her ways. But anyone who didn't fit in with Society's idea of perfection was labeled an outcast. Or, in Eleanor's case, an *oddity*. In Henrietta's experience, she had never once seen anyone ask Eleanor to dance, whereas Eleanor's younger sister, Juliette, had no end of suitors clamoring to fill her dance card.

"I could ask Johnny," Henrietta said, nodding to where a blond-haired young man stood holding an empty glass. "He'd be happy to give you a turn about the room."

"Don't you want to dance with him yourself?" Eleanor asked.

"Heavens, no!" Henrietta laughed. "Johnny's a friend—and he views me as too much of a tomboy to be seen partnering me on the dancefloor. There's nobody here I wish to dance with or secure the admiration of. But Johnny would dance with *you* if I made the introduction."

Eleanor shook her head. "I-I can't. I remember the steps if I practice in the mirror—but I can't seem to make my body listen to my head when dancing for real. Besides, I see little point in dancing—though I wish I could enjoy it like everyone else."

"Those who dance at a Society ball aren't doing it for the love of dancing," Lavinia said. "The men use the power of choice in order to sample prospective wives, and the ladies seek only to outdo their rivals in the sport of competitive dance-card filling."

Eleanor gave a snort that sounded like a suppressed giggle. "Juliette declared herself triumphant earlier when she showed me her dance card," she said. "That is, until I told her that Lady Irma Fairchild had filled hers before she even stepped foot in the ballroom."

"I'll wager Juliette didn't like *that*," Lavinia said.

Eleanor sighed. "She made such a point of the lack of names on my own card, that I couldn't help myself."

"Serves her right," Henrietta said.

Juliette Howard was one of the prettiest young women of the Season, but with the foulest disposition. Henrietta had witnessed her taunting Eleanor over her lack of suitors on her third Season. With luck, Juliette would be married soon, and Eleanor would be free of her spite.

"I think it's time I went exploring," Lavinia said. "Aunt Edna is, at last, looking the other way. You don't mind, do you?"

Henrietta shook her head. "Eleanor and I will take care of each other in your absence," she said. "You can be assured we'll not be captured by any sharks tonight." She looked across the dancefloor and caught sight of her Aunt Agnes, settled in a chair—if having squeezed her voluminous frame into it could be called *settled*—next to Lavinia's chaperone, Lady Edna Yates. Both women were too occupied with gossip and punch to take any notice of their charges.

Lavinia rose to her feet, slipped into the crowd, and disappeared.

Shortly after, a young man approached them.

"Hen! Are you well?" he asked.

"Perfectly so," Henrietta said. "Have you met my friend, Eleanor Howard?"

"Charmed." Johnny bowed.

Eleanor colored and looked away. "I don't want to dance," she whispered. Johnny stared at her, straightened his stance, and left.

"Sorry." Eleanor fidgeted with her scrap of lace.

"No, you must forgive *me*," Henrietta replied. "I only wanted to introduce you."

Henrietta's gut twisted with guilt as her friend's body seemed to vibrate with distress, and she took Eleanor's hand.

"Shall I bring you something to drink? And I can procure some of Lady Houghton's biscuits, assuming my Aunt Agnes hasn't eaten them all."

Eleanor nodded and gave a watery smile.

Henrietta rose to her feet and weaved her way around the

edge of the dance floor, toward the half-empty punchbowl beside which a solitary footman stood to attention. His staid expression morphed into one of relief as he saw her approach. Poor fellow—Lord and Lady Houghton, and, in fact, most members of Society, were rich enough to afford to pay men and women to stand still for an entire evening, their boredom relieved by the occasional request for a drink. Though capable of helping herself, Henrietta had no wish to deprive him of the opportunity to move.

"Two glasses, please."

The enthusiasm with which the footman filled the glasses could almost be laughable were it not so tragic. He presented them to her, and she rewarded him with a smile and a word of thanks—something which, if his reaction was anything to go by, was in short supply among the guests.

As Henrietta picked her way round the edge of the ballroom on her return journey, the dance came to an end, and a ripple of gloved applause threaded through the company. She caught Aunt Agnes's familiar tones.

"*There* you are, young lady!"

Oh, heavens! Doubtless Aunt was about to resume her quest to shackle her to some man for the rest of the evening. Aunt considered Henrietta, at twenty years old, to be in danger of heading for spinsterhood unless she found a husband quickly, and she'd been threatening to introduce her to Lord Tippey—a gentleman of a sickly disposition and with breath sour enough to wither an oak tree at fifty paces. Lord Tippey was a viscount, from an old family, and his late wife had been Aunt's dearest friend—and that, in Aunt's eyes, rendered him an eligible suitor for Henrietta.

Which meant he must be avoided at all costs.

Henrietta increased her pace, making her way toward Eleanor. The musicians began tuning their instruments, and the couples lined up for the next dance.

"Where has she got to, now?"

Henrietta flinched. Aunt Agnes's voice was loud enough to

penetrate through a stone wall, and it bore that note of exasperation which had begun to grate on Henrietta's nerves this past year. It was almost worth getting married to free herself from an aunt who, though she professed to have Henrietta's best interests at heart, could only ever be seen as her gaoler.

Marriage would introduce her to a worse kind of gaoler.

The dancing began, but Henrietta could swear she heard Aunt's voice following her. She increased the pace and glanced over her shoulder. But, to her relief, she spotted Aunt striding toward the punchbowl—which usually meant she'd be too inebriated for matchmaking and, with luck, too indisposed tomorrow morning to criticize Henrietta's unladylike demeanor.

Henrietta was free—at least for the rest of the evening.

She had almost reached her destination when to avoid a dancing couple, she veered to one side—and collided with a solid wall of muscle.

"Oh!" She let out a shriek and jerked backward, losing her balance. Strong hands grasped her wrists to stem her fall, and the contents of her glasses soared in the air, forming a graceful arc, before spilling down the front of her dress in a dark, red shower, complete with slices of peach and strawberry, some of which settled on her bosom.

She stared open-mouthed at her soaked gown—Aunt Agnes would have a fit of apoplexy when she saw it.

But at least she could have some sport with the clumsy buffoon responsible for ruining her dress. Suppressing the desire to laugh, she waited for whatever ridiculous excuse for an apology he'd bestow on her.

But no apology was forthcoming.

Flicking a slice of peach off her chest, she molded her features into the haughtiest expression she could muster and lifted her gaze.

A pair of cold blue eyes stared back at her, framed by an aggressively handsome face—a strong brow, straight nose, and cheekbones which looked as if they'd been chiseled from marble, and a mouth…a mouth which was full and sensual, with a firm, square jaw.

It was a face she knew as well as her own—a face that invaded her dreams and which she'd both hoped and feared to see again. Her fingers itched to be buried in the thick, dark hair that brushed the tips of his ears and curled round the base of his jawline.

His eyes narrowed as if he read her thoughts. Her cheeks warming with humiliation, Henrietta averted her gaze. But everywhere she looked, her senses were assaulted by the sheer masculinity that engulfed her—the long, lean fingers curled round her wrists, the finely tailored suit that fitted his body—his very *male* body—to perfection.

And the intoxicating aroma of male spices brought back the memory of one man.

The man standing before her now.

Giles.

Earl Thorpe.

The boy from the neighboring estate who had always looked upon her with disdain as she'd grown up, calling her a grubby urchin—even though he was barely four years older than her—until that one glorious moment, when he'd awakened her senses with a kiss.

It had been almost two years since she'd last seen him. Back then, he'd dismissed her as an annoyance—until that one kiss, when she'd seen the desire in his eyes.

"Giles…"

She looked up and fixed her gaze on him. He continued to stare at her, his expression impassive. Perhaps he didn't recognize her. The tomboy he used to taunt had been transformed by her overbearing aunt into a debutante.

"Don't you know me?" she whispered.

A spark of longing flared in his expression, and a small pulse of anticipation rippled through her.

He lowered his gaze to her gown and curled his lip into a

sneer.

"I'd have known *you* anywhere, Miss Redford."

Before she could respond, he brushed past her and strode toward the elegant form of Lady Irma Fairchild, where he offered the lady his arm and disappeared among the dancers, as if Henrietta had never existed.

Henrietta's cheeks burned with shame—not from the humiliation of having ruined her dress in public—but from the fact that, while she had always declared that no man would stir her senses into oblivion, there was one exception.

Giles Thorpe.

The man who had just treated her as if she was nothing more than an insect, to be stepped on and flicked aside.

CHAPTER ONE

Surrey, September 1812

"Can you see anything, Henry?"

"Not yet."

Two identical faces peered up at Henrietta through the leaves. The Meredith twins—Phillip and Johnny—were hopeless at climbing trees compared to her. Her long-limbed form gave her a greater reach, something they continually teased her about.

Few people could tell the twins apart—their golden-haired, blue-eyed features were almost identical. But their eyes distinguished them from each other. Most of the time, Johnny wore a vacant look, as if he'd forgotten something, and could never quite remember what it was. His older brother Phillip's expression was sharp, almost cunning. But, as the heir, perhaps he needed to develop a predatory nature. Heirs carried the weight of responsibility on their shoulders and couldn't be seen grubbing about in the dirt—and Phillip always seemed to have the knack of evading trouble at the expense of his younger brother.

And often at Henrietta's expense. From the moment they'd begun playing together as children, the twins had declared her to be an honorary boy, and thus fit to be a member of their little trio. They had encouraged, rather than objected to, her tomboyish nature, showing her all the best spots in the surrounding countryside to indulge in her love of the outdoors.

And climbing—she loved climbing. It was an activity in which she felt comfortable and at home—considerably more enjoyable than stitching cushions or drawing bland little landscapes to hang above the fireplaces in dull parlors.

She placed her foot on the branch, tested her weight, then hauled herself further up into the tree. The branches were thinning out, and she'd be unable to climb much higher. Her heart was still racing from the snapped branch lower down, where she almost lost her footing.

The next branch overhung the grounds of Thorpe Hall, almost touching the building. Henrietta swung her leg up to sit astride the branch as if she were mounting Papa's horse. Grasping the branch with her hands, she shuffled forward. The branch creaked and dipped under her weight.

"Careful, Hen!" Johnny cried. "You'll fall!"

"Don't be a baby, Johnny!" Phillip said. "She's more of a boy than you."

"Henry's still a *girl*, Phillip, and she'll be a young lady when she has her come-out. That's what Mama said."

Phillip snorted. "She's no lady, are you—*Miss Redford?*"

Though Henrietta agreed, she detected the sneer in Phillip's tone. But she didn't care.

Ladies were ridiculous creatures, all frills and no substance. Why would she want to be one?

Because you must, now you've turned eighteen, Henrietta my love. All children grow up—boys into men and girls into ladies.

She shook her head to dispel Papa's words and shuffled further along the branch.

But Papa was right. Boys grew into men. Phillip and Johnny had already begun to change. The time for playing was drawing to a close. Each time they returned from Harrow for vacation, they were less amendable to games. And now they were readying for Oxford, they talked more of taking mistresses and getting married. They had both—especially Phillip—made it abundantly clear that they didn't view her as even remotely desirable to fulfill either position. They wanted wives who were *pretty*.

Which was something of a relief, for she wanted neither a husband nor a lover. She wanted to work with Papa and learn to run his business. Her father was a veritable genius at furniture design. His pieces could be found in grand homes all over the country and were good enough to grace the royal palaces. The perfect combination between practicality and art form, his cabinets were adorned with the most exquisite inlay work, forming intricate designs and realistic likenesses.

When she'd been younger, Papa had shown her how to stain each piece of wood in order to give the images depth and character, and she dreamed of designing her own pieces and immortalizing the world around her.

But it wasn't a daughter's place to run a business—at least not according to Aunt Agnes. A daughter's responsibility was to secure a good marriage in order to elevate her family's social status, not sully her fingers with wood stains. And Papa always listened to Aunt Agnes. As Mama's sister, she considered herself the mistress of Henrietta's fate. The daughter of a baronet outranked a furniture merchant, no matter how prosperous he might be, and of late, her father had been deferring to her aunt more frequently.

Aunt had threatened Henrietta with a London Season, and while Henrietta had managed to persuade Papa to prevent that particular Damoclean sword from falling upon her head, it would not stay suspended forever. She was growing up, as were her friends, and she didn't like it one bit.

But Papa had promised to let her enjoy one more year of freedom before sending her to Aunt Agnes for lessons in deportment and other fripperies.

And she meant to make the best of her freedom by getting her revenge on the miserable brute next door.

Giles Thorpe.

Though he was only four years older, he'd always looked down on her as if she were an infant. Johnny and Phillip were still boys, but there was nothing boyish about Giles Thorpe.

He was all man.

Where the twins could be considered handsome by those who deemed that sort of thing worth their notice, Giles Thorpe was a god—a Herculean god. He was as dark as they were golden, his hair as black as a raven's wing. And his features were so unlike the soft, round faces of Johnny and Phillip. Giles's features were harsh, angular, as if a stonemason had chiseled them out of granite.

And his eyes…

Though they were blue, like the twins' eyes, the similarity ended there. For they reminded her of a deep, treacherous ocean—endless, like an abyss, into which the unwary would drown.

Something in his gaze always unsettled her, the way his eyes seemed to breach her defenses and see right through to her soul.

Yet, like a moth drawn to a flame, she yearned to feel his gaze, yet feared it at the same time, as if it might burn her. But, to him, she was nothing more than an annoyance, a brat. At least, on the days when he bothered to notice her at all.

Well, today, he'd have no choice *but* to notice her.

Brat. That's what he'd called her, words uttered with such disdain.

She'd show *him*.

Gripping the branch with her knees, she pulled out the sheet of paper she'd tucked up her sleeve and, after making several careful folds, fashioned it into the shape of a cube.

A perfect vessel to contain water. All she need do now was wait until the man himself walked beneath the tree, and ambush him from above. She giggled to herself at the image of him soaked through, his perfect jacket dripping with water. It might be childish, and not the behavior of a young lady, but what did she care? Ladies had no fun. Once she'd been married off, her freedom would be curtailed, so she may as well enjoy it now.

From her vantage point on the branch, she was almost close

enough to touch the main building of Thorpe Hall. She parted the leaves to get a better look. The rays of the afternoon sun shone on the building, illuminating the red bricks and reflecting off the edge of a half-open sash window on the second floor, level with her eyes. She shuffled closer until the window came into full view.

The room inside was lined with wooden-paneled walls, dotted with candle sconces. At one end she could make out a door, and beside it, a stone fireplace, in which a fire glowed. A solitary wingback chair occupied the center of the room, its back to the window, and beside the chair was a small, round table, bearing a single glass.

The room looked stark and cheerless.

Perhaps it was one of the servants' chambers.

The door opened, and Henrietta shrank back, though the fading light meant that anyone inside the room would struggle to see her. A middle-aged woman in a maid's uniform entered and curtseyed.

A figure rose from the chair. Tall and thin and dressed in a white shift and black lace shawl, it looked like a ghost. The maid approached the figure and curtseyed again.

The room's occupant must be the dowager Lady Thorpe—an invalid, and rumored to be blind, having almost died in the coaching accident which had killed her husband, the old earl, five years ago. Papa had told Henrietta once that Lord and Lady Thorpe were a sociable couple who held many riotous parties. Lady Thorpe in particular had a reputation for being fun-loving and adventurous. But since the accident which claimed her husband, she'd become a recluse. Giles, as the heir, had seen fit to lock her away, perhaps as punishment. Henrietta had never set eyes on her.

Until today.

But, rather than an elegant, adventurous countess, the woman in the room reminded Henrietta of a prisoner—a creature to be pitied.

"Can you see him yet?" Phillip's voice called out.

"Hush!" she hissed, shrinking back. But the room's occupants showed no sign of having heard. Clinging to the maid's arm, Lady Thorpe shuffled across the room, out of sight. Shortly after, the maid reappeared. She approached the window and pulled it shut, then she extinguished the candles and the room plunged into darkness save the dying embers of the fire.

Tears stung Henrietta's eyes. Was that what awaited all women? To be defined by their husbands, locked away out of sight, when they were deemed to be of no further use?

Was that how Giles Thorpe valued his mother?

Henrietta curled her hands into fists. To think—she would have given anything to have her dear Mama alive, yet Giles valued his mother so little that he kept her prisoner.

How could he be so cruel? A makeshift water bomb was the least he deserved. It might not be much, but it was something she could do to restore the imbalance in a world that favored men and pushed women to the background.

As if Fate had answered her prayer, footsteps crunched on the gravel path below. The path followed a route that brought it close enough to the tree—at least, within throwing distance.

With luck, she'd manage a direct hit.

Holding the water bottle she'd tied to her waist earlier, she uncorked it and poured its contents into the makeshift paper vessel. Then, cradling her missile in her hands, she waited as the footsteps came closer.

A familiar figure approached. She'd recognize him anywhere. The very air seemed to tremble around him as if the world understood his magnificence and bent to his will.

How could such magnificence live together with such a sour disposition?

He drew near, walked past the tree, continuing on the path, his back to her.

In a swift, smooth underarm gesture, she launched her missile into the air. It sailed through the leaves and flew in an arc toward her target.

Her aim wasn't true, but it sufficed. The missile glanced off his shoulder, exploded on impact, and fell to the ground.

"What the devil?" a deep voice cried.

Most of the water splashed onto the ground, but some had hit the target. Through the leaves, she could discern a dark stain on the sleeve of his jacket.

He picked up the remnants of paper at his feet. Then he turned, his body vibrating with fury. Though shielded by the foliage, Henrietta felt horribly exposed as he strode back along the path and stopped beside the tree.

"Who's there!" he roared.

Below her, she heard snorts of laughter, and she issued a silent plea.

Johnny, be quiet!

Phillip was the more composed of the two, but his younger brother could never control his mirth. This was why Johnny always took the blame for their escapades, while Phillip feigned innocence to perfection.

Shortly after, she heard footsteps scuttling away. Her friends had left her to face the enemy alone.

"I know you're there!" Thorpe cried. "Come out, you little coward!"

She shivered at the raw fury in his voice.

"Cursed Meredith boys, you deserve to be thrashed! Wait till I get my hands on you!" He approached the tree and looked up, and her heart shuddered. Slowly, she curled her legs up, shrinking back against the tree trunk.

"I can see you!" he cried. "Come down and face me like a man! I'll have you whipped raw!"

She held her breath, willing her trembling limbs to still. Eyes narrowed, he looked about the tree but didn't fix his gaze on her.

He couldn't see her at all. He'd lied in an attempt to flush her out. If she remained still, he wouldn't spot her. But her heart was pounding in her ears; surely he could hear it.

He shook his head. "Bloody brat. I'll wager it's *her* doing."

Brat—how dare he!

Unable to resist the temptation, she held out the water bottle and tipped out the last few drops. He blinked and shook his head, then spoke more softly, as if to himself.

"That girl's a bad influence on everyone she comes into contact with. Worthless creature—she'll come to no good. I pity her poor father and the burden he bears."

He ran a hand through his hair to dispel the water droplets, sighed, and continued along the path, disappearing round the building.

The resigned tone of his voice did more to shame her than his fury. She took pleasure from seeing him riled up as retribution for insulting her, but while the fury of those she sought to irk might be a reward, she could not weather their disappointment. For disappointment implied that they considered her unworthy of their interest—unworthy of her place in the world.

As for Papa...

Was she a burden to him? She craved her independence, but Papa had tried to explain, many times, that in order to survive in the world she must find her place in it. He loved her dearly, and he trusted her to keep her promise—to set aside her tomboyish ways when the time came for her debut. Though he'd never taken his hand to her, there was always a place of no return, a boundary which, if she crossed, he would have no choice.

Perhaps he feared that if she continued to indulge in tomboyish activities, she would end up like Lady Thorpe—locked away in a dreary room, forgotten forever.

Is that what men did to their wives and mothers when they disapproved of them?

She shuffled back along the branch, shivering as she glanced toward the window of Lady Thorpe's room. No woman deserved that poor lady's fate. Perhaps she should turn her efforts toward something far better than simply irking Giles Thorpe.

The twins had disappeared. Most likely they'd run home,

abandoning her to face whatever punishment Thorpe would mete out.

But he'd never catch *her*.

She climbed back down the tree, jumping the final few feet, and landing on the soft ground. She winced at a tearing sound and, on inspecting her gown, noticed a small rend in the skirt. Small enough for her to mend without Papa noticing it.

She was alone—and free. With nobody to judge or chastise, she broke into a run, jogging and skipping across the grass, taking the shortcut home through Thorpe Hall's stable yard, plucking an apple from the orchard on the way.

As she approached the stable buildings, she heard the familiar snort of Thunder, Thorpe's stallion. A beautiful animal—she'd made secret friends with him, and he would appreciate her gift today. Thunder liked apples, and she loved stroking his nose and chattering to him while he plucked the fruit from her palm with his big velvet-soft lips.

But, before she reached the stables, a rider emerged, sitting astride Thunder. He steered the animal as if he and it were one, and she stopped in her tracks, the breath catching in her throat. Back straight, muscular thighs pressed against the animal's flank, the rider exuded raw male power. Mouth set in a grim line, his mouth a dark slash, he stared at her, his eyes darkening with anger.

Giles Thorpe.

He lowered his gaze to the riding crop in his right hand, then lifted it again to stare directly at her.

"Aye," he said tonelessly. "I pity him."

Henrietta's gut twisted in fear.

He'd known it was her in the tree.

An overwhelming urge struck her, to plead with him not to tell Papa. If she must be thrashed, let it be done now, so she'd be spared Papa's disappointment.

To her shame, tears stung her eyes, and she blinked, letting them splash onto her cheeks. She wouldn't give him the satisfaction of seeing her wipe them away.

As if he understood her anguish, his lips curled in a smile of cold satisfaction. He gave her a curt nod, steered his horse in a tight circle, and rode away.

CHAPTER TWO

SITTING ASTRIDE HIS horse, his steward beside him, Giles cast his gaze over the farmhouse.

"The building looks sound to me, Mr. Wilmot," he said. "Save a few missing tiles on the roof, I see nothing wrong. Surely there's no need for further expense?"

"The tiles can be replaced, Lord Thorpe, but that's the least of your worries." The steward pointed to the building. "See the chimney stack? There's a stone missing near the base. That happened during the frosts in February."

"Then why hasn't Brummitt replaced the stones?" Giles asked. "Heavens, man, must I be hauled out here for every trivial problem you encounter?"

"It's not so trivial," the steward replied. "There's a crack running right through the chimney. One harsh winter—one high wind—and the whole thing could collapse, taking the roof with it."

"Then employ a stonemason."

"I already have, sir, but he'll want payment in advance this time."

Of course he bloody would. So, that was why Wilmot had seen fit to drag him all the way over here—to convince him to open up the purse strings and delve into his almost-exhausted coffers.

Dear God—there seemed to be a never-ending swath of problems needing his attention of late. And with so few funds, he spent most of his time lurching from one disaster to the next, fighting the worst, while the smaller problems grew insidiously, ready to strike when he'd averted the latest crisis.

He tipped his head to the sky and uttered a silent curse.

This is all your fault, Father.

His late grandmother had been right—good sense always skipped a generation. Only Grandmother had been able to curb Father's excesses. The sternest of matriarchs—once lady-in-waiting to the queen—she'd been the most desirable debutante in her day and had caught Grandfather's attention with her no-nonsense, practical approach to life. She struck fear into the heart of every man who disappointed her—as Father, and Giles himself, did on several occasions. And she wasn't averse to smacking Father with her fan if he spoke out of turn.

But, beneath the stern exterior, she possessed a kind heart and a wealth of good sense which was sorely lacking in the world. Banished from court for making her disapproval of the Regent's excesses known, she had retired to Thorpe Hall and held court there. But, after Grandfather's death, her influence had waned. While Father and Mother indulged in the fruits of Grandmother's thrift and economy, she was left to raise Giles to be the earl his father never could.

But, by the time the earldom passed to him, Father had frittered away the fortune on trinkets, gambling, and mistresses, leaving behind a crumbling estate and a resentful son.

Giles had seen too much of the fruits of excess to wish to indulge in it himself. He needed to follow Grandmother's example—rein in the spending and focus on the essentials.

As for frivolities, he had the delectable Betty to service those needs, once a month, when he visited London. But, as an independent, worldly wise widow, his mistress was sensible enough to understand that her tenure in his bed would come to an end when he married.

And he intended to marry the right woman—a sensible, level-headed girl of good family. A woman who would provide him with an heir with little fuss and maintain Thorpe Hall in as economical a manner as possible, leaving him to restore the fortunes of the estate.

A young wife would, perhaps, be preferable. Some innocent debutante, grateful for his attention and willing to be molded into doing his bidding.

But, at any cost, she would be ladylike and demure, and not at all adventurous—the opposite of...

The opposite of *her*.

Henrietta Redford.

The urchin from the neighboring manor had a particular talent for making his blood boil. Her laughter always seemed to invade his thoughts and ensnare his senses, until all rational thoughts flew from his mind. It wasn't the dainty titter of laughter deemed so desirable in the fairer sex—but a great big belly laugh of pure unadulterated mirth. Filled with such joy and delicious abandon, it was the laughter of someone with no responsibility on their shoulders—someone who lived for the pure joy of *living*.

And it stirred unwelcome desires in him.

She was a siren, an other-worldly creature, who rose from the boiling ocean in a storm to tempt and deceive—to lure unsuspecting men to their destruction, dash them to pieces against the rocks.

From the moment he'd first seen her, he knew she was trouble. The long-limbed tomboy who was either dangling upside-down from a tree, riding her horse astride, or playing at sword-fights. The fire in her eyes spoke of bedevilment. Wild and free, she represented everything he feared—adventure, daring, temptation, and ruination.

But she cared so little of others' opinions of her. Free from the shackles of nicety and responsibility, she weathered his criticisms with laughter and seemed to take delight in his disdain. Nothing fazed her. When he'd encountered her by the lakeside, a mud stain on the front of her gown, she'd pulled a face at his scolding and dived headfirst into the lake. Then, she had risen from the water like a nymph, the fabric of her gown clinging scandalously to her body, and a hot flare of desire had almost incapacitated him. But she'd merely mocked his discomfort and ran away, her laughter echoing in his ears.

No woman—or even man—of his acquaintance possessed such spirit. And now, she was growing into a young woman…

No. She was a risk not worth taking, no matter how much she set his dreams alight. When he lay in bed alone, the chores of the day complete, he could indulge in a brief respite from the realities of his world and dream of *her*.

But he could do no more than dream.

"Lord Thorpe?"

The steward's inquiry brought him back to the present.

"Instruct the stonemason to start immediately," he said. "You have permission to pay him in full."

Leaving the steward gaping at him open mouthed, Giles turned his mount in a tight circle and spurred the animal into a gallop, letting the cool air on his cheeks dampen the desire which burned in his blood.

But, Fate—always the temptress—had other plans. As he took the path in the woods that led back to the stables, he spotted three figures ahead—two identical males and a young woman. He drew in a sharp breath at the twinge of jealousy.

Whenever he saw the Meredith twins, *she* was never far away.

One of the twins—he was damned if he could tell them apart—sat on a pile of logs, while the other, and Miss Redford, circled each other, holding wooden sticks aloft.

The Meredith boy pranced about, swinging his makeshift sword while Miss Redford moved in a more measured, fluid motion, her wooden sword seeming to be an extension of her arm.

And no wonder—Giles had often spied her practicing her

lunges, thrusting her makeshift sword into hay bales in the barn on his estate. Perhaps she fancied herself a Medieval knight. With her speed, deadly accuracy, and sheer force of will, she might have brought armies to their knees had she been born five hundred years ago—and had she been born a man.

She stopped and turned as if she sensed him. Did she know he watched her while she practiced, thinking herself unobserved? Or that he'd seen her dancing in the rain and whooping with joy to herself?

Did she know that, to him, she was the most extraordinary creature—someone he desired above all others?

Shit…

Where had *that* notion come from?

He couldn't…*didn't*…desire her.

Not at all.

She lowered her sword and stared at him, her liquid brown eyes almost black in the shade of the woods. While she was distracted, her sparring partner rushed toward her and lunged forward with his stick. She whirled on her feet and leaped to one side like a deer, then let out a laugh.

"Very ungallant of you, Johnny!" she cried. "Think you can best me by cheating?"

"Don't be a baby!"

He rushed again, but even Giles, with his untrained eye, could see he'd left his side exposed. With a blur of movement, she thrust her sword and smacked him square in the chest. He toppled backward with a cry.

"Now who's the baby!" She laughed.

Her opponent struggled to his feet, wiping the dust from his breeches.

"What have you done, you fool!" he cried. "You've torn my jacket."

"*You* tore it when you fell flat on your behind," she said, holding out her hand. "Come on—shake on it like gentlemen?"

"You're no gentleman!" he sneered.

"Nor a lady," said his brother, rising to his feet. "Come along, Johnny, Mrs. White will mend that for you in no time."

Arm-in-arm, the twins strode away.

"Why don't you get her to wipe your nose while she's at it?" she cried at their retreating backs. "But don't worry, you'll soon have doting little wives to tend to your every whim. I pity the ladies you choose!"

"Whereas I pity you," the elder twin said over his shoulder. "You're such a brat—who'd ever want *you?*"

She curled her hands into fists, and for a moment, a flicker of pain crossed her expression, and she let out a laugh. She stood still, watching them until they'd disappeared out of sight. Then she sighed and threw her stick to the ground, wiping her hands.

"Did you like what you saw, Lord Thorpe?" Her voice came out in a sneer, though he detected a slight huskiness, as if she were controlling her emotions.

"Not particularly." He steered his mount closer, and she took a step back and folded her arms.

"Be on your way," she said.

Uncivil creature!

"I think you'll find this is *my* land."

Her eyes narrowed, and Giles cursed his churlishness.

She approached him, and his breath caught at the sight of her—cheeks flushed, eyes bright with exercise, her body vibrating with vitality.

She turned her attention to his horse.

"Hello, Thunder," she said. "I have a gift for you—would you like it?"

The horse's ears pricked up, and she rubbed his nose. Then she smiled, and it was like the sunshine breaking through a cloud. It was the first time he'd seen her smile—she'd laughed at him many times during their encounters over the years, but a soft smile of friendship—and love—was something he'd not seen before.

His heart was lost.

But the smile was not for him.

She drew an apple from her pocket and held it out. The animal took it and swished his tail.

"Beautiful boy!" she whispered, rubbing the animal's nose again.

Giles couldn't help smiling at her audacity, for she'd been stealing apples from his orchard again and had the cheek to give it to his horse right under his nose.

"It's late," he said. "Shall I take you home?"

"I know the way."

"It's over a mile away, through the fields."

"I'm no fine lady needing to be pampered."

He couldn't help laughing. "No, that you're not."

She stepped back, her smile fading. Then she lowered herself into a mock curtsey.

"Please consider yourself free of any obligation."

Before he could reply, she turned her back and walked off.

The Meredith boy was wrong. Someone did want Miss Redford. Very much.

But duty came before desire. It was his misfortune that the one woman he wanted was the most inappropriate match. He'd need to take action before he fell completely under her spell.

CHAPTER THREE

HENRIETTA HAULED HERSELF up into the tree, taking care to avoid the loose branch. Phillip and Johnny had gone to London with their father for the rest of their vacation. She had to acknowledge a sense of relief. Their teasing, which had always been good-natured, had taken a sour note lately, particularly after Phillip had blamed her for ripping Johnny's jacket.

Lord Meredith had a fearsome reputation, and for two days, she'd waited anxiously for the twins' father to turn up on her doorstep and demand she be thrashed.

But she needn't have worried. Lord Meredith was so strict that he would have beaten his sons black and blue for their part, and they were both—especially Phillip—the most insufferable cowards.

Today was not a day for games or japes. Today, she had a mission.

To help Lady Thorpe, the prisoner in the mansion.

She'd spotted Giles riding across the fields on Thunder, presumably to impose his tyranny on his tenants, which gave Henrietta enough time to ascertain whether Lady Thorpe was in need of help.

The window was half open as before, but, as it was the morning, the sun shone directly into the room, picking out the furnishings—the occasional flash of gilt on the woodwork and the brass fireplace surround.

Henrietta crawled further along the branch to get a closer look.

The wingback chair had been moved sideways, and its occupant was visible in profile. It was the same woman Henrietta had seen before. Save for the blanket draped over her knees, there was an air of abandonment in the room, as if she'd been tended to at the beginning of the day, then conveniently forgotten about.

She held a book in one hand and an eyeglass in the other, her brow creased into a frown as she leaned over the book.

Henrietta moved further along the branch, until she reached the window, and froze as the branch shuddered beneath her with a creak. Trembling, she reached toward the window frame and pulled herself onto the ledge.

The woman continued studying her book, but distress shone in her eyes. She lifted the book, bringing it closer to her face, and it slipped out of her grasp and fell to the floor. She let out a soft cry and sank back into the chair, her eyes glistening with tears.

An invisible knife sliced through Henrietta's heart. This poor lady was wasting away with no one to help her, save a solitary maid who turned her chair to the window, so she could be taunted by the image of the world she was excluded from.

Life was to be lived, not frittered away in a darkened room, abandoned and alone.

"Who's that?"

The woman sat up and looked straight at Henrietta.

"Is someone there? Who are you?"

The frailty in the woman's voice stirred Henrietta's heart. Crouching on the ledge, she stuck her head through the gap in the window.

"I'm a friend."

"You're a *girl!*" The woman strained further forward, blinking. She shook her head. "All my friends are gone."

"May I come in? I mean you no harm."

"Why are you here?" Pale blue eyes stared out at her, but they showed no sign of recognition.

"I-I saw you a few days ago," Henrietta said. "And I came to see if you needed anything."

"Through my window?"

"I climbed the tree just outside."

The woman's face broke into a smile. "My—what an adventurous young lady you are! Do you live nearby?"

"At Portdown Lodge."

"Oh! You must be Mr. Redford's girl. We have one of his cabinets in the dining room. It's quite beautiful—at least, as far as I can recall. The last time I saw you, you were still in leading strings, though I doubt you remember. I'm Lady Thorpe. Forgive me if I don't get up—I find it so difficult these days, and one must be careful."

"Can't you walk?" Henrietta asked.

"My son thinks it best if I remain here," came the reply. "My accident…" She shook her head. "Forgive me, it was so long ago, but I remember as if it were yesterday. He knows what's best for me."

"What, shut up in this gloomy old room?"

"He says I must remain indoors to prevent further damage to my eyes and rest to preserve my strength. And I'm comfortable enough, no longer in pain. My son becomes so distressed when I'm in pain. He's working hard for everyone here, and it distresses me to know I'm such a burden."

How could this poor creature be a burden to anyone?

"My dear," Lady Thorpe said, "would you be so kind as to find my book? I've mislaid it, and Annie won't be here until the afternoon."

Henrietta picked up the book and flicked through it. "Shakespeare's sonnets," she said. "Which one were you reading?"

"I-I can't recall."

"Shall *I* read to you?"

Lady Thorpe's expression lit up, then she sank back and shook her head. "No, I'm sure you should be getting along. Won't your papa wonder where you are?"

"He's at his offices today," Henrietta said. "He's always telling me how hopeless I am at both reading and elocution. Perhaps you might help me, Lady Thorpe?"

Lady Thorpe smiled. "Pull up a chair, my dear. I believe we can help each other."

BY THE TIME Henrietta had finished reading, the sun had moved to the south side of the building and no longer shone directly into the window. Lady Thorpe seemed to have blossomed in the short while she'd been there. Her cheeks, which were a papery white, now showed a little color, and though her eyes still held the faraway expression of the partially sighted, they shone with delight.

"Oh, what joy to hear Shakespeare's words again!" she cried. "You have a very clear voice, my dear."

"I'll come and read to you every day," Henrietta said. "I could bring some flowers next time, to brighten up your room."

"I shan't be able to see them properly, my dear—my eyes are so weak. It would be such a waste!"

Henrietta's heart almost broke at the matter-of-fact way in which Lady Thorpe dismissed herself. "It's no waste," she said firmly. "You have a fine rose garden here at Thorpe Hall, and I'm sure you'd appreciate the scent. I'll bring some tomorrow—that is, if you'd like me to visit again."

Lady Thorpe closed her eyes and sighed as if reliving a precious memory. "Oh, the roses..." she whispered. "How I miss their bright colors!" She shook her head. "I wouldn't want you to go to any trouble, my dear, though I must admit I've enjoyed the company."

"Do you spend every day here alone?" Henrietta asked. "Surely you could have a companion."

"Dear Annie does her best, but she's always so busy around

the house, and I wouldn't dream of putting my son to such inconvenience, not when he did so much when I was ill. I couldn't burden him further."

Henrietta's body shook with anger. What the devil was Giles Thorpe playing at?

"How could anyone see you as a burden, Lady Thorpe?" she cried.

"Oh, no, dear, you quite mistake me," the lady replied. "My son does what he can. He found the very best doctor, who visits me each week, all the way from Harley Street. But Dr. Odgers is so very…" Her voice trailed off, and she colored and turned her head away.

Expensive.

Henrietta took Lady Thorpe's hand and glanced about the room, taking in the shabbiness of the décor.

So, despite the finery, the title, and the grand house, the Thorpes lacked money. A little devil on her shoulder laughed. What justification did he have to look down on her when he couldn't afford a companion for his mother?

But it wasn't an affliction to laugh at. He might be an arrogant fool, but a sour disposition was the least of his problems. And though Henrietta might thoroughly dislike him, she had no wish to see him suffer.

A clock chimed in the distance, twelve times.

"That's noon," Lady Thorpe said. "Annie will be here soon with my tray."

Henrietta rose to her feet. "I should go. You won't tell them I've come to visit, will you? I don't think your son would approve."

"Nonsense!" Lady Thorpe laughed, then she stopped, surprise in her expression. "I can't recall the last time I laughed."

"I'll come again tomorrow," Henrietta said, "but only if you promise not to tell."

Lady Thorpe shook her head. "I can't deceive my son. It's wrong to keep secrets."

"I could take you outside."

"Oh, no, my dear! My son wouldn't hear of it. Dr. Odgers has advised against it, you see—on account of my disposition. He said my nerves wouldn't be up to it. I-I'm too fragile, he says. And my eyes—they're so weak. He said I must preserve what little sight I have left. The daylight could destroy it completely."

"If you're not permitted to venture outside this room," Henrietta said, "what is your sight being preserved for?"

"Dr. Odgers is a very clever man."

Henrietta snorted. Dr. Odgers sounded like a complete fool. Lady Thorpe was a little frail and had poor sight, but she hardly seemed so delicate that the world outside presented a danger to her life. By confining her to her room, Dr. Odgers had perpetuated both her condition and his income, which was, most likely, his objective.

"Wouldn't you like to see your roses?" she suggested. "Just once to venture outside and feel the sun on your face?"

Desire flickered in Lady Thorpe's eyes, and she shook her head. "My son wouldn't approve."

"You're the mistress of the house," Henrietta said. "It should be your decision and yours alone. I could take you."

"I don't know…"

"Of course, I wouldn't want to upset the earl by questioning his judgment," Henrietta said, "but what if the doctor's wrong? I see no harm from a little turn about the rose garden on a warm day. If it doesn't suit your constitution, I can bring you straight back inside, and nobody would be any the wiser. But, imagine, if a walk outside were to improve your health, imagine how delighted your son would be!"

Lady Thorpe cocked her head to one side, as if in thought.

"Of course," Henrietta continued, "the earl is right in that you shouldn't entertain the notion of going outdoors in bad weather. That would be preposterous. If you asked me to take you outside in the rain, I'd have to refuse. But on a warm, sunny day, I might overlook any scruples. And, as your newest friend, I would be willing to do anything you asked of me."

She took Lady Thorpe's hand.

"Anything at all."

She withdrew her hand. "I must be going, your ladyship," she said. "I'll bring a book of mine tomorrow. I have a hankering to read *A Midsummer Night's Dream*, if you'd like to assist me in my study?"

"I'd like that very much…" Lady Thorpe hesitated. "Forgive me, what is your name, my dear?"

"It's Henrietta—but my friends call me Henry."

Lady Thorpe laughed. "Henry! A name for kings, but some-how, it suits you."

Henrietta rose to her feet and dipped into a curtsey. "Good-bye, Lady Thorpe," she said.

"Call me Euphramia," came the reply. "We're friends now, are we not?"

"Until tomorrow, Euphramia."

Henrietta approached the window and climbed onto the ledge just as footsteps approached the chamber door. She slipped through the gap and lowered herself onto the branch, wincing as it gave a loud creak.

Voices filtered through the window—Lady Thorpe's soft tones, together with that of another woman—presumably the maid.

Would she tell the maid that an intruder had entered her chamber?

She waited for the maid to fling open the window and shoo her away. But, after a while, the voices faded. She lifted her head and peered through the window. Lady Thorpe's chair had been moved away from the window, and a table placed in front of her with a plate of food at which the lady picked with a fork.

Smiling to herself, Henrietta crawled back to the center of the tree and descended, jumping from the lowest branch onto the ground.

Her new friend had not betrayed her.

CHAPTER FOUR

GILES KNOCKED ON Mother's chamber door and waited. A soft voice called out, and he slipped inside.

"Giles, darling."

"Mother, I'm come to take my leave before I ride for London."

She held out her hands, and he approached her, taking her hands in his and bending down to kiss her forehead.

His heart sank each time he saw her. Dr. Odgers said she wasn't improving, and his only hope was to maintain her present state and prevent further deterioration.

But, today, she seemed a little better, animated, even. Her smile reached her eyes.

"You're looking well, Mother," he said. "Annie tells me you ate all your luncheon."

"Thank you, dear," she said. "You're too kind."

He shook his head. "If only I could do more."

She patted his hand. "My dear boy, you have enough with the managing of the estate, to concern yourself with my troubles. But, I do wonder, perhaps you could ask Dr. West to attend me instead of Dr. Odgers?"

He shook his head. "I told you I'd find you the best doctor in Harley Street, and that's the one thing I refuse to compromise on."

"Not even if I wish it?" she asked. "Dr. West is a perfectly good doctor, and he lives close by, rather than in London. Annie was telling me the other day how he tended so beautifully to her niece in her confinement."

"But your condition is so much more severe," he said. "Oh, Mother, are you concerned about the expense? I assure you it's no trouble."

"Why are you riding to London to see your lawyer rather than summoning him here, like you summon Dr. Odgers?"

"I've a number of errands to complete in London," he said. "There's the townhouse to see to, and I've secured a meeting with my banker."

"Oh, Giles!" she cried. "Not another loan? Why can't you marry?"

"I'm not that desperate yet."

"You'll need to find a wife eventually."

"I'll take a wife when I'm ready."

"The estate needs an heir, Giles," she said. "It would break my heart, and your dear papa would turn in his grave if the title were to become extinct."

Bloody Father—if it weren't for the title and his desire to display it in the form of such extravagance, there'd be no need for loans. Sometimes, he cursed the earldom, which brought him nothing but misery and expectation. Why had he not been born a commoner like Redford? A successful merchant, he enjoyed the trappings of wealth without the shackles of a title.

As for Redford's daughter…

Giles shook his head.

A few days in London would do him good, perhaps cure him of his obsession—the inability to shake *her* from his thoughts.

He glanced around the chamber, and his gaze fell upon a single rose in a vase by the window.

"Find yourself a wife while you're in London," Mother said. "Dowries, unlike loans, don't have to be paid back."

He caressed her hand. Her skin was paper thin.

"If only I could do more for you, Mother," he said.

"You do too much, my dear," she said. "I am willing to forego the extravagance of Dr. Odgers."

He shook his head. "Some expenses are worth paying."

"Such as a mistress?"

"Mother, I…"

"Don't try to deny it, Giles, dear," she said. "I may be an invalid, but I'm no fool. All men have mistresses—and Lady Elizabeth Grey's reputation is not just confined to London. Does she make you happy?"

"How did you know…"

She let out a laugh. "I know, my boy," she said. "You always had such a serious little voice until you spoke of your favorite toys. It's just the same with your acquaintances. You speak about most of them in the matter-of-fact tone I've come to know well over the years. But, occasionally, your voice changes, when you have something on your mind or when you're tired after a day on the estate. And, when you speak of Lady Elizabeth Grey…" She shook her head. "I can't describe it, but you lower some of the walls you've fashioned around yourself."

"It matters not," he said. "Lady Betty knows how the world works."

She squeezed his hand.

"Do you love her?"

"It's of no consequence if I do."

"Perhaps not to your title or your estate, but the consequence to your heart cannot be ignored."

Giles sighed. He was fond of Betty, though he didn't love her. But, while he was determined to be a faithful husband, Betty would always hold a piece of his heart, for she was that rare beast, a woman who gave more than she took.

Their affair was reaching a natural conclusion. And the last time he'd seen her, his mind had been plagued by a spirited creature who defied him at every turn, who was able to get under his skin and chip away at his heart, until her image was indelibly etched onto it.

He needed a wife, not only to satisfy Mother and perpetuate the family lineage but to drive the indomitable Miss Redford from his mind once and for all. One more glorious weekend with Betty and they could part company as good friends, to meet in the future as acquaintances, but no longer lovers.

"My heart is safe, Mother," he said. "I'll not be so foolish as to fall in love with Lady Elizabeth Grey. Or," he added, "with the woman I choose to marry, beyond what's expected of a husband."

How soulless that sounded! But falling in love was not a path he intended to follow.

"I always said you were a sensible boy," Mother said, "unlikely to be weakened by foolish notions of love. So, that's settled. You'll find yourself a woman of good family and good fortune who is capable of overseeing the household and applying economy to the home."

"And," he added, "she must meet with your approval."

A smile illuminated her features. "I look forward to meeting this paragon when you've found her."

He kissed her forehead, then exited the chamber.

Mother was right, of course. He needed to find a wife, a dull, dependable sort of girl.

He shook his head. In London, he'd be able to forget about Miss Redford. And, with her debut on the horizon, she'd soon be married off herself, and he'd never see her again.

But he couldn't help the needle of jealousy that stabbed at his heart, at the notion of her belonging to another. Would her wings be clipped, her spirit caged? Or would she find someone to love, someone who'd enable her to soar into the heavens?

Whoever he was, he'd better appreciate what a damn lucky bastard he'd be.

CHAPTER FIVE

FROM HER VANTAGE point halfway up the tree, Henrietta watched the lone rider disappear down the tree-lined drive, heading away from Thorpe Hall.

She smiled to herself. Giles Thorpe's tall frame was unmistakable, even atop a horse.

Which meant she was in no danger of getting caught today. Checking her bag was secure over her shoulder, she swung herself up onto the next branch and edged toward Lady Thorpe's window.

Her new friend was waiting for her. Lady Thorpe's face broke into a smile as Henrietta squeezed through the half-open window and climbed into the chamber, dusting down her skirts.

"I wondered if you'd visit me today, my dear."

"Didn't I promise?" Henrietta fished a book out of her bag. "I've something I think you'll like."

"More Shakespeare?"

"No," Henrietta said. "It's Bewick's *History of British Birds*. Do you know of it?"

Lady Thorpe shook her head. Henrietta drew up a chair next to her and opened the book, flicking through the pages until she reached an illustration of a swan.

"If you cannot venture outside, then I'll bring some of the outdoors to you," Henrietta said. "See the detail in the illustration?"

Lady Thorpe narrowed her eyes in concentration.

"Can you see it?" Henrietta asked.

"With difficulty, my dear. The shapes are so blurry that they merge into one another."

"Let me help."

Henrietta took Lady Thorpe's hand. "Hold out your finger, point at the page…"

When her friend obliged, Henrietta guided her hand in order to trace the outline of the bird with her forefinger.

"There's the beak," she said, "and if you follow the line along the neck…" she guided Lady Thorpe's finger across the page, "…you reach the back, where he's spreading his wings."

Lady Thorpe's smile broadened, and delight shone in her eyes. "Oh yes!" she cried. "I can discern his shape. We have swans in our lake, you know." Her smile faded. "At least, we *did*."

"They're still there," Henrietta said. "I can see them from the top of the tree, and I've heard them often. Wouldn't you like to see them again?"

"How can I?"

"Why don't you let me take you outside?" Henrietta suggested. "Just a short stroll, nobody need know." She hesitated. "Is Lord Thorpe at home?"

The lady shook her head. "No, my dear, my son's left. He'll not be back until the weekend."

Henrietta drew in a sharp breath at the twinge of disappointment, though why she'd be disappointed at the prospect of not seeing that disagreeable man, she couldn't fathom.

"He's gone away?"

"My son has business to attend to." Lady Thorpe leaned forward. "Are you all right, my dear? You sound a little out of sorts."

"Y-yes," Henrietta said. "He must be a very busy man."

"He is." Lady Thorpe gave the indulgent smile of a besotted mother. "He's such a good boy—he works very hard. I do hope his trip is successful. He's gone to London, you see."

"Oh?"

"To find a wife."

Henrietta caught her breath as her heart flip-flopped in her chest.

Why should the prospect of him marrying disconcert her?

"And..." she hesitated, "...is he likely to succeed?"

"He's bound to." Lady Thorpe smiled. "I know he's my own son, but he'd make a fine husband, and the Thorpe name dates back to the Norman conquest. He only needs the right partner, a genteel lady of good sense, good family, and, of course, the right temperament."

Henrietta sighed inwardly.

Everything I am not.

"My dear, are you quite sure you're all right?"

"Of course," Henrietta said, forcing a smile. She snapped the book shut. "I think it's time I took you outside. The weather is glorious."

An expression of longing glowed in Lady Thorpe's eyes. "How can I venture out in my nightgown? It would be most improper."

"There's nobody to see us," Henrietta said. "I could help you dress."

"Good heavens, no!" Lady Thorpe cried. "I know you're no *lady*, but it still wouldn't do to have you dress me as if you were a servant."

You're no lady...

Henrietta's heart sank. Lady Thorpe had meant no offense, but, to all women of her class, the world was separated into two species, those with titles and those without.

She took Lady Thorpe's arm. "Permit me to indulge in the next best thing," she said. "Can you stand?"

"I cannot go outside."

"You can, at least indulge in its delights," Henrietta said. "Let me show you."

The lady stood, and Henrietta led her toward the window.

She pushed the sash fully up.

"There!" she cried. "Why not lean out and feel the sun on your face?"

Lady Thorpe complied. The sun illuminated her eyes, which shimmered like pale sapphires. Then she closed her eyes and smiled.

"Wonderful…" she breathed.

"Can you see much?" Henrietta asked.

She opened her eyes. "I can see the light and shapes. The dark green of the tree to the right, and, straight ahead…" she squinted and cocked her head to one side, "…I can discern a color—something pink. Yes, that's it—pink."

"That's the rose garden," Henrietta said.

"Oh!" Sorrow flickered across Lady Thorpe's expression. "How I miss it!"

"Shall I describe it?" Henrietta suggested.

"Oh, please."

"The roses are in full bloom, bright pinks and reds against the glossy dark green of the leaves, except for the far end of the garden, where the roses are white."

"Is there a statue?"

Henrietta nodded. "A woman holding an urn. She's surrounded by the white roses."

"Ah, Antheia." Lady Thorpe sighed.

"The goddess of gardens."

"Oh!" Lady Thorpe cried. "How do you know…" She broke off and colored. "I meant no offense."

Henrietta laughed. "Papa taught me the classics," she said. "In our society and in modern literature, women are depicted as frail creatures who need to be tended, whose only objective is to find a man to own them. But, in ancient Greece, women had the power to raise armies or launch a thousand ships. Women changed the course of history."

"Are you fond of studying rather than accomplishment?"

"Accomplishment in the eyes of Society is a woman's ability

to sew pretty cushion covers or paint adorable little landscapes in order to elicit sighs among dowagers in the drawing room," Henrietta said.

Lady Thorpe laughed. "My dear child! How you amuse me. Your ideas are so *modern*. I can't decide whether you're unlike every other young woman in the world or whether the whole of society has changed in my absence."

You're nothing but a grubby little urchin...

His words taunted her. "I believe that young ladies are as elegant as they ever were, Lady Thorpe. I am, however, nothing like them."

"Call me *Euphramia*, my dear, please," Lady Thorpe said. She reached for Henrietta's hand, her grip surprisingly firm.

"Forgive me, I meant no insult. I find your frankness refreshing, especially when I'm afforded such little company, and when my son and Dr. Odgers always see fit to refrain from telling me the truth." She lowered her voice. "I sometimes wonder if my days are numbered."

"I have no wish to speak out of turn, *Euphramia*," Henrietta said, "but I cannot believe that. You're not in any pain, are you? It seems as if the doctor has prescribed you nothing but incarceration and tonics, not once considering the benefit of company and fresh air. Don't you wish to venture out into the gardens you once loved so much?"

"I-I don't know..."

A flicker of fear showed in Lady Thorpe's eyes, and Henrietta's blood boiled with anger.

How dare they! How many years had this poor woman been locked away, such that she was too afraid even to step out of her own door, lest she fall dead in an instant?

A distant call echoed through the air.

"Oh!" Lady Thorpe cried. "Was that the swans?"

Henrietta leaned out of the window. "I can't see the lake," she said, "but I'm sure they're there."

Lady Thorpe sighed, and Henrietta squeezed her hand. "I'll

take no refusal, Euphramia," she said. "I insist you accompany me outside to walk among the roses and to greet the swans."

Thin, bony fingers tightened their grip on her wrist, and Lady Thorpe turned her face toward the window, determination in her expression.

"Perhaps a small venture," she said, lowering her voice as if they were about to commit a transgression. "And," she added, a smile of mischief on her lips, "since my son is not at home, you can leave the house in a more conventional manner today. Through the front door, like a guest." She nodded as if in determination. "And you *are* my guest, are you not?"

Victory! Henrietta glanced about the room, and her gaze landed on a shawl draped over the bed. But before they could move, the door opened and a woman appeared. Henrietta recognized the maid who'd been tending to Lady Thorpe before.

The maid let out a shriek.

"Who the devil are you?" she cried. "Take your hands off her ladyship!"

"It's all right, Annie," Lady Thorpe said. "Miss Redford is my guest."

"Miss Redford?" The maid shook her head. "Oh, no, that simply won't do."

"Why ever not?" Lady Thorpe asked.

"The master wouldn't approve, he's said that…" The maid hesitated and stared at Henrietta.

"Do go on," Lady Thorpe said.

"Forgive me for saying so, your ladyship, but he's spoken of Miss Redford before, and how he disapproves of her, for being a little—wild."

Henrietta's cheeks flushed with warmth. *How dare he!* But, given his overt disdain of her, should she have expected anything different?

Perhaps not, but a twinge of pain twisted in her gut at how readily he shared his poor opinion of her to all and sundry, even the servants.

But, in Lady Thorpe, Henrietta had a champion.

"Annie, my dear, Miss Redford is a little adventurous, to be sure, but I have found her company to be a great tonic."

The maid looked as if she were about to faint. "Oh, dear, your ladyship, do you mean she's been here before?"

"Yes," Henrietta said, unable to resist the temptation to shock the maid further. "I climbed in through Euphramia's window."

The maid drew in a sharp breath at the familiar address.

"As you see," Henrietta continued, "I am no lady, but I have your mistress's best interests at heart. I am convinced that a brief turn about the gardens on a warm day, such as today, will be beneficial to her health."

The maid looked from Henrietta to Lady Thorpe and back and shook her head as if trying to comprehend what was happening.

"Lady Thorpe's welfare and health are of the utmost importance to me," Henrietta said. "I'm sure we are of one mind on *that* matter, even if not on the suitability of my mode of entry into this house."

Lady Thorpe gave a delicate snort as if to hide her laughter, and the maid's eyes widened in surprise.

"Well, I've never seen the like!" she cried. "Your ladyship does seem happier today."

"And it is my wish that she remain so," Henrietta said.

"The master should be told."

"There's no need to trouble my son," Lady Thorpe said. "He's enough worries to deal with. I ask for your discretion, Annie. After all, what harm can come from a stroll in the garden?"

"Much if you have no wish to be caught," the maid said. "The master's steward is in the study, and the window overlooks the garden, as you know."

"What the devil is Mr. Wilmot doing here today?"

"He's settling the stonemason's account for the Brummitt farm in the master's absence."

"So many accounts..." Lady Thorpe shook her head. She

leaned against Henrietta, as if in need of support.

"Lady Thorpe, are you well?" Henrietta asked. "Let me help you to your chair. Here, take my arm."

They shuffled toward the chair, the maid taking Lady Thorpe's other arm, and settled her in. Henrietta reached for the shawl on the bed and placed it over her friend's lap.

"I'm afraid our walk will have to wait, my dear," Lady Thorpe said. "Such a shame!"

She clung to Henrietta's hand, her thin fingers clutching onto her wrist as if her life depended on it.

"Please, your ladyship, do not distress yourself!" Annie cried.

Henrietta's heart pained at the anguish in the maid's voice. No matter what Lord Thorpe or the doctor were up to—Annie, at least, cared deeply for her mistress.

"I should go," Henrietta said. "Forgive me, I didn't mean to distress you. But perhaps, if you're feeling better, might I call tomorrow? You can tell me which pictures in Bewick's book are your favorites."

Lady Thorpe nodded and smiled. "Please do. I so look forward to your visits. Let us venture outside tomorrow. Annie can help me to find something more appropriate to wear, won't you, Annie, dear?"

"Yes, your ladyship."

"And perhaps you would be so kind as to see Miss Redford out? You can take her through the kitchen garden, so there's no danger of being seen."

The maid bobbed a curtsey. "Of course, your ladyship."

"I'll take my leave," Henrietta said.

"Dear Henry!" Lady Thorpe lifted Henrietta's hand to her lips and kissed it.

Henrietta let the maid lead her out of the chamber, into a wooden-paneled corridor, at the end of which was a narrow staircase that led to the kitchen. Though the kitchen was enormous, with a huge range occupying most of one wall, the atmosphere was cold and damp—so unlike her kitchen at home in which a fire always burned brightly.

The kitchen was as forlorn and neglected as Lady Thorpe herself.

"This way, Miss." A door led outside to a garden, where vegetables grew in neat rows.

"Shall I await you here tomorrow?" the maid asked. "It seems more appropriate than climbing in through the window."

"Despite what your master says. I want to help Lady Thorpe, who seems rather neglected."

The maid blushed and averted her gaze. Henrietta took her hand. "Rest assured that I mean her ladyship no harm."

The maid nodded. "Of course, Miss. Forgive me for speaking out of turn. For my part, I'll say that you don't seem quite the wild thing I've been led to believe. I'll wait here for you at noon tomorrow. You mustn't endanger yourself by climbing that old tree."

Henrietta opened her mouth to protest, but she closed it and nodded instead.

"Very well," she said. "Until tomorrow."

"And, rest assured, your secret's safe with me." She bobbed another curtsey, then closed the door.

Henrietta crossed the kitchen garden and skirted the building until she reached the front lawn. Two statues dominated the view, standing on either side of the main doors—sentinels on guard, waiting for their master to return.

She approached the statues. They had been carved with an expert hand, but their expressions lacked warmth—soulless faces staring haughtily out over the main drive. The statues reminded her of their owner, ready to sneer in contempt at every visitor they deemed beneath them. What might they look like with a chamber pot on their heads!

Giggling to herself, she ran across the lawn and didn't stop until she reached home. The sight of the Thorpe Hall kitchen, in all its stark desolation, had given her an idea—to bake some biscuits for Lady Thorpe. If she could persuade Mrs. Briggs to let her take over a corner of the kitchen tonight, they'd be ready for tomorrow, and she could take her new friend for a picnic by the lake.

CHAPTER SIX

"YOU SEEM OUT of sorts, Giles, darling."

Giles leaned back in his chair, stretched out his long limbs, then closed his eyes. Betty possessed the uncanny ability to read his mind. Her expression, always so searching, penetrated a man's soul. Which, presumably, explained why she had thrived in her new station in life.

Widowed in her twenties, Lady Betty Grey could have succumbed to melancholy and grown old before her time. But, with shrewd intelligence and a love of life, she triumphed under adversity, lived within her means, and turned her late husband's annuity into a substantial enough income to send her son to Harrow and now, Oxford. Rumor abounded that she had turned down the hand of no less than two viscounts, preferring her independence, and she had gained herself a reputation for being one of the most sought-after and discerning companions in London society.

Companion was a far more respectable term for a woman of good family, exquisite taste, and known to be the epitome of discretion.

She had the countenance and temperament of an angel. And, by heaven, he would miss her. An uncomplicated woman who served his physical needs without demanding his heart.

She picked up the decanter and glided across the room to refill his glass. He took a sip and sighed.

"Where do you get your brandy from, Betty? I've never tasted the like."

"From a friend."

"Which friend?"

"A wine merchant. I've known him for years. Don't be jealous, darling."

"I'm not." Giles took another sip. "May I stay tonight?"

She placed a hand on his shoulder and shook her head. "Darling, much as I love your company, I don't think it a good idea."

"Why not? You've never refused me before." Giles winced at the peevishness in his tone.

"Because," she said, "when an affair comes to an end, it must always be on *my* terms."

How the devil did she know he was planning to end their affair?

She let out a laugh. "Oh, darling! You've much to learn about women—and about yourself. I could tell from your demeanor, the moment you arrived on my doorstep today, that you intended this to be our final encounter, at least as lovers." She nodded to the vase on the side table. "And, you've never brought me roses before, let alone a dozen of them." She gave him a rueful smile. "Why is it that a man considers roses to be a sign of affection, whereas, in reality, they represent guilt? I suppose this means you're looking for a wife."

He couldn't deny it, not to her. She deserved the truth.

"Forgive me, Betty."

"There's nothing to forgive," she replied. "I have nothing but good memories of our liaison, and I'm glad we can part as friends." She kneeled at his feet and placed her head on his lap, and he caressed her hair, as he had done on countless other nights when they'd talked in front of the crackling fire in her parlor before he'd carried her upstairs and made love to her all night.

"Why can't we spend one last night together as friends?" he asked.

"But it wouldn't be just one night," she said. "Would it?"

"Would it matter? We love each other, don't we?"

She stiffened and lifted her head to look directly at him. "*Do you love me?*" she asked. "Enough to commit yourself to me tonight and every night thereafter? When you look at every other woman, do you see me?"

He opened his mouth to reply, then closed it.

In truth, each time he looked at a woman, even Betty, all he could think of was a very different creature. A hellion.

But he must turn aside all thoughts of Betty—and of *her*—and do his duty.

"I'm fond of you, Betty," he said. "I admire your independence and your love of life."

She took his hand, interlocking her fingers with his, then she kissed each of his knuckles. "My poor, Giles," she said. "You're determined *not* to enjoy life because of your father. I only hope that the woman you eventually choose will bring some light into your life."

"Mother wants me to wed sensibly."

She let out an unladylike snort. "So, you must find yourself a dull wife with a dowry and a title, one who'll do your bidding at every turn and provide you with a litter of heirs."

"Perhaps."

"Trust me, that's the last sort of woman to make you happy," she said. "You need an independent spirit, otherwise you'll bore easily. And—an honorable man such as yourself is unlikely to do what most bored husbands do. Which means you'll be miserable for the rest of your life, and you'll live a life of resentment and regret."

"A little melodramatic, don't you think, Betty?"

She rose to her feet, then settled herself on his lap, and drew him into her arms. Then she placed a soft kiss on his forehead. He breathed in her sweet scent, the faint overtones of rose and honey.

Sweet heaven, how he'd miss her! Betty understood how to bring him to the peak of physical pleasure like no other woman of his acquaintance. But he would, most of all, miss her companionship and their easy conversation. She always knew when to fill the emptiness with chatter and when to remain silent.

"So," she said, her voice bright, "when am I to be introduced to the woman of your choosing?"

"I have yet to find her."

"If you're eager to be married quickly, the Duke of Sandcombe's daughter is a pleasant enough creature," she said. "Or, if you're after an ornament and are prepared to wait, Lord and Lady Fairchild's youngest is having her come-out next Season. She's rumored to be even prettier than her sister, who managed to snare a viscount."

"The very same viscount you turned down, if I recall."

"*One* of them." Her lips curled in a smile of mischief.

Someone knocked on a door in the distance, and Giles glanced at the clock. "It's past ten—have you supplanted me already with another?"

"No, darling," she laughed. "Etiquette demands that I wait until my current lover is at least out of the house before inviting his replacement in."

The parlor door opened, and a footman stood in the doorway, holding a letter.

"What is it, Tippet?" Betty asked.

"Forgive me, your ladyship," he said, "I've an urgent message for Lord Thorpe."

Giles's heart tightened in his chest.

"Mother…"

Had she been taken ill? Dr. Odgers had warned him of the possibility of a seizure if she didn't remain quiet, and Mother had looked animated of late, as if she'd been over-exerting herself.

The footman handed over the letter. Giles tore it open, his hands trembling, then read the first paragraph.

It wasn't Mother—thank goodness—but his aunt and uncle. They had been killed that afternoon in a coaching accident, leaving his cousin Beatrice—a girl of fifteen—an orphan.

Who was, according to the letter, now his ward.

Shit.

As if he didn't have enough responsibility.

He admonished himself. The poor child had just lost her parents. An incident—that was, to him, an inconvenience—had shattered her world.

"Giles?" Betty placed a light hand on his arm and pressed a glass into his hand. "Drink this for the shock. Your mother…?"

He shook his head. "It's from my uncle's solicitor. My aunt and uncle have been…" He hesitated. "Little Beatrice…the last time I saw her she must have been five years old, at most."

He handed the note to Betty, and she read it. "Oh, poor child!" she cried. "What will you do?"

"I must honor Uncle's wish," he said. "I'm her guardian, now." He folded the letter and placed it in his pocket.

"What shall I tell your man?" the footman said. "He's waiting for you outside."

"Tell him I'll come directly," Giles said. "It seems I must cut short my stay in London and delay any thought of matrimony." He took Betty's hand. "Forgive me for leaving so abruptly."

She placed a kiss on his cheek. "Of course," she said. "I trust that when I next see you, it'll be a happier circumstance—at your wedding."

He smiled ruefully. "I'll have to delay searching for a wife, now, but, rest assured, you'll be first on the guest list.

He pressed his lips to hers, knowing that it would be their final kiss, then bade his leave, stepping out into the night.

CHAPTER SEVEN

"**O**H, HENRIETTA—MY DEAR—YOU cannot imagine how glorious this is!"

Lady Thorpe bent over the rose bush, her eyes shining with exhilaration as she inhaled their delicate scent. Standing in the center of the walled rose garden, dressed in an intricately embroidered redingote of vivid blue silk over a pale-yellow gown, she looked like a very different creature from the invalid Henrietta had first glimpsed a month before.

The dress was a little loose on her thin frame, but she looked every part the elegant dowager countess, and the style, though a little old-fashioned, reminded Henrietta of a Gainsborough painting.

How graceful Lady Thorpe must have been in her prime! And, how despicable a crime it was to have confined her to a darkened room.

But her incarceration was at an end, now she had Henrietta to champion her cause.

Lady Thorpe closed her eyes and smiled.

"Can you hear it?" she whispered. "The sounds of nature and life. Oh, how I've missed it!" She reached out and took Henrietta's hand. "Here, close your eyes and listen."

Henrietta closed her eyes, concentrating on the sounds of the outdoors. The wind in the trees, the gentle hum of insects, punctuated by the occasional cry of a water bird in the distance.

"Is that a swan?" Lady Thorpe asked.

"No, I think it's a moorhen," Henrietta said.

"Shall we go to the lake and find them?" she suggested. "Perhaps we'll glimpse the swans, also. We can have our picnic by the water's edge."

"Ooh, a picnic!" Lady Thorpe gave a cry like an excited child.

That morning, Henrietta had procured a few treats from Papa's kitchen and a bottle of lemonade, which rested in her basket, tucked beneath a plaid blanket in a bright red and green pattern.

"Do you mind sitting on the ground?" Henrietta asked. "I've brought a blanket and a cushion for you."

"I can't think of anything more delightful."

Arm in arm, they followed the path through the walled garden, until they emerged through a stone archway onto the well-clipped lawn that sloped gently down to the lake. A breeze rippled across the lake, sending sparkles of reflected light pirouetting across the surface.

"Oh!" Lady Thorpe cried, "I can see the lights on the water, like nymphs dancing!"

Henrietta led her to the water's edge, where the ground leveled out. She unfolded the blanket and spread it over the ground and helped her friend to sit and then set out the picnic things.

"It's nothing special, I'm afraid," she said, pouring a glass of lemonade and handing it to Lady Thorpe. "Just some bread and cheese, a few shortbread biscuits—which I made myself last night—and some of our cook's lemonade."

"That sounds delightful," Lady Thorpe said. "Food always tastes so much better when eaten out of doors, don't you think?"

"Absolutely." Given that most of the food Henrietta ate outdoors was stolen from Thorpe Hall's orchard and that stolen fruit was always the most delicious, she had to agree.

"And, if it's been made by a friend, so much the better," Lady Thorpe continued. She sipped her drink. "This lemonade is delicious. Our cook makes it too sweet, and I cannot abide overly sweet things."

"Perhaps that's why you're able to tolerate *my* company."

"Dear Henry!" Lady Thorpe laughed. "I adore your company, but shouldn't you have friends your own age? There must be many young ladies hereabouts."

"I doubt they'd like me," Henrietta replied. "I'm not what a young lady ought to be."

"I'm aware of that," Lady Thorpe said. "Annie tells me that my son disapproves of you. But I should be permitted to choose my own friends whether he dislikes them or not, and *I* think you're charming."

Henrietta fixed her gaze on the water that stretched ahead of her, to the distant shore, where a marble folly nestled among rhododendron bushes. A favorite haunt of hers, where she played hide and seek as a child.

Lady Thorpe was right—she didn't fit in, and almost everyone disapproved of her.

But to hear it from her friend's lips, voiced so explicitly…

To hear that *he* disliked her…

She drew in a sharp breath. She'd made no attempt to ingratiate him, in fact, she'd taken delight from vexing him at every turn, from eliciting a reaction from him, even if it was fury.

Why, then, did the confirmation of his dislike affect her?

Two white shapes swam into view at the far end of the lake and glided smoothly across the surface.

"There they are!" Henrietta cried, swallowing her melancholy. "Can you see them?"

Lady Thorpe leaned forward, squinting her eyes. "I can just make them out," she said. "How delightful! I wonder if it's the same pair I used to give bread to…" She frowned as if concentrating, "…it must be almost ten years ago."

"Is that likely?" Henrietta asked.

"If they're well-tended to, they can live for many years."

"How can you be sure it's the same *pair*?"

"Swans mate for life," Lady Thorpe said. "They're like us in that respect. When you find your one true love, nobody else will do." She wiped a tear with her sleeve.

Henrietta took her hand. "I'm sorry. I didn't mean to bring back painful memories."

"Oh, but we need the pain in order to remember the joy," Lady Thorpe said. "My dear Gerald, for all his faults, was my one true mate. Of course, he often irritated me beyond belief, and at times I wanted to push him into the lake, but that's what kept our love *alive*."

She turned her gaze to Henrietta. "You'll know your one true love the moment you set eyes on him."

"Will I?"

"If you have good luck, you will. That is why you must widen your acquaintance. Consider the likelihood of finding your perfect partner when your circle of acquaintance is so restricted! But you must select the right partner who is destined to make you happy—and never mistake contentment for happiness."

"What do you mean?"

"A partnership for life must be nurtured," Lady Thorpe said. "Consider the rose bush, the sweet, soft petals, delicate aroma, and bright colors combined with the prickly thorns. *That* is how a relationship should be, a myriad of textures and layers."

"It all sounds rather uncomfortable," Henrietta said.

"You don't strike me as the sort of young woman who minds a little discomfort. In fact, I'll wager you thrive on it. You should never settle for a man who flatters and admires you. Flattery is the manifestation of insincerity and treachery. No, I'm convinced that if a man infuriates you beyond belief, but you're drawn to him, he's the one for you."

As Lady Thorpe fixed her gaze on Henrietta, the sunlight caught her eyes, emphasizing their clear blue color.

Henrietta's breath caught in her throat, as the revelation struck her.

Lady Thorpe had just described her son.

Giles…

Henrietta turned her face toward the lake, catching the breeze that cooled her burning cheeks. Thank heavens Lady Thorpe had such poor sight, or the blush spreading across her face might betray her.

The memory of his voice swirled in her mind. Even when raised in anger, it set her senses ablaze, as if her soul fed on his passion.

What the devil are you doing?

His angry words echoed in her ears, cutting through the tranquil air. She shook her head to dispel the noise, but the voice grew in intensity, accompanied by footsteps.

"I *said*, what the devil are you doing with my mother?"

She turned toward the voice, and her gut twisted in fear.

Striding across the lawn, Annie stumbling behind him, was her nemesis.

Giles Thorpe.

Henrietta leaped to her feet.

"Dear God!" he cried. "It's worse than I thought. You little *hellcat!*"

"Giles!" Lady Thorpe let out a cry. Henrietta took her hand and helped her up.

"Take your hands off my mother!" he roared. Henrietta jumped at the force in his voice.

She had never seen him so angry.

"Is this what you do in my absence, abduct my mother and subject her to whatever godforsaken scheme you've dreamed up?"

Annie burst into tears. "I'm ever so sorry, ma'am!"

"Stop your wailing," he snarled. "Take Mother inside. Then send for Dr. Odgers. I should have you dismissed for this!"

"Giles, darling," Lady Thorpe said. "There's no harm in…"

"There's every harm!" he cried. "Do you have any idea how much damage you might have done to yourself?"

"Oh, don't be an ass!" Henrietta cried. "Lady Thorpe is perfectly well. The fresh air has done her a world of…"

"Who are you to advise on my mother's state of health?" He moved toward Henrietta, his big body blocking out the sunlight. Though his face was in the shade, his eyes glittered with rage.

He curled his hands into fists, his body shaking with barely controlled fury, and he spoke through gritted teeth.

"Annie—take Mother inside, now, before I have you whipped. Mother—do as I bid. I'll deal with you later."

"Giles, I really think…"

"Mother, you *don't* think," he said. "That's the problem. Have you forgotten what happened to you as a result of Father's recklessness?"

Henrietta shook her head. Surely, he wouldn't be so insensitive as to mention the accident which had taken his father's life?

Lady Thorpe's eyes widened. "That was an accident, Giles, it…"

"It was no accident, Mother, and you well know it," he said. "Do you know why I'm home from London earlier than expected? It's because Uncle and Aunt have been killed in just such an accident."

"Sweet heaven! Not dear John and Amelia?"

"The very same," he replied. "And, through their recklessness, their daughter is now an orphan with no one to protect her."

Lady Thorpe gave a cry. "Little Beatrice?"

"Aye, Beatrice," he said. "Do you now understand my concern? While you've been tempted into recklessness by this…" he waved a dismissive hand at Henrietta, "…this *hellion*, a young girl's life has been all but destroyed."

"What will become of Beatrice?"

"She's now under my guardianship and will be arriving here in two days if you have no objection to her coming to live with us."

"Of course, I've no objection," Lady Thorpe replied.

"Good, it's settled," he said. "And, of course, you understand that you must be more discerning in your choice of companions from now on." He gave Henrietta a look of disdain. "Beatrice must not associate with those I deem to be beneath her."

"Giles, I…"

"That's enough, Mother," he said. "Annie, take your mistress inside unless you wish to be dismissed."

Sniffing, the maid bobbed a curtsey and linked her arm round Lady Thorpe's, then set off toward the house.

"Lady Thorpe, I…" Henrietta began, but a strong hand clasped her wrist, and she looked up into a pair of cold blue eyes.

"You're *not* to speak to my mother again," he said. "Don't you think you've distressed her enough?"

"I've distressed her?" she cried. "Your mother and I were having a perfectly pleasant day until you arrived. I'm sorry for your loss, but you could have broken the news to your mother in a less distressing manner."

"Had she been safely tucked away in her chamber, I would have been able to do just that."

Henrietta let out a snort. "Safely tucked away, indeed! Your poor mother's been a prisoner these past ten years, abandoned and alone, while you spend your days strutting about the place, looking down your nose at the rest of us. Did she look distressed or unwell to you, today? No, she was laughing. Fresh air, exercise, and the opportunity to laugh—*that's* what your mother needs, not some tonic prescribed by a London charlatan who only wishes to augment his income."

"Dr. Odgers is no charlatan," he said. "He's one of the most respected doctors in Harley Street."

"That merely means he's one of the most expensive," Henrietta said. "But a man's expertise is not determined by price alone."

He curled his lips into a sneer. "Perhaps you could remind me where you studied medicine?"

"I know little about medicine," she said, "but I'll wager I know more about your mother than Dr. Odgers or perhaps even you, seeing as you've forsaken her."

He stepped closer, his body shaking with fury.

"How dare…"

"I do dare!" she cried. "Your mother needs company and conversation, she needs friendship and love."

"Mother needs rest and quiet."

"So, she's to be abandoned again?"

"Beatrice will be company enough for her," he said. "*You* are not to visit again. I don't want Mother further distressed. As for Beatrice, I'll not have her tainted by your influence."

"Tainted?"

"Aye," he said. "My cousin is due to be presented at court, and as such, she must be schooled in the manner befitting her station. Grubbing around in the dirt with the local urchin is hardly a fitting education for a young woman of her sensibilities."

The arrow, shaped by his words, hit home. Orphaned she may be, but this Beatrice, who Lord Thorpe clearly deemed the epitome of ladylike perfection, did not sound like the sort of creature Henrietta would want as a friend. In fact, she was determined to hate her.

"Better an urchin who grubs around in the dirt than a pompous ass who treats the world with contempt," she said.

"You're hardly a paragon," he replied. "You're either wallowing in the mud, diving into the lake, or shinning up trees like some godforsaken guttersnipe. It's most unladylike for a young woman your age. What sort of a man is your father, to let you run wild like this? You ought to be thrashed. I should drag you to your father and insist he does it himself."

"Why don't you!" she cried. "Why not destroy me like you've destroyed your mother?"

"You little hellcat!" he cried. "I ought to throw you off my land."

"Try it," she challenged, "if you're man enough."

She raised her fist, and he caught her wrist and pulled her hard against him. She struggled in his grip, but he held her firm, while she grasped his arms and strained to pull free. Panting, she tilted her head back and met his gaze. Their bodies pressed against each other, the faint rhythm of his heartbeat pulsing against her chest.

A flare of passion ignited in the depths of his eyes, and he lowered his mouth to hers.

At first, she resisted, then she clutched at his sleeve, while his warm lips slid over hers. The tip of his tongue stroked the seam of her mouth—at first gently, then, with more insistence, almost desperation, as if he were a man dying of thirst.

With a sigh, she granted him entrance, and he slipped his tongue between her lips, stroking the inside of her mouth, claiming every inch of her, marking her as his.

And she *was* his. Her body thrummed with life, and a wave of passion rose deep within her. Strong, dominant hands held her firm as if invisible chains bound her to him.

He hesitated, uncertainty in his expression. The wave receded, and a little mewl of frustration escaped her. Clutching his sleeve, she pulled him closer and curled her tongue round his.

What the devil was she doing?

She stiffened in his arms and pulled free. He released his hold and stepped back, the passion in his eyes no more than dying embers. Passion she had longed to see.

Then the passion turned to regret and disgust.

"Forgive me," he said, shaking his head. "I shouldn't have done that—not with *you*, of all women."

Her gut twisted in shame. Did he find her so repulsive?

She lifted her hand to strike him, but he caught her wrist.

"You'll have to be quicker than that, Miss Hellcat, if you're to best me."

Hellcat, was it?

Anger flared at the arrogance of his tone, and she struck him, clawing at his face.

"Ouch—you little *ruffian!*" he cried, releasing her. "I'll thrash you myself!"

Before he could catch her, she lifted her skirts and set off at a sprint, while his curses echoed across the lawn. She didn't stop running until she reached home.

Curse him! Why did he have the power to unsettle her, to make her hate him, yet want to kiss him at the same time?

Papa wasn't at home, he must still be at his offices, but she could hear the cook bustling about in the kitchen. In her haste, she'd abandoned her basket, and Cook was bound to admonish her over the missing plate, not to mention the bottle of lemonade. But the woman adored her. With a few smiles, she'd be able to avoid punishment.

She slipped into the library, glancing at the empty space on the bookshelf, which had once housed Bewick's *History of British Birds*. She might be forgiven the loss of a bottle of lemonade, but the missing book was another matter. If she were not permitted to visit Lady Thorpe again, how would she ever get it back?

CHAPTER EIGHT

T HE FIRST RAYS of the morning sun slid across the landscape as Henrietta walked along the hedgerow. Everything looked better in the morning.

Last night during supper, she'd waited for Papa to demand what had happened to his missing book. But, after discussing her studies and his activities for the day, he excused himself and disappeared into his study with a bottle of port and a stack of letters to answer.

Later that evening, he'd joined her for tea in the drawing room and listened to her attempts at the pianoforte. He made all the right noises of encouragement that an indulgent Papa did to a daughter with little to no talent for music, then he retired, bidding her goodnight.

Her little adventure was over, and her father was none the wiser. Though Henrietta would miss Lady Thorpe, she still had plenty to enjoy. Perhaps, when the twins returned from their first term at Oxford, they'd be amenable to another bout of fencing. Johnny certainly would. Phillip always fancied himself the best of the three of them, though he'd always shied away from sparring with her.

Henrietta knew how to use an adversary's strength against him.

Except for *him*...

Last night, Giles Thorpe had plagued her dreams as usual.

But this time, rather than fight with her, he'd held her close, told her that he loved her above all others, then kissed her. She closed her eyes, imagining scenes filled with passion, where they wept and sighed in each other's arms.

Infuriating man!

If a man infuriates you beyond belief…then he's the one for you.

Lady Thorpe's words swirled in her mind.

But he wasn't the one for her. Or, at least, she wasn't the one for him. He'd made that abundantly clear yesterday.

After he had kissed her…

…and set her body ablaze with need…

"No," she whispered to herself. She must be strong and steer clear of him. The man who visited her dreams in all his glory was a different creature from the man who clearly loathed her. Most likely he'd be turning his attention on the prissy young cousin of his—*what was her name?*—and counting his blessings that he could enjoy the company of a young woman of such superior quality to the hellion from the neighboring property.

The morning mist had dissipated by the time she reached home, and her stomach growled at the faint aroma of smoked fish and the prospect of Cook's kedgeree. She slipped through the front door, made her way to the breakfast room, and froze.

On the bureau beside the door to Papa's study was a book.

Bewick's *History of British Birds*.

And, on the chair, someone had placed a basket, containing a neatly folded red and green plaid blanket.

Papa's voice called out from within the study.

"Is that you, daughter?"

Daughter.

Not Hen—or even Henrietta—but *daughter*.

An address he usually reserved for an admonishment.

She retreated on tiptoe, but before she could escape, the door opened.

"Ah, *there* you are. At last." Papa's expression was as grim as his tone. "Come in. I wish to speak with you."

"With?" she asked. "Or *at?*"

His expression darkened, and he stepped aside.

He wasn't alone. His guest sat with his back to her. As she entered the room, he rose and turned to face her.

Compared to the anger in Papa's eyes, the man before her showed no emotion, no sign of the fury he'd displayed yesterday—nothing, in fact, save cold contempt.

"I hear you've been trespassing and molesting Lady Thorpe," Papa said.

"You're mistaken," she replied. "Lady Thorpe is my…"

Papa took her wrist and she winced. "Do *not* interrupt me, child, when I'm speaking to you! Have you been wandering about Thorpe Hall uninvited and disturbing Lady Thorpe's rest?"

"Papa, you don't understand…"

"Did you take Lady Thorpe outside, knowing that it was against her doctor's advice?" Papa asked. "Yes or no?"

"Lady Thorpe said I could…"

He tightened his grip. "Yes. Or no."

"Yes," she whispered.

He released his hold, and she stepped back, rubbing her wrist. Then he sighed and shook his head. The anger in his eyes disappeared and was replaced by the one emotion which had the power to destroy her.

Disappointment.

"I've been a poor father," he said, weariness in his voice. "I should have known that after your dear mama passed you needed the guidance that only a lady could provide. But I honestly believed that you would respect my wishes and the boundaries I'd set."

"Mr. Redford, you shouldn't blame yourself," a deep voice said. "Any parent would have struggled under the circumstances."

Henrietta eyed Lord Thorpe with distaste.

Pompous, condescending man—how dare he!

"I see now the mistake I made in giving you too much freedom," Papa continued. "I had hoped that you'd treat your freedom with the respect it deserved. But, alas, it was not to be."

Lord Thorpe moved toward her, stepping into the light of the morning sun, and she caught sight of his face.

Three parallel lines ran diagonally across his left cheek. He raised his hand and rubbed his cheek.

"You should have that seen to," Papa said. "How came you by such an injury?"

Would he betray her? Papa was angry enough—who knew what punishment he'd hand out if he knew she was responsible?

"I was scratched by a wild animal."

Henrietta stifled a giggle, disguising it with a cough.

"But," he continued, "I believe the creature will soon be caged and dealt with accordingly. As to your daughter, Mr. Redford, I'd advise a firmer hand. Perhaps a little parental discipline will teach her the benefits of respecting her betters. A good strapping is the only way to temper such savagery."

Papa hesitated. He always said that he'd never raise his hand to her. And he was a man of his word.

"Or, perhaps *I* could…" Lord Thorpe reached toward her, but she jumped back.

"You wouldn't dare!" she cried. "If you so much as touch me, I'll emasculate you with my sword!"

"Henrietta!" Papa roared. "You forget yourself. Lord Thorpe is right—I've been far too lenient with you. But no longer."

"Are you going to thrash me?"

He shook his head. "No, I don't believe you'd learn anything from a thrashing, but I can think of a far more appropriate punishment."

Her stomach clenched in fear. The air of calm resignation in Papa's voice did more to frighten her than any threats of a beating.

"I shall take your sword from you," Papa said, "and everything I deem inappropriate."

Inwardly, she sighed with relief. Her sword she could manage without. And short of locking her in her chamber—something he'd never do—Papa couldn't prevent her from going outside.

"And today," he said, flexing his fingers, "I shall write to your Aunt Agnes to tell her that you're going to stay with her, so she can complete your education in whatever manner she sees fit."

Her heart sank. Papa looked up to his sister-in-law because she had noble blood in her veins. But, Aunt Agnes was known for having a will of iron. Unlike Papa's easy-going nature, she had the temperament of a general.

"Could you not beat me instead?" she asked.

"The very fact that you ask it of me, confirms it would have little effect in correcting your behavior," Papa said. "But, rest assured, if I catch you within fifty paces of Thorpe Hall again, I *will* thrash you."

He nodded as if to convince himself that he'd made the right decision. Behind him, Lord Thorpe continued to stare at her, an expression of satisfaction on his face.

Papa turned to their guest. "I must thank you, Lord Thorpe, in bringing my daughter's behavior to my attention. I only trust that she'll learn obedience under the tutelage of her aunt rather than learn it the hard way at the hands of her husband."

A ripple of fear threaded through her. "H-husband?"

"Aye," Papa said, his voice grim.

"Yes, but I don't want…"

"I care *not* what you want!" he cried. "You're eighteen, Henrietta—and of marriageable age. It's high time you did your duty. I should have sent you to your aunt last year, but you persuaded me otherwise, and I yielded, like the fool I was. But no more. Your aunt will prepare you for the Season and ensure that you're married off to the first man who offers."

The breath caught in her throat as her chest tightened in panic.

"No…"

"I have nothing more to say on the matter," Papa said. "Lord Thorpe, let me see you out. Daughter, wait here until I return."

He pushed her toward the chair Lord Thorpe had just vacated. Her legs no longer able to support her, they gave way, and she slumped into the seat.

Dear God—what had she done?

CHAPTER NINE

B Y THE TIME Giles returned to Thorpe Hall, his conscience had begun to needle him.

The conviction that he was right, that justice needed to be served, had melted at the sight of her stricken face.

Henrietta…

A spark had shone in her eyes when he'd suggested he beat her—anger, defiance, and spirit as if she relished the prospect of a fight. And the blood had rushed to his groin at the notion of going into battle with her.

She was so unlike every other woman! And she was a woman now. He'd seen it in her eyes—the primal need which reflected his own debilitating desire for her.

But her spark had dulled at her father's words. Not at the prospect of being beaten but at the promise of curtailment. When her father had told her that he was packing her off to her aunt with a view to marrying her off as soon as possible, the light in her eyes had died.

Marrying her off…

His gut twisted at the notion of her being sold in marriage— of that free spirit being caged. He wasn't so foolish as to lack understanding of the world or of marriage. He himself was looking for a biddable wife to meet his needs and produce an heir with the least amount of fuss.

But, for her…

Marriage would erode her soul. Some man, some damnable lucky bastard, would claim her as his without understanding the treasure he'd won. She would be forced to pledge obedience to him, and that fire he so admired would be doused.

And the real tragedy was—that man wouldn't be *him*.

He shook his head.

Bloody hell…

She bewitched him. Even the thought of her eroded his reason, causing the primal beast within him to roar with need of her.

Which just went to prove that she was the very last woman to make him a suitable wife.

He had no wish to consider the faintest prospect of having her in his life…

And in his bed.

Stop it!

He couldn't afford to think of his own selfish desires. He had another to consider.

Beatrice—his sweet, young cousin—the impressionable child who needed him most. It was Beatrice he needed to place at the forefront of his mind—to provide her with the love and guidance of a parent and to complete her education and entrée into Society.

He reached the main doors of Thorpe Hall, and they opened to reveal a single footman, who bowed. Giles allowed himself a wry smile as he entered. This Aunt Agnes, whoever she was, would have her hands full trying to shape Henrietta Redford into a debutante. Whereas his gentle cousin Beatrice would provide him with few challenges. A sweet, unassuming child eager to please was a far better prospect than a stubborn, headstrong hellion, who had, most likely, set Mother's recovery back several years with her recklessness.

But I'd rather have the hellion…

Silencing the treacherous voice which whispered of his innermost desires, he crossed the hallway and ascended the main staircase in search of his mother.

You've abandoned her.

The little hellion's words pricked at his conscience. Perhaps she was right. Having believed that the best treatment was the attention of the most expensive Harley Street doctor, Miss Redford's words made Giles doubt his wisdom. She challenged him—his ideals and purposes. But, yesterday, the challenge had struck home and pierced his conscience, needling at him last night when he lay in his bedchamber, trying not to think of her…

…or the sweet taste of her lips and that lush, ripe body…

…the pebbly little nipples that brushed against his arm as he held her close.

He reached the door leading to Mother's bedchamber and knocked.

Silence.

She must still be asleep—exhausted from her ordeal. He pushed the door open and drew a sharp breath.

The bedchamber was empty.

A ripple of fear threaded through him. Where was she? Had she succumbed to recklessness? He shook his head to dispel the vision of her broken body, but it remained in his mind's eye, as vivid as if it were yesterday.

His heart shuddered, and he reached out to the wall to steady himself, unable to fight the image which assaulted him.

Papa, his body twisted and crumpled beneath the carriage wheel— bloodied and battered, his head at an unnatural angle.

Sightless eyes staring up at him, their expression frozen with shock, mouth open in an airless scream.

Mother's body crumpled beside Father, trapped beneath the wreckage of the carriage, her face smeared with blood—the only evidence of life, her chest rising and falling in a shuddering breath while soft whimpers of pain escaped her lips.

Those whimpers had turned into wails of pain and despair as his once vibrant mother found herself a heartbroken, bedridden widow.

From that day he'd vowed to protect her and never to let her out again, lest she endanger herself. His mission had been to ensure she had the very best of care that money could buy, while he restored the estate from the near ruination it had suffered at Father's hands.

Sweet Lord—when her maid had tearfully confessed yesterday that she'd ventured into the garden, together with that reckless hellion who thought nothing of hanging upside down from the topmost branches of a tree or throwing herself into the lake…

"Mother!"

His voice echoed through the passage, bouncing off the walls as if to mock him.

He ran to the window overlooking the gardens, but there was no sign of her. Retracing his steps, he descended the main staircase. Then he heard it.

Voices and laughter.

Mother's laugh.

He followed the voices until he reached the door leading to the orangery. What the devil was going on? Like much of Thorpe Hall, the orangery had been closed off in favor of other more pressing matters, such as the constant cycle of repairs needed on the tenants' cottages.

But when he pushed the door open, he did not find an abandoned room. The orangery was filled with light and warmth.

The deep green foliage of orange trees lined the main wall—trees that Father had brought back from his travels—and Giles breathed in the sharp scent of citrus. Sunlight streamed across the orangery, illuminating the black and white tiles on the floor, which sparkled and shone. Through the windows, he could see the main garden, the bushes in need of clipping. Beyond, the landscape fell away in a gentle slope, leading to the forest on the horizon, and, in the distance, the hills were shrouded in a blue haze.

A round table laden with breakfast things occupied the center of the room, at which his mother sat, her back to him, her maid beside her.

He almost didn't recognize her. Dressed in an elegant silk gown, covered in a soft, white shawl, her hair had been piled atop her head in a series of elaborate curls.

She looked like she was hosting a tea party.

Like the vibrant woman he'd remembered as a boy—before the accident that had destroyed her life.

The maid picked up a teapot to fill her mistress's cup.

Giles stepped forward, his boots clicking against the tiles, and the two women looked round. The maid gave a shriek, and droplets of tea splashed onto her gown.

"L-lord Thorpe!" she cried. "Forgive me. We…or, rather, I…"

Mother held up her hand. "Annie, my dear, there's no need to be so flustered." She gestured toward Giles, squinting. "Come here, my boy. Won't you join us for breakfast?"

"You're dining with your maid?" Giles flinched at the peevish tone of his voice.

"You expect me to dine alone?"

He stood, rooted to the spot, and she gave a sigh of exasperation—a sigh she'd often turned on him when he was a child, being stubborn over something or other, usually when he'd been unable to get his own way.

"Are you going to stand there all morning?" she asked. "You'll make the place look dreadfully untidy. And it's most inconsiderate of you to expect me to have to turn around to address you. Come and sit where I can see you properly."

He hesitated, and she let out a huff. "Infuriating boy! Why must you always be so single-minded? Can't you indulge me just this once?"

He approached the table and took the empty chair. The table had been set for three.

"Have you been expecting me?" he asked.

"I wouldn't presume to expect *anything* from you," she said, "but I hoped you'd join me. I see so little of you and, infuriating though you are, I wish to remedy that." She gestured to the teapot. "Tea?" she asked. "Assuming, of course, dear Annie's left any. You gave her quite the fright, didn't he, Annie, dear?"

Annie flushed and rose to her feet. "Forgive me, your ladyship, I must see to my duties."

"Oh, very well." Mother sighed. Giles stood, then he winced as she slapped his arm.

"Not so fast, young man," she said. "You're always rushing about. Can't you spare a few minutes for your mother?"

"I have much to do," he said, "not least of which is to send for Dr. Odgers."

"For what purpose?"

"To examine you for any ill effects after yesterday," he said, "When I saw you outside, I…"

"But, you *didn't* see me," she said. "Not with any clarity."

"I only want the best for you, Mother," he said. "Dr. Odgers is the best…"

"Yes, yes," she said, exasperation in her tone. "He's the best surgeon in Harley Street, comes highly recommended, and costs a small fortune. But should *I* not have a say in my welfare? Yesterday was one of the happiest days I've spent here since your dear papa's passing, thanks to that lovely young woman. Yet, you chased her off the grounds as if she were a common criminal."

He opened his mouth to protest, then stopped. Mother was right. Henrietta Redford had, he conceded, acted out of kindness, not out of any desire to make mischief. It had been easier to convince himself that she'd intended to cause trouble. But the only trouble was the maelstrom of desire swirling in his mind.

His desire for her.

It was for *that* that he had sought vengeance and betrayed her to her father, knowing she'd be punished for it. Not because he believed her to be evil, but because he wanted her to suffer the punishment for his own desire.

And, given the stricken look in her eyes, he'd succeeded.

A delicate hand touched his arm, and he looked up into Mother's blue gaze.

"My dear son," she said, moisture glistening in her eyes. "I know you want the best for me, and I love you for it. But I ask you to trust me to decide for myself what's best."

"Which is?"

"Air," she said. "Air and light." She gestured about the orangery. "Do you know I can see enough in here to move about on my own? The shapes are blurred, aye, but the contrast of light and dark, together with memories of this room, enables me to find my way about. And yesterday…" she broke off, and a tear splashed onto her cheek, "Yesterday, I saw the water on the lake—the flashes of light, forming patterns which danced like faeries in the wind."

"Would you like to go outside today?" he asked.

"Yes," she said. "And tomorrow—and each day thereafter. I want to breathe the air again and feel alive."

He shook his head. "Dr. Odgers…"

"…can remain in London for all I care," she interrupted. "We have a perfectly good man in Dr. West in the village who, I'm sure, would oblige me on occasion should I need medicine. I need laughter and light, Giles. And company."

"But what of the danger to your health?"

She gave an unladylike snort. "We all risk our health simply by getting out of bed each morning. The world is filled with danger. But, as your dear papa and I taught you as a child, the way to grow strong is to face that danger head-on. If you hide away, then it has conquered you."

"But we must be wary of danger," he said.

She smiled. "I'm not saying that danger shouldn't be respected, Giles. I think we can both agree that your papa—God rest his soul—courted danger. But we must all take risks if we are to truly *live*." She patted his hand. "Even you."

"You wish me to place you in danger?"

"Of course not!" She laughed.

His heart leaped with joy to hear her laugh—the rich sound of mirth that he'd always loved when he was a boy. It was her laugh which had ensnared Father's heart. Father had once told him that from the moment he'd heard Mother laugh, he'd vowed that there was no other woman for him.

For a fleeting moment, the laugh of another reverberated in his mind—the laugh of pure joy emanating from the uppermost branches of a tree.

Her laugh—his little tomboy hellion.

"When does poor Beatrice arrive?" Mother asked.

"Tomorrow."

"Methinks she'll have as much need for fresh air and laughter as I, poor child. Will she have her come-out this Season?"

"I thought to defer it to next year," he said. "Given the circumstances, it seems cruel to remove her from the only home she's ever known, to thrust her into the marriage mart shortly after. I would not have her believe she's unwelcome in our home."

"Of course not," she said. "Dear, sweet child! Perhaps, when she has her come-out, I can accompany you both to London. She will, after all, require a chaperone. And widowed aunts make the best chaperones. I only hope she'll not mind having an invalid for company."

"Mother, you're no invalid."

And she wasn't—not anymore. Today, and, he had to admit, yesterday, he'd caught a glimpse of what his mother once was.

And he had one person to thank for that.

Henrietta Redford—the person who, most likely, irrevocably hated him.

CHAPTER TEN

HENRIETTA STARED AT her half-filled trunk, a pair of slippers in her hand, then she cast her gaze about her chamber.

Would she ever see it again? Tomorrow, she was to be packed off to Aunt Agnes, and from there, taken to London to prepare for her enslavement.

Or, as Aunt Agnes called it, a *respectable marriage*.

Curse him!

She flung the slippers at the wall just as the door opened.

Papa stood in the doorway and flinched as they narrowly missed his head.

"I see you've yet to finish packing."

She sat on the bed with a sigh.

"I only want what's best for you," he said. "Please understand."

"But I don't want to go to Aunt's," she protested. "I don't want to learn how to walk properly in a pretty dress just to attract the attention of a man."

"It's the world we live in, Hen."

Hen. He'd called her Hen. His anger had softened—perhaps enough to persuade him to change his mind.

She held out her hand, and he took it.

"Papa…"

"No."

"You don't know what I was going to say."

"I do," he said. "I can see it in your face. You've never been able to conceal your emotions, Henrietta." He patted her hand, then sat on the bed and drew his arm round her.

"That's one thing you will learn at your aunt's."

She snorted. "What—subterfuge?"

"If you wish to call it so," he said. "There's much to be said for brutal honesty, but as you reach adulthood, you'll learn that total frankness can be taken advantage of by the unscrupulous, particularly in London."

"Then why must I go?"

"You want to have a home and children of your own, don't you? For that, you need a husband."

"I don't want a husband who needs to be deceived in order to like me."

He let out a laugh. "My dear child, who said anything about deceit? I would not have you married off to a rake who will make you unhappy or a man who wants you only for your fortune. I want you to marry a good, honest man."

"Then should I not apply honesty myself?"

"It is not for the purposes of securing a man that I wish you to be schooled in the customs of Society, my dear," he said, "but out of a wish to protect you from men who would otherwise take advantage. There is merit in protecting your heart and your reputation by concealing your true feelings."

"I don't see why I should marry at all."

"Because I have no son," he said. "You need a good, honest husband whom I can trust to run the business and take care of you when I'm gone."

"I can shift for myself," she replied, "and I can run the business. You said yourself I had mastered the art of inlaying wood."

"There's more to running a business than marquetry," he said. "Running a business comes with a huge responsibility, not only to yourself but to others. And you're too reckless."

"I thought that's what you loved about me."

He smiled, but the sadness remained in his eyes. "I do love

you, Hen," he said. "A little spirit is all well and good, but you must learn to temper your wildness in order to survive. The world is a den of wolves, and you, my dear, are a little rabbit who seeks to stray too far from the warren. I would not have you devoured."

She withdrew her hand. "You make it sound like I'm weak."

"No, not weak, Henrietta," he said softly, "but a woman in a man's world is considered easy prey. Your aunt is the best person to teach you how to navigate the murky waters of Society in order to survive it."

"Can you not reconsider?" she asked. "Give me another chance. Let me prove to you that I can temper my behavior. Let me help you with your work. I'd rather learn about the manufacture of furniture than how to walk properly in a pretty gown. Then I can help you with the business."

He shook his head. "No, my dear. As Lord Thorpe pointed out, you're not a child anymore. I've neglected that fact for far too long already. You're a young woman, and it's time that young woman was turned into a lady."

He rose to his feet.

"Why don't you go for a walk outside?" he suggested. "It's a beautiful day. I'll ask Tilly to finish your packing."

"One last day of freedom?"

He sighed. "One day you'll understand that by equipping you for the real world, I'm giving you freedom, not taking it away."

She reached for her shawl, and he caught her hand.

"You're my only child, Henrietta, and I love you. I would not have you married to a beast."

"Then why have me marry at all?"

"It's the way of the world." He kissed her forehead, then exited the room.

The way of the world!

Aye—the world of men. Men such as Giles Thorpe.

How could she both hate and desire him at the same time?

All her frustrations and fury at her situation centered around him. If it weren't for him, she might have remained here—free, at the home she loved.

Very well—he'd succeeded in having her banished, but not before she took vengeance, no matter how petty.

She caught sight of the chamber pot beneath her bed and smiled to herself as an idea formed in her mind.

She picked up the chamber pot, exited her bedchamber, then stepped outside.

If Papa had given her a few more hours of freedom, then she'd use them to her full advantage.

As she walked along the lane leading to Thorpe Hall, she caught sight of two familiar figures.

"Henry!" they cried in unison.

"I thought you were in London," she said.

"We're home for the weekend before traveling to Oxford," Johnny said. "I hear you're off to your aunt's to learn how to be a lady."

"*Lady!*" Phillip scoffed. "As if *you* could ever be turned into a lady!"

"As if I'd *want* to!" she retorted, giving him a push. "You only find ladies desirable because they're biddable little weaklings who'll cater to your every whim."

"That's not very friendly," he replied. "We came to say good-bye."

"To wish you luck," Johnny added. "Do you fancy one last adventure before you become a lady and forget all about us?"

"I'm embarking on an adventure of my own," she said.

"Is that why you're carrying that piss-pot?" Phillip wrinkled his nose.

"What do you intend to do with it?" Johnny asked.

"I'm going to stick it on the head of the statue at the entrance to Thorpe Hall."

Johnny let out a laugh, but Phillip shook his head. "Rather childish, isn't it?"

"As if I care!" she cried."

"You'll get into trouble. He'll know it's you."

"I cannot think of a worse punishment than the one that's already being meted out," she said. "So, I might as well have some fun. There's nothing more they can do to me."

She eyed Phillip with suspicion. "You won't tell on me, would you?"

"Of course not," Phillip said. "I'm a man of honor. If you like, we'll be your lookouts. Besides, you'll need help. Those statues are awfully tall."

"I don't know…" She hesitated.

"Come on," Johnny coaxed, linking his arm through hers. "One last adventure before we all grow up. Phillip, carry the piss-pot, will you?"

Phillip took the chamber pot, and the three of them set off toward Thorpe Hall.

The building looked even more imposing approaching it from the main drive—the window a row of eyes that frowned darkly at the three of them. As they drew near, Henrietta's resolve almost crumbled, but Johnny's enthusiasm spurred her on. The twins might not be perfect, but they were the only friends she had.

The statues stood impassive, staring out at them, blissfully unaware of their fate.

"All right, shall we advance?" Johnny asked.

Phillip handed the chamber pot back to Henrietta.

"I'll stay here."

"Too scared to come closer?" Johnny taunted.

"I can see the windows from here," Phillip replied. "I'm the lookout, aren't I?"

"Come on, Johnny," Henrietta said. "If Phillip's too much of a coward, then we don't want him with us."

She approached one of the two statues and eyed up the plinth.

"Do you want a bunk up?" Johnny asked. "You can climb on my shoulders. I won't look up your skirt—promise."

"I'll hit you over the head with this pot if you do," she retorted. "You can give me a bunk up with your hands, as if I were mounting a horse. I should be able to get a purchase higher up, on the shoulders."

"Get on with it, you cowards!" Phillip hissed.

"*Cowards*, eh?" Johnny scoffed. "Says the one who's hiding at a safe distance while others do the derring-do. Come on, Henry."

He bent over and cupped his hands, lacing his fingers together. Placing a hand on his shoulder, Henrietta stepped into the makeshift stirrup and launched herself upward, grasping onto the statue's shoulders, wrapping her legs round the torso to keep herself from slipping.

"Are you secure?" he asked.

"Yes," she said. "Pass me the pot."

He handed it up to her. Squeezing her thighs round the statue's torso, she reached up with both hands and placed the chamber pot on the statue's head.

Then she froze. She was at eye level with the statue, and for the first time, she looked at his face. Cold featureless eyes met her gaze, and a thread of apprehension rippled through her.

The statue was the image of Giles Thorpe.

It was not unheard of for families to adorn their estates with statues of themselves or of their ancestors, but the notion hadn't unsettled her.

Until now.

She stared defiantly back, as if the statue were the embodiment of her nemesis.

"What did you expect?" she said.

The statue stared blankly at her, as if Lord Thorpe himself faced her, and she could swear she saw an expression of contempt in its eyes.

"I'll never be a debutante," she hissed. "I'll fight it, no matter who tries to oppress me—Papa, Aunt, or you. I pray that I'll never lose my liberty, and..." she pulled a face, "...whatever unfortunate woman you choose for a wife—I pray she'll give you hell."

If it were me…

Her heart shuddered, and with a cry, she lost her grip and slipped, but she regained her purchase and clung to the statue.

"What are you doing?" Johnny asked.

"Practicing deportment," she retorted. "What the devil do you think I'm doing you fool!"

"Johnny!" Phillip's voice echoed across the lawn.

"It's all right, she's not fallen off!" Johnny replied.

"Someone's coming! A man on a horse. Come quick—it's Thorpe!"

Johnny turned and broke into a run toward his brother.

"Hey!" Henrietta cried out. "Come back and help me down!"

But when she glanced over her shoulder, all she could see were two retreating figures. There was nothing for it, so she had to jump.

Releasing her grip on the statue, she let herself fall, bending her knees as she landed to lessen the impact. But a spike of pain shot through her left ankle, and she pitched forward and tumbled onto the gravel path.

She struggled to her feet, wincing, as she wiped her hands. Small shards of gravel were embedded in her palm.

"Hey! What are you doing?" a voice roared in anger. She glanced toward the drive. The unmistakable silhouette of Giles Thorpe dominated the view, sitting atop his horse, Thunder.

But his attention wasn't focused on her. He was addressing two figures standing side by side. She slipped behind the statue. With luck, he'd not notice her.

But luck was not her friend today. One of the figures—Phillip, most likely—gestured in her direction. Then the two of them sprinted off. The rider spurred his horse toward Henrietta, and she ran for her life.

Her escape route down the drive was cut off, so she ran round the side of the building, until she entered a side garden, surrounded by a tall wall overlooked by her tree.

As she reached the wall, footsteps crunched on the gravel

path behind her. Hitching up her skirts, she climbed onto the wall, digging her fingers in the gaps around the stones to gain a purchase. The indents in the wall were just large enough to fit the toe of her boots, though they'd be horribly scratched. Papa would be furious, but with a little of Tilly's boot polish, he'd be none the wiser.

The footsteps drew nearer, and a voice called out. Despite trying to convince herself of her defiance and determination, she had no wish to be caught.

Not by him.

Her foot slipped against the wall, and she cursed herself.

Concentrate, you fool!

Why did the mere thought of him distract her from rational thought—even when she needed to escape?

She looked up and almost cried with relief. A branch was nearly within reach. Just a little further up the wall and she'd have it in her grasp. She launched herself upward, grasped the branch, and hauled herself up and swinging her legs over until she straddled it.

It was the same branch that overlooked Lady Thorpe's window.

For a brief moment, a sense of shame overcame her. Though she relished the notion of needling Giles Thorpe, she had no wish to upset his mother.

And, while she might declare to the world that she cared little for what the rest of Society thought of her, she found that she cared a great deal for Lady Thorpe's good opinion.

The footsteps came closer.

But she was safe. With a laugh of triumph, she shuffled along the branch, toward the tree trunk. In a matter of moments, she'd overlook the other side of the wall and could jump down and run to safety unobserved.

Crack!

The branch gave way beneath her.

With a cry, she reached forward, fingers clawing in the air in a futile attempt to reach the next branch, but there was nothing but air in front of her. The branch swung out and crashed against the wall, and she slid to the ground.

The last thing she saw was the dappled light through the leaves before she landed on the ground with a jolt, and an explosion of pain cast her into oblivion.

CHAPTER ELEVEN

WHEN HENRIETTA OPENED her eyes, she was surrounded by darkness. Panic overcame her, and she tried to move, but a sharp spike of pain tore through her head, and she let out a whimper.

A gentle hand touched her shoulder.

Henrietta blinked, and her eyes adjusted to the light. A face stared back at her.

But it was not the face she both feared and yearned to see.

It was a woman dressed in a plain gray gown with soft brown hair tied in a neat bun and kindness twinkling in her hazel eyes. She looked familiar, but Henrietta couldn't place her.

"What's happened?" she asked. "Who…who are you?"

"Shh, my dear," the woman said in hushed tones. "I'm the doctor's wife. I don't believe we've been properly introduced."

"Mrs. West?"

The woman nodded. "Aye, that's right."

Henrietta let out a giggle. Aunt Agnes would likely have a fit of apoplexy at the impropriety of being introduced in such a manner.

The woman eyed her with suspicion. "You've taken a nasty tumble and hit your head."

"I'm of sound mind if that's what you're concerned about," Henrietta said. "I was just wondering what my aunt would think of me behaving improperly."

"Ah." Mrs. West nodded, and she gave a warm smile that illuminated her features. "Is not throwing oneself out of a tree a skill that a young lady needs to perfect?"

Henrietta struggled to sit up. "How did you know…?"

"Here—let me."

Mrs. West placed her arm around Henrietta and helped her to sit.

Henrietta eyed her surroundings. She was in a bedchamber. The room was small and furnished in soft muted tones. A vase of roses by the window was the only splash of color.

Most ladies would, no doubt, criticize the room for being plain and unadorned. But Henrietta loved its simplicity.

Her shawl lay at the foot of the bed, neatly folded, and her boots had been placed on the floor side by side—with no evidence of a scuff on the toes.

Next to the bed was a washstand and bowl and a small vial. The woman reached for the vial and shook it.

"Are you in pain?"

"A slight headache, that's all." Henrietta eyed the bottle. "I don't need laudanum. How did I get here?"

"You were found after your accident."

"Who found me?"

"I'm afraid I can't say that. But you're in safe hands with me."

"Is Dr. West…"

"My husband's out, I'm afraid," the woman said. "He's tending to Lady Thorpe."

"*Lady Thorpe?*" Henrietta asked. "But I thought Dr. Odgers…"

"It's a new appointment—just yesterday, in fact." Mrs. West looked as if she was going to continue, then she shook her head.

Henrietta shifted position and winced at a spike of pain in her foot. She pulled her skirt up.

Her ankle had been neatly bandaged.

"It's just a sprain," Mrs. West said, "but you may want to keep the bandage on for a few days."

"Thank you."

"Would you like some tea?"

Henrietta shook her head. "I should be getting home. Papa will be worried."

"There's no need," the woman said. "I've sent my house-keeper with a message to say that you took a tumble and I invited you in to shelter from the weather." She gestured to the window where the rain was forming rivulets of water which trickled down in jagged paths. A twinkle of mischief shone in her gaze. "As you see, 'tis the truth."

What was the woman about?

Mrs. West let out a laugh. "There's no harm in a little adventure. Of course, my Simon and I are biased in that respect. I relish my freedom and sense of adventure and find it refreshing to see that spirit in a young woman."

"But you're *married!*" Henrietta exclaimed.

"Do you think the marriage state curbs a woman's sense of adventure?"

"My freedom will be curtailed as soon as I don a bridal gown."

Mrs. West shook her head. "Not necessarily, my dear. You just need to make sure you accomplish one objective."

"Which is?"

"Choose the right husband."

"If only it were that simple!"

"There's plenty of sensible young men in the world," Mrs. West said. "Granted, they take a little more rooting out among all the coxcombs and rakes, but they exist, nonetheless. Take my Simon, for example. Kind, honorable, and more than willing to take my advice. Had I married a gentleman, I might have festered in a drawing room somewhere. But in marrying a kind, hard-working man, I was able to stretch my boundaries, not restrict them." She took Henrietta's hand. "You seem a sensible and intelligent young woman," she said. "Use that good sense to make the right choices—those born of reason, rather than emotion. Only then will you be able to retain your freedom.

Adventure can be attained in moderation."

"How do you know all this?" Henrietta asked. "I've not met you before today."

Mrs. West averted her gaze. "My husband has spoken of you," she said. "He told me that one of his first tasks after he came to live here was to tend to your mother in her confinement—and that you were a handful even then. He also said that he tended to you when you broke your leg, when you were a child, though you were, perhaps, too young to remember." She took Henrietta's hand. "It was, I believe, shortly after your mother passed."

A distant memory rippled through Henrietta's mind...the desperate need to secure Papa's attention after Mama had gone...the staircase...the feeling of exhilaration as she'd bumped down the stairs as if flying through the air...then an explosion of pain...the doctor's kind brown eyes...and gentle hands carrying her to her chamber.

She closed her eyes, and her mind was assaulted by another image, an image that was closer, somehow ...clear blue eyes staring at her with intensity...concern shimmering in their depths, followed by an expression of such tenderness, that it made her heart ache...

...and those soft, whispered words.

Be still, my little hellion. You're safe with me, my love.

She shook her head, cursing her weakness. It was a dream, that was all—a silly dream, born of a childish wish fulfillment.

Heat spread across her cheeks. What must Mrs. West think of her? Papa was right. She needed to curb her recklessness—learn how to survive in a world where adventure in a woman was frowned upon.

Very well—she would succumb to Aunt's tutelage and learn how to preen, pose, and dance.

But on her own terms. Short of chaining her to her bed or locking her in her chamber, Aunt could not prevent her from seeking a little adventure. Papa had indulged her as a child. She only needed to discover what could be used to persuade her aunt to indulge her as a young woman.

She swung her legs over the edge of the bed and stood up, testing her balance. Save a slight throbbing in her head and a dull ache in her ankle, she was unharmed.

"Thank you, Mrs. West," she said. "I must return home."

"The weather's frightful outside. I'm sure your father would never forgive me if I allowed you to place yourself in danger."

"I don't mind the rain," Henrietta said. "And besides, you've done me more good than you know. When Dr. West returns, please thank him for carrying me here."

"But he didn't..." Mrs. West hesitated, then nodded. "Of course, I will," she said. "And he'd never forgive me if I didn't accompany you home." She met Henrietta's gaze, and the smile of mischief returned. "Your Papa will wish to have a full account of your little adventure today. We might go now if you'd like to make yourself ready?"

Henrietta nodded, and Mrs. West exited the chamber.

She reached for her boots and put them on, barely wincing as she slipped her bandaged foot in. While she laced them up, Mrs. West returned with two umbrellas, and they set off for home.

Though she'd been reckless in her final adventure, Henrietta had to admit it had taught her a useful lesson.

That it might be possible to maintain her freedom. Perhaps, if she showed Aunt that she was willing to learn how to behave in Society, then her surrender to captivity might be deferred.

DAWN HAD BROKEN over an hour ago.

If only life were that simple! If a man needed only to secure his territory, defend it against marauders, and find a mate for life.

Like the swans on the lake.

Granted, his fate was better than most. With a title from

ancient lineage and an expansive estate, Giles was aware that he was the target of many grasping mamas who'd be fighting to secure his attention on behalf of their daughters. He'd have the pick of the dowries to restore Thorpe Hall with.

Uncle's bequest was enough to begin the works. And, in little Beatrice, he'd be able to provide Mother with a companion. Beatrice would bring youth and merriment—tempered with good breeding, of course—to Thorpe Hall. And Mother would school her into the perfect debutante. His cousin would be the jewel of the Season, and he'd have his pick of brides.

Why, then, did he feel like a swan whose true mate had been ripped from him?

And at his own hand?

But he had another to think of now. Beatrice needed him, and he was on his way to bring her to Thorpe Hall. It was just a coincidence that he happened to set off today when he knew that *she* was leaving to stay with her aunt.

You're deluding yourself.

He silenced the voice in his mind and steered his mount to-ward Portdown Lodge, Mr. Redford's home. As he turned the corner in the lane, he spotted a coach-and-four. Two footmen were securing a trunk to the back with straps, while the horses stamped on the ground, puffs of mist dissipating from their nostrils in the cold morning air.

Then she emerged from the house, dressed in a white muslin gown and a dark blue redingote in a military style. Instead of the miserable girl he'd expected to see, he was rewarded with another sight entirely—a fierce woman sallying forth with her head held high.

There's my hellion.

He smiled to himself. Any pity he might have felt for her was replaced by pity for her aunt.

Her father appeared beside her and led her to the carriage. She clung to his arm, favoring her right foot, and climbed in, then he followed.

Then the carriage set off. Giles guided his mount into the verge and watched them approach. The driver slowed the horses as the carriage passed alongside him. Giles glanced at the window, but the reflection of the sunlight obscured the view within.

Did she see him? Did those chocolate eyes blaze with anger? Or had she turned her head away in indifference, looking toward her future?

He raised his hand in salute. Once past him, the driver picked up the pace.

Just before the carriage reached the turn in the lane, he caught a glimpse of a hand, pushing the window open, and a head appeared, followed by a pair of shoulders as one of the occupants leaned out. Though she was silhouetted against the sunlight, he'd recognize her anywhere.

Then the carriage turned at the end of the lane and disappeared.

She was no longer his concern.

And a good thing, too. Who would want such a hellion in his life, plaguing him day and night?

I would.

"No," he whispered to himself, fighting the treacherous voice in his mind. He had another to concern himself with. Beatrice.

Miss Redford was a distraction he could never afford. In all likelihood, he'd never see her again.

CHAPTER TWELVE

London, July 1814

"SIT UP STRAIGHT, child! How many times must I tell you?"

Henrietta rolled her eyes and shifted uncomfortably in her chair. After a week of rain, the day had dawned bright and fresh, yet Aunt Agnes was only concerned with deportment and decorum. Henrietta ached to venture outside for a walk in the park, and at this hour, there would be nobody about to see her or chastise her for going unchaperoned.

But Aunt, as usual, insisted she remain indoors—"to preserve your complexion, though I quite despair of those freckles on your nose."

She reached for another slice of bacon.

"Henrietta!" Aunt cried. "You've had four slices already. Why would you need a fifth?"

"I don't know, Aunt," Henrietta said. "Might it be because I'm hungry?"

"Hen," Papa growled, though a smile twinkled in his eyes.

"I *am* hungry."

"Henrietta is rather tall, Agnes," Papa said, "and she's always had a healthy appetite."

Aunt Agnes tutted. "You're too soft on her, Benjamin. A lady should not be seen to eat too much."

"Why not?"

"Because it's improper. A lady must rise above the baser animal instincts observed in the lower classes."

Henrietta giggled. "You mean instincts such as…"

"Hen!" Papa cried.

"Benjamin, she'll never become a lady if she doesn't learn proper decorum," Aunt said.

"She'll make do," Papa replied.

He exchanged a smile with Henrietta. After more than a year under Aunt's watchful eyes, she had learned how to walk, talk, eat properly, and to squeeze her frame into the tightest of corsets. Aunt declared that she almost found her "quite pretty," but that she was too *athletic* to attract the notice of a man of any worth. Men of worth wanted women who were soulless, colorless, characterless, and small enough to dwindle into nothing when their husbands so desired. Whereas Henrietta, no matter how much powder Aunt applied on her face, always had flushed cheeks, eyes that were overly bright, and she fidgeted too much.

Papa had, eventually, relented a little, concluding that Henrietta could never fully temper her free spirit—or, her *unruly savagery*, as Aunt put it. And, in turn, she had promised to behave—in public, at least—in a manner befitting a young lady, and to accede to any of Papa's requests.

Which meant that, provided she did as he asked, Papa turned a blind eye to her indulging in an occasional unchaperoned walk or—heaven forbid—practicing with her sword in their garden, away from prying eyes, as long as Aunt Agnes never found out.

The two of them, Henrietta and Papa, had reached a truce. On recognizing the folly of having too much freedom, she had earned herself the benefit of having a little freedom—provided she used it wisely. And, as Papa pointed out to her, therein lay the difference between a child and an adult.

So, she indulged Aunt Agnes's little whims, by presenting herself at parties and balls and smiling at the appropriate moments.

Mrs. West's words from two years ago still echoed in her

mind—words to live by.

Choose the right husband.

And it certainly wouldn't be Giles Thorpe. She flushed with shame at the memory of their encounter last night, at Lady Houghton's ball—not just because of the wine stain on her gown, which Aunt Agnes had said brought about the necessity for yet another visit to the modiste—but because of the unwelcome, yet delicious sensations he'd stirred in her.

And, of course, his disdain and indifference.

Curse him!

Giles Thorpe…

"Lord Thorpe…"

She glanced up at the mention of his name. Aunt Agnes sliced through her bacon—her *seventh* slice—with relish.

"He's the catch of the Season," Aunt said. "He's already rumored to have secured the attention of the Fairchild girl."

"Who?" Papa spoke in a bored tone as he picked up his paper. Society gossip was never his favorite topic. But Aunt, who had long despaired of Henrietta showing any interest in who courted whom, was determined to find an audience.

"Oh, *you* know, Benjamin. Lord Fairchild's youngest. Irma, I believe her name is. She's rumored to have thirty thousand, so will be first in the running."

"Oh," Father said. "That plain little thing I saw in the park last week."

"She's quite pretty," Aunt said.

Papa winked at Henrietta, then rustled his paper. "Don't you recall my saying what a forgettable-looking creature she was, Agnes?"

"Benjamin, I recall no such thing!"

"Perhaps her beauty is enhanced by her thirty thousand?" Henrietta suggested.

"She has a title," Aunt said. "Which is why *you*, my dear child, must work harder at securing a match, lest you be known only for your shortcomings."

Ignoring the insult, Henrietta reached for another slice of bacon. "Irma has a rival," she said. "I saw Lord Thorpe strutting around with the youngest Miss Howard at the ball last night."

Papa lowered his paper and met her gaze. "You didn't tell me you'd seen him. Is he well?"

"He seemed so, in health at least…" Henrietta said, "…if not in temper," she muttered to herself.

"How many times have I told you not to mumble!" Aunt Agnes cried. "Enunciate your words properly." She picked up her teacup, took a delicate sip, then set it aside.

"Miss Juliette Howard is a beautiful creature," she said. "I'll wager she'll make a match before her elder sister."

"Eleanor?" Henrietta asked.

"That's the one," Aunt said. "Now, *there's* an unpleasant creature. Always frowning, and no conversation about her."

"Eleanor is my friend, Aunt."

"You'll not go far in Society with friends like *that*," Aunt said. "You'd do better if Lady Irma permitted you into her circle. Or perhaps the Thorpe girl, now she's been presented at court."

"Lord Thorpe's cousin?" Papa asked.

"Yes," Aunt replied. "Lady Beatrice. She's already being raved about. By all accounts, she's the epitome of elegance and grace and is bound to upstage even Lady Irma at her first dance. I'm sure she'll not be averse to befriending *you*, Henrietta, if you only made a little more effort. Perhaps we could invite her for tea?"

Henrietta snorted. The last thing she wanted was to befriend a prim, pampered little miss whom all of Society raved about.

"What do you think, Benjamin?" Aunt persisted. "Did you see anything of her over the winter?"

"I did, actually," Papa said. "She seemed a very pleasant, well-mannered young woman." He nodded toward Henrietta. "You could do far worse in your choice of friend, you know."

"But…"

"Henrietta," he interrupted. "Remember our agreement. I think you should cultivate a friendship with Lady Beatrice. After all, we're neighbors in Surrey. And, of course, as an orphan, she commands our compassion."

"Are you saying I should befriend her out of *pity*?"

"You should befriend her in order to further your advancement in Society," Aunt Agnes said.

Henrietta let out a laugh, and Papa struggled to hide a smile.

Aunt narrowed her eyes, then pushed back her chair and rose to her feet in a dramatic gesture.

"I have a megrim," she said.

Which was Papa's cue to take her aside, out of Henrietta's earshot, in order to listen to a catalogue of Henrietta's faults and Aunt's proposals for their rectification.

"You must take your rest, Agnes," Papa replied, setting his paper down. "Come, let me escort you to your chamber."

"You're too kind, Benjamin."

Papa stood and offered his arm to Aunt Agnes, who clung to it with an exaggerated gesture. Before they exited the breakfast room, he glanced back at Henrietta and winked.

Henrietta waited five minutes, then grabbed her shawl and slipped outside. If Papa could weather Aunt's many criticisms of her and keep her occupied while Henrietta indulged in a little freedom in the park, then she'd willingly befriend any young lady of Papa's choosing.

Even the unpalatable Lady Beatrice Thorpe.

As Henrietta had anticipated, the park was almost empty at this hour. Henrietta made her way to the secluded corner where she had previously discovered a delightful oak tree with sturdy branches. The lowest branch was beyond even the reach of the tallest man, but a split in the tree trunk about three feet off the ground would, she was certain, provide her with a foothold to enable her to climb high enough to reach the branch, and swing herself up into the center of the tree.

She pressed her palm against the trunk, running her fingertips over the contours of the bark. Her body vibrated with pent-up energy and the urge to swing herself up among the branches. But she hesitated. Aunt had lectured her on the dangers of improper behavior in public and though, to Henrietta, Society and its rules was something to laugh at rather than adhere to, she had no wish to disappoint Papa. She would have to seek out adventure where she could, in the knowledge that her circle of freedom was considerably more restricted in London than in the country.

With a sigh, she leaned against the tree trunk. Then, she closed her eyes and grew still, savoring the sensations of the park—the texture of the bark under her fingertips, the rush of the wind in the trees, and the occasional cry of a water bird in the distance. It provided a much-needed respite from the sharp twitterings of ladies in drawing rooms or Aunt's needling admonishments.

After a while, she heard voices—early visitors to the park. It was time to return home. Aunt should have finished relaying all her faults to Papa by now and might be looking for her. She had secured an appointment with the modiste later that morning, and it was worth avoiding a scolding not to be late.

Sighing, she stepped back from the tree and wiped the dust off her hands. Then she froze.

The voices were coming closer.

She backed away, then heard footsteps approach.

She was cut off, with nowhere to hide.

She slipped between two rhododendron bushes, and pushed through to the other side, emerging on the main path which led to the exit.

That was close.

She rounded a corner, then collided with what felt like a solid wall.

"Watch where you're going!" a voice cried. A deep voice. A familiar voice.

Two strong hands clasped her shoulders, and Henrietta found herself face to face with a broad male chest.

No—it can't be…

Surely she couldn't be that unlucky.

But the fluttering of her heart said otherwise. Her body had always reacted to his closeness.

Giles Thorpe.

She tilted her head back and looked up into a pair of eyes the color of cold sapphires, bearing the same expression of contempt she'd seen last night at Lady Houghton's ball.

Heat bloomed in her cheeks, and she became painfully aware of a smudge of dirt on her gown.

"Miss Redford. I might have known."

She lowered her gaze, and her humiliation intensified as she caught sight of a rhododendron leaf poking out from the neckline of her gown. With as much dignity as she could muster, she plucked it out from between her breasts and tossed it aside.

Then a female voice spoke—sharp and shrewish, laced with disdain.

"Aren't you going to introduce me to your…*friend?*"

Oh Lord…

Lord Thorpe was not alone. A woman clung to his arm.

She was the most beautiful creature Henrietta had seen. Her delicate features and porcelain skin doubtless attracted the attention of every suitor in London. Sharp blue eyes glared at her, and a pretty elfin-like nose wrinkled in disgust. Honey-gold hair had been fashioned into an elaborate hairstyle, dotted with flowers, with a single thick curl trailing down her neck and perfectly placed on her shoulder, in stark contrast to Henrietta's hair which had already worked loose. Standing behind the couple was an older woman dressed in a plain blue gown, her iron-gray hair scraped back into a severe style.

There was no need for introductions. Juliette Howard outshone every other woman in London with her exquisite beauty. Henrietta had already suffered her company when she'd visited

Eleanor Howard for tea. She glanced at the older woman—Juliette's chaperone, presumably. An old governess, perhaps?

Poor woman—to have spent her years in the company of that unpleasant creature!

"Miss Redford," Lord Thorpe said, "may I have the honor of introducing you to Miss Juliette Howard?"

He did not introduce Juliette's chaperone—most likely because, like all aristocrats, he considered individuals who earned their own living to be beneath him.

"I've already been overwhelmed by the honor," Henrietta said. "But perhaps Miss Howard has forgotten."

She dipped into a curtsey, but Juliette merely inclined her head and wrinkled her nose further.

"Are you enjoying a walk in the park, Miss Howard?" Henrietta asked.

"We are, indeed," Juliette replied, spite glittering in her expression. "The wildlife in particular is an intriguing sight. Even in the midst of London, one can never predict from which bush the next animal will spring."

The insult was not unexpected, but, perhaps with his scrupulousness when it came to propriety, Lord Thorpe might admonish his companion.

Instead, a smile spread across his lips—the lips which had once kissed her.

Not only did he dislike her, but he had no qualms about showing his contempt in public.

CHAPTER THIRTEEN

G ILES DREW IN a deep breath.

The sight of that untamed creature bursting from the midst of the bushes had set his pulse racing.

His breeches had grown uncomfortably tight, and as she collided with him, he was unable to resist the urge to grasp her by the shoulders.

Desire overcame him, along with an aftertaste of shame at the way he'd treated her last night at Lady Houghton's ball. First, he had knocked into her, causing her to spill punch down her dress, then he'd dismissed her with contempt.

But he'd done it to curb the surge of powerful lust which had almost overcome him when he'd caught sight of the shadowy nipples beneath her soaked gown—delicious little peaks which made his mouth water.

What might it have been like to taste them!

And they were before him now. Her chest rose and fell with each breath, causing the two little peaks to shift against her gown, just below the neckline. He had only to dip his finger between them to feel their smoothness…

Then Miss Howard interrupted, demanding an introduction, even though she knew perfectly well who Miss Redford was.

But, as alluring as Henrietta Redford was, she lacked propriety. Part of him admired her spirit, but another part compared her to his cousin Beatrice and found her wanting.

"Does your father know you're roaming the streets unaccompanied?" he asked. "Or your aunt?"

"Why do you ask?" she retorted. "Do you wish to betray me again, or perhaps offer to beat me, like you did before?"

Miss Howard gasped and lifted her hand to her mouth in exaggerated horror.

"What do you think, Miss Howard?" Miss Redford asked, laughter in her voice. "Do I merit a beating?"

Miss Howard curled her lip in a sneer. "If Lord Thorpe says so, then I agree with him. Untamed young women must be disciplined properly if they wish to marry well."

"Then I consider myself free from the obligation, for I have since risen above the base need to marry well," Henrietta said. "Or, at all."

"That must be a relief for *you*," Miss Howard said, "given your prospects. I suggest you count your blessings."

"And I suggest you keep your sharp nose to yourself."

Giles suppressed a laugh at the horror in Miss Howard's expression. Doubtless, she surrounded herself with sycophants and rarely experienced incivility. Whereas he knew full well how sharp Miss Redford's tongue was.

But Miss Redford's lack of reverence was refreshing. She wasn't afraid to speak her mind, even if it resulted in punishment. Such honesty was rare in a young woman.

But she was no ordinary young woman.

Miss Redford met his gaze once more, then she dipped into a curtsey.

"Lord Thorpe, Miss Howard, if you'll forgive me, I have other people to shock with my inappropriate behavior."

Before he could reply, she turned her back and disappeared through the gates leading out of the park.

"Well, really!" Miss Howard exclaimed. "What an unpleasant creature. That's one acquaintance I have no intention of furthering. How the devil do you know her?"

"She lives close to Thorpe Hall."

"What is she doing in London?"

"She's having a Season like every other young lady," he replied. "Did you not see her at Lady Houghton's ball last night? She spent much of the evening with your sister Eleanor."

"Oh, *her*. I daresay they suit each other." The spite in Miss Howard's voice would have taken him aback, but he'd grown used to it over the past few days. Beautiful a creature as she was, her character was quite the opposite.

"I think perhaps it's time to return," he said. "I'll escort you home," he nodded toward Miss Howard's chaperone, "and Miss Lynott, of course."

"But I thought we were to take luncheon…"

"Forgive me, I'd quite forgotten I have a prior engagement. Perhaps another time."

She frowned at the slight, but he'd already had enough of her spite for the day.

After taking her home and enduring her silence—which she may have deemed a punishment, but he saw as a relief—he returned to his townhouse.

He found Beatrice in the morning room, occupied with her embroidery. After weathering the grief at losing her parents, his cousin had blossomed into a delightful, young woman. Her sunny nature and optimistic outlook on life contrasted with his serious nature. At least, that's what Mother kept saying. But Mother spoke the truth. Since Beatrice had entered his life, he'd had more occasion to laugh. Mother had found a new lease of life, and despite her poor sight, she'd been able to accompany Beatrice on several excursions around London.

His cousin looked up as he entered the morning room, then leaned to one side, as if trying to peer round him.

"Are you alone?"

He nodded, and she visibly relaxed.

"That's a relief," she said. "I'm glad you've not brought that horrid woman back with you."

"What horrid woman?"

"Juliette Howard. You'd threatened to bring her here for luncheon."

"She's considered one of the most beautiful ladies in London," he said, "and an excellent conversationalist. Many would argue that she'd be a fine companion for you during the Season."

"Pah!" Beatrice exclaimed, tossing her embroidery to one side. "I daresay if I wished to spend every waking moment discussing the latest expensive silks, or whether it's better to secure the hand of a duke or a viscount, I might enjoy her company. As it is, I find nothing to like in her. Nothing at all."

"Aren't you being a little harsh?"

She shook her head. "The other day, she ticked me off for not sitting up straight enough. If you marry her, I'll elope with the first man who asks me, just to get away from her."

"Do that, and you'll be ruined," he said. "I guarantee such a fate would be worse than putting up with Miss Howard's company."

She pulled a face.

"My dear cousin," he said. "Rest assured, I have no intention of marrying Miss Howard."

"Then I'll refrain from eloping, for the present."

He nodded toward the abandoned embroidery. "How are you getting on with your needlework?"

"It's almost done," she said. "I don't enjoy it. I'd rather be out of doors, especially on a day like today. But it's for Aunt Euphramia, so I'm determined to finish it."

"Good girl," he said. "But you mustn't work all the time. How about we go for a walk in the park later?"

"Why not now?"

"I have some letters to write. Perhaps Mother could take you."

"She's resting," Beatrice said. "I wish I had a friend here."

"There are plenty of amiable young women in London," he said.

Her smile slipped, and he squeezed her hand. Despite being

tall for her age, Beatrice suffered from shyness and a lack of confidence. She lacked the ruthlessness which most debutantes possessed. In that respect, she was almost the exact opposite of Juliette Howard.

Which could only ever be considered a virtue.

In many ways, she resembled Miss Redford.

He cursed himself. Why did his thoughts always turn to *her*? As much as he tried to surround himself with women who were her opposite—the beautiful Miss Howard, the elegant Lady Irma—he could never quite wipe the image of Henrietta Redford from his mind.

CHAPTER FOURTEEN

"**M**Y SISTER TOLD me she saw you last week."

Henrietta glanced up at her friend, whose arm was linked with hers as they strode through the park on their way to take tea. Aunt Agnes followed a few steps behind, her cane tap-tapping on the path.

"Heaven help me, Eleanor," Henrietta said. "Don't tell me we're going to be blessed with Juliette's company at tea this afternoon."

"No—she's visiting Lady Irma Fairchild."

Henrietta let out a laugh. "Keeping her enemies close, is she? The charming Lady Irma must be her main rival this Season. But I'm being unfair to your poor sister." She gave a smile of mischief. "I'm sure she was very complimentary when she spoke of me."

"No more than usual."

"Let me hazard a guess," Henrietta said before raising her voice in pitch to emulate Juliette's shrewish tone. "Oh, Eleanor dearest, you won't secure a good match if you associate with *guttersnipes.*"

Aunt Agnes's disapproving voice cut through their laughter.

"Young lady!" she cried. "How many times have I warned you not to play the fool, particularly in public?"

"Sorry, Aunt," Henrietta said before lowering her voice and leaning toward her friend.

"She's warned me fifty times at the last count," she whispered. "Aunt quite despairs of me."

"Whereas Juliette relishes my awkwardness," Eleanor said with a sigh.

Poor Eleanor! She couldn't help her nature. She was terrified of even the smallest social occasion, having confessed to Henrietta that she never knew what to say to anyone. But, rather than help her sister, Juliette took advantage of Eleanor's affliction by placing herself first at every occasion, despite being the younger, and securing the limelight and the admiration of impressionable ladies by ridiculing her sister at every opportunity.

"She called you a *grubby little urchin*," Eleanor said with a giggle. "I told her I was most impressed that she'd increased her vocabulary since the last time she insulted one of my friends."

Henrietta stiffened.

Grubby little urchin.

Only one person described her thus.

Giles Thorpe.

He must have discussed his dislike of her with Juliette Howard.

Beast! Did he hate her that much?

"Henrietta?" Eleanor's voice cut through her anger, and she turned to see her friend staring at her, fear in her eyes.

"I-I'm sorry, Henrietta," she whispered. "I meant no offense."

Henrietta placed her hand over her friend's and squeezed it lightly. "You've done nothing wrong, Ellie."

"Sometimes I don't know whether I've said the right thing or not. The last thing I want to do is upset a friend."

"Believe me, Ellie, I'd never be upset at anything you might say. It's not your fault that your sister's such a harridan." She let out a laugh. "She'll do very well for him—they deserve each other."

"Who?"

"Lord Thorpe. She was looking all doe-eyed at him when I saw them in the park."

Eleanor laughed. "I think he's about to be supplanted," she

said. "Juliette doesn't think I notice, but she's set her sights on the Duke of Dunton."

"That old lecher?"

"Lord Thorpe is her backup strategy. She's planning it like a military campaign. If Dunton doesn't succumb to her advances, she'll set her cap at Thorpe. After all, a duke is worth more than an earl."

"Only if you value a title," Henrietta said.

"Which my sister does. She's determined to marry better than me." Eleanor shook her head. "Of course, I'm the least likely person to attract the attention of any man, so it's not much of a victory."

"You're bound to catch someone's eye," Henrietta said. "Perhaps you'll find your perfect match at Lady Allen's ball."

Eleanor shivered. "I hope not. I have never liked being looked at. I always fear that my innermost thoughts will betray me."

"What if you see someone you admire?"

"I prefer to admire from a distance," Eleanor said. "If I see someone I like the look of, I seem to lose all reason. I'm so afraid of making a fool of myself that I run and hide like a little girl. I dislike handsome men in particular. I always think they'll laugh at me for having the audacity to look at them, dowdy as I am."

"You think too little of yourself," Henrietta said. "The best thing about you is that you're like me—a misfit. From the moment we were introduced, I knew we'd be friends."

"Even though I can never be elegant?"

Henrietta snorted. "There's nothing I'd like worse than an elegant female for a friend."

"Such as *her*."

"Who?"

"Her over there—by the water's edge."

Eleanor pointed to a tall young woman who stood beside the Serpentine, watching a pair of swans gliding along the water. Clinging to her arm, was a gray-haired woman dressed in an old-fashioned gown and redingote.

The young woman turned as they approached, and Henrietta was struck by how exquisitely beautiful she was. Glossy black hair piled up in an unassuming style, framed a face with delicate features and warm, liquid brown eyes. Though she was tall and elegantly attired, she lacked the ostentation of Juliette Howard or the sneering air of Lady Irma Fairchild.

Nevertheless, she looked a paragon—the sort of young lady who made someone like Henrietta feel grubby and ungainly.

Eleanor leaned close. "Juliette was raving about her last week," she said. "About how elegant she was and how she wished to befriend her. Of course, she has her own reasons for that, which have nothing to do with friendship."

"What reasons?" Henrietta asked.

"She wishes to ingratiate herself with the family," Eleanor said.

"I don't understand."

"The young woman you see over there is Lady Beatrice Thorpe."

Henrietta looked at the object of their discussion with re-newed interest.

So, this was the epitome of elegance she compared so unfavorably to! Then, the woman with her must be…

"Lady Thorpe!" Aunt Agnes let out a cry. "How delightful! And this must be Lady Beatrice."

The older woman turned and lifted her hand to shield her eyes against the glare of the sun. Henrietta hardly recognized her friend. No longer the thin, frail woman she'd first caught sight of through the window at Thorpe Hall, Lady Thorpe looked the picture of health, her cheeks blooming with vitality.

"Lady Agnes? Is that you?"

"It is."

"Of course!" Lady Thorpe cried. "I'd recognize your voice anywhere. Forgive me, my eyesight is not what it was."

"Have you recently arrived in Town?" Aunt asked.

"My niece and I have not been here a week," Lady Thorpe

replied, "but already I feel at home. The beauty of London is that while it never changes, there's always something new to see."

"How is your health?" Aunt asked.

"Much improved. Dr. McIver is an absolute treasure! He's prescribed a tonic in the morning, plenty of fresh air, and a little brandy at night if I have trouble sleeping. It's worked wonders, and I feel renewed. And dear Beatrice is always so attentive."

Eleanor tightened her grip on Henrietta's arm. Lady Beatrice was staring at them, an earnest expression in her dark eyes.

"Lady Thorpe, may I present my niece?" Aunt Agnes asked. "Henrietta, this is…"

"Oh!" Lady Thorpe cried. "Do forgive me for not recognizing you. How are you, my dear?"

Lady Beatrice's eyes widened, and she continued to stare at Henrietta.

"I'm very well, Lady Thorpe," Henrietta said, "and you look well yourself."

Lady Thorpe reached out for Henrietta's hand. Then she smiled. "Ah yes, I can see it's you, now. Dear Henry! And I've told you before, call me Euphramia."

Lady Beatrice raised her eyebrows but said nothing. Doubtless, the conceited little miss considered Henrietta to be beneath her.

"Have you met my niece?" Lady Thorpe continued. "Beatrice, my dear, this is Miss Henrietta Redford, whom I've said so much about."

The young woman dipped into a curtsey, and Henrietta mirrored the gesture.

"Pleased to meet you, Miss Henrietta."

"And I, Miss Beatrice."

"Henrietta!" Aunt Agnes cried, and Henrietta felt a sharp sting as Aunt smacked her arm with her fan. "*Lady* Beatrice if you please. Do forgive me, Lady Beatrice. My niece has much to learn about etiquette." She turned her attention to Eleanor. "This is Miss Howard…"

"We're already acquainted," Lady Beatrice said, turning her gaze toward Eleanor, who tightened her grip on Henrietta's arm.

"What do you think of my niece?" Lady Thorpe asked. "Isn't she a fine young woman? It would be my dearest wish if she were to find a special friend in London. She cannot always be saddled with her invalid old aunt."

"Aunt, you're no invalid," Beatrice said quietly. "I enjoy your company. Giles says…"

"Oh, Giles says rather too much," Lady Thorpe said. "Which reminds me, he didn't want us tarrying too long in the park. The Fairchilds are coming for supper, and you'll need to practice your instrument beforehand." She turned toward Henrietta. "My niece is quite the proficient, you know. You should come and hear her play. I've never heard anything the like!"

Lady Beatrice frowned. "Aunt, please, I'd rather not."

"Oh, very well," Lady Thorpe said. "Forgive me for wanting the whole world to hear you play. You do, of course, have the right to be discerning and choose your audience. And now, we really must be going. Giles will be worrying about you. You know how anxious he is to ensure you shine in Society."

Lady Beatrice turned her head away as if bored by the conversation.

Lady Thorpe dipped into a curtsey. "Lady Agnes, Miss Redford, I hope I shall see more of you while we're in London."

Henrietta and Eleanor curtseyed in unison and watched as Lady Thorpe and her niece continued along the path.

After their walk, they returned to Eleanor's home, where a liveried footman greeted them at the main doors.

"I wonder," Eleanor said, handing her pelisse to the footman, "should I have invited Lady Beatrice to tea?"

"It wouldn't have been appropriate," Aunt Agnes said. "I only hope Henrietta hasn't damaged your chances of friendship by her inappropriate address."

"No friend of mine would be bothered about whether I addressed them properly," Henrietta said.

Aunt gave a huff. "And that's why you'll always attract the wrong sort of friends."

Eleanor blushed and drew in a sharp breath. Oblivious to the insult she'd just issued, Aunt Agnes continued.

"I'm determined to ensure Lady Beatrice befriends you. If we pay due reverence, she'll forgive your slight. I must speak to your father about it when we return. Perhaps we can call on her tomorrow." She turned to Eleanor. "Where is your dear mama? I thought I could spend some time with her while you young ladies take your tea."

"She'll be in her parlor at this hour," Eleanor said. "James, please take Lady Agnes to Mama, then Miss Redford and I will be ready to take tea." Her blush deepened as it always did when giving orders or making long speeches.

"Very good, Miss Eleanor." The footman bowed. "Lady Agnes, would you care to follow me?"

After Aunt Agnes was safely out of sight, Henrietta let out a sigh and followed Eleanor into the parlor that was her friend's private haven. Most young ladies would have described the room as cluttered or dull. It was an eccentric combination of order and chaos, filled with books, sketchbooks, and artist's materials, and the smell of paint lingered in the air.

Eleanor took a seat, and Henrietta flopped down in a nearby armchair.

"Sweet heaven!" she cried. "Aunt's idea of *the right friends* leaves a lot to be desired. Did you see how the precious Lady Beatrice slighted us? Not that I'd want to be invited to hear her play her silly instrument, no matter how proficient she is."

"Perhaps she's shy?" Eleanor suggested.

Henrietta snorted. "I doubt it. Her sort are never uncomfortable in public. She had no wish to taint herself with our presence. And just as well. She has no conversation about her. I dare say she spends her life being praised and flattered such that she only needs to nod her pretty little head for everyone to sigh with rapture at her elegance."

"You're determined to hate her?"

"Hate is a strong word," Henrietta said. "Dislike, yes, but hatred I reserve for those who actively seek to harm us. Lady Beatrice, I presume, is an unfortunate product of her titled ancestry, and her guardian's contempt for anyone and anything he considers beneath him." She leaned forward. "Don't tell me you *liked* her, Ellie?"

Eleanor shook her head. "I find her disconcerting," she replied. "She has this habit of staring directly at you. Like her guardian."

"Lord Thorpe?"

"Aye," Eleanor said. "He's called on Juliette, and a few minutes in his company was more than enough for me. I'm a little afraid of him."

"You're afraid of all men," Henrietta said.

"Just the handsome ones." Eleanor grinned. "Want to see my latest sketches?"

"Oh yes!"

The world might think young women such as Lady Beatrice or Irma Fairchild were the epitome of accomplishment, but they possessed only a mediocre talent—enough to entertain shallow ladies and gentlemen in drawing rooms.

But Eleanor possessed a talent the likes of which Henrietta had never seen. She was an accomplished artist. But, unlike her sister Juliette, who painted delicate little landscapes and was therefore deemed by Society to be a great proficient, Eleanor's sketches were bold and disconcerting. They made the observer *think*.

Which, in Henrietta's opinion, was the mark of a true artist.

Eleanor picked up a sketchbook and flicked through the pages. Then she held it up.

"What do you think?"

Henrietta drew in a sharp breath.

"It's me!"

The sketch had been produced with uncanny accuracy, and

Henrietta could almost have believed she was looking into a mirror.

"When did you draw this?"

"Last night."

Henrietta shook her head. "But—how?"

"From memory."

"But the detail! How did you manage to recall it, right down to the freckles on my nose—and the mole on my chin that Aunt's always telling me to conceal with powder."

Eleanor shrugged. "I don't know," she said. "When I close my eyes, I picture the subject as if they're standing before me. I thought everybody did it, until I mentioned it to Juliette."

"What did she say?"

"She called me a freak."

"Have you sketched her?"

"No," Eleanor said. "But this is what I wanted to show you."

She flicked through the pages and stopped at a sketch of Lady Beatrice. The likeness was extraordinary—from the rosebud mouth to the pert little nose, and the furrowed brow and those intense, deep-set eyes.

"I find her stare disconcerting, don't you?" Eleanor said.

"Then why immortalize it on paper?" Henrietta asked.

"So I can practice looking."

"Practice?"

Eleanor nodded. "I cannot abide it when people look at me," she said. "But if I spend my time looking at the floor, which is my preference, I seem to gain even more attention. So, I practice looking at the images of people who make me uncomfortable, so that when I look at them for real, I can hold their gaze without flinching."

"Is it working?"

"Sometimes." She flicked through pages again, hesitating at one likeness—a strong-featured man Henrietta didn't recognize. Then she turned the page, and Henrietta's heart jolted in her chest.

Giles Thorpe.

His gaze seemed to leap off the page and penetrate her mind. Brow furrowed, he stared directly at her, disapproval in his eyes, as if he were about to issue an admonishment.

Then Eleanor turned the page again to reveal a very different Giles Thorpe.

This one was smiling. His mouth curved upward, and laughter lines creased in the corners of his eyes, which twinkled with warmth and depth. They were eyes to drown in—the eyes which had penetrated her dreams when she lay alone at night, strange sensations fluttering inside her stomach when she thought of the kiss they shared...

An uncomfortable heat prickled her skin, and she sat back.

"Sweet heaven..." she whispered.

"I decided to engage in a little transformation," Eleanor said. "I lack the power to influence anyone myself, but, in my mind, I can see how they'd look if they viewed the world differently. Lord Thorpe is an unpleasant sort of fellow, but his unpleasantness doesn't seem to originate from a poor character—but rather, that he has yet to understand the meaning of joy. I merely wondered what he might look like if joy came into his life—or, perhaps, if he fell in love."

What might he look like, indeed?

Henrietta continued to observe the sketch, her gaze lingering on his features.

Eleanor let out a snort. "Of course, I've never seen him look like this. If he spends much more time with my sister, he'll never smile again! But I sometimes indulge myself in wondering what a man must look like if he's in love."

The despair in her friend's voice tore through Henrietta's heart. Did Eleanor believe herself to be entirely unlovable, merely because she was a little eccentric and viewed the world differently to others?

The door opened, and a maid entered carrying a tea tray. She bobbed a curtsey and set it on a table before scuttling off, closing the door behind her. While Eleanor poured the tea, Henrietta resumed her attention on the sketch.

The realization dawned on her like a punch in the gut. The expression in his eyes, that of desire and love…

It was the expression she'd seen, for a fleeting moment, the day he'd kissed her.

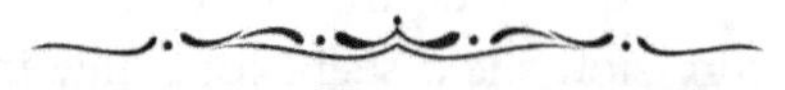

CHAPTER FIFTEEN

"WHAT DID YOU think of the Fairchild girl?"

Giles looked up from his paper. But Mother was addressing Beatrice, not him.

Which was just as well.

Elegant as the young lady was, he'd found her a little too willing to follow the opinions of those her overbearing mama wished to ingratiate herself with.

In other words, she had the makings of the perfect, biddable wife. She was the kind of woman who'd produce an heir and a couple of spares within the first three years of marriage—having lain back and thought of her duty during the process—then retire to the country and turn a blind eye to her husband securing a mistress to indulge in the bodily pleasures that she found so disgusting to her person.

"Pleasant enough, I suppose," Beatrice said, "and very civil. But she's so elegant, I didn't know what to say to her."

"That's because her mama did most of the talking," Mother said, reaching for the teapot.

"Here—let me." Beatrice picked up the teapot and refilled Mother's cup, then she gave Giles a shy smile, a hint of wickedness in their expression.

"She seemed to like *you*, Giles," Mother said.

"And," Beatrice added, "she agreed with you on an astonishing number of matters agricultural."

He suppressed a laugh. "She did seem to have a keen interest in the goings-on at the Brummitt farm."

"Is that what you were talking about in earnest after dinner?" Mother asked. "The two of you seemed to be getting on well."

"I asked her opinion on a great many things," Giles said, "and was rewarded with exactly the kind of responses I expected."

"Is that a good thing?"

"It is, in that it helped me form an opinion of her."

"She seems agreeable," Mother said.

"A little *too* agreeable," Giles replied, "in that she was all too apt to agree with everything I said."

"Don't you want that in a wife?"

"What—to be agreed with on every little matter, never to be challenged?" he asked. "She even nodded and smiled when I asked her opinion on whether or not sheep should wear breeches in order to keep themselves warm in winter."

Beatrice let out a giggle.

"Child!" Mother admonished, though she, too, suppressed a laugh. "We must make allowances. Lady Irma is not acquainted with the ways of the country. I think it rather touching that she's eager to embrace your ideas. You wouldn't want to spend your life arguing with your partner, would you?"

He shook his head. "No, but I'd prefer a woman who has a mind of her own. Otherwise, I'm constantly in danger of making poor decisions with nobody to challenge them."

"As if *you'd* make poor decisions!" Mother laughed. "You're the most sensible man I know. You have far more sense than your dear papa had."

"Lady Irma wouldn't be any fun," Beatrice said, sipping her tea.

Giles set his paper aside. "Marriages are not about *fun*."

Beatrice sighed. "Then, if you're seeking a dull wife, you should ask her. You can then be dull together."

"Perhaps I will," Giles said.

"I like her better than Juliette Howard," Beatrice continued.

"But then, I like everyone better than *that* creature.

"Beatrice!" Mother cried. "You forget your manners."

"Juliette's sister Eleanor seems more interesting," Beatrice continued, "though I can't make her out. She doesn't speak much. We saw her yesterday in the park, didn't we Aunt? She was with her friend, but I don't think she likes me."

"Which one?" Mother asked. "Miss Howard or Miss Redford?"

Giles caught his breath. "Miss Redford?"

"Oh, didn't you know? She's in Town," Mother said. "She looks well and has turned out quite a pretty thing. Of course, she lacks the elegance of the Fairchild girl, but I'll always admire her spirit. She was very kind to me. But I know you disapprove of her, Giles."

Beatrice leaned forward, an eager expression in her eyes. "You do? Why's that?"

"Because she's a hellion," he said. "If Lady Irma is the epitome of elegance, Miss Redford is the opposite. Uncouth, all too apt to run about the place like an urchin, and intent on disagreeing with everybody in order to rile them. Her father sent her away in disgrace because she was too unruly."

"Giles, you're being unfair," Mother said. "Mr. Redford sent his daughter to her aunt's to prepare her for her come-out. She may be a little spirited, but she's a pleasant young woman, and I wish her well. So should you."

"She sounds interesting," Beatrice said. "I should like to know her better."

"You'll do no such thing!" Giles said. "She was always getting herself into scrapes. She'll land herself and everyone who associates with her in trouble. Mark my words."

"You seem determined to hate her," Beatrice said. "What has she done to anger you so much? Has she disagreed with your suggestion of putting ballgowns on cows?"

"She placed a chamber pot on the statue of your great-grandfather."

Rather than express horror, his cousin let out a snort, and her body shook with mirth.

"It's not a laughing matter!" he cried. "That sort of behavior can ruin a young woman's reputation. When she was younger, she was always up some tree or other—and did you know I saw her running about the park unchaperoned last week? Her aunt's taught her nothing. Once a hellion, always a hellion. And *you*, Beatrice…" he pointed his finger at his cousin, "…are to keep well away from her."

Beatrice scowled, then reached for Mother's hand.

"May I be excused, Aunt?" she asked.

"Of course, my dear."

Beatrice rose and exited the breakfast room.

"You're too hard on the child," Mother said as soon as the door clicked shut.

"She's got to learn," Giles said. "I don't want her making a fool of herself. A young woman's reputation is everything."

"I know that, Giles, but if you tighten the bit and bridle too much, the horse will bolt at the first opportunity. Beatrice is impetuous. She wants adventure, and if you tell her to do something, she'll go out of her way to do the opposite. Forbidden fruit is, after all, the sweetest."

"I understand," he said, "but I'm within my rights to prevent her from fraternizing with those I deem to be a bad influence."

"Such as Henrietta Redford?"

"*She* is more likely to lead Beatrice into trouble than anyone else in the whole of London."

Mother let out a laugh. "All because she used to climb trees and played a practical joke on you, two years ago?" She shook her head. "I fail to understand why you dislike her so much."

"I don't dislike her. I just don't think she's a suitable companion for Beatrice."

"Which amounts to the same thing."

He resumed his attention on his paper—a signal that the conversation was over. But though he read the words on the page, his mind was now occupied with another subject…

A defiant hellion, a woman with a mind of her own.

A woman who would ensure that any marriage would be *fun*.

CHAPTER SIXTEEN

LADY ALLEN HAD spared no expense for her ball. As Henrietta entered the main hall, her senses were assaulted by the light of what must have been over a thousand candles. Bowls of fruit filled the tables, each one topped by a pineapple. The lady herself was resplendent in a peacock-blue silk gown and a headdress topped with feathers and studded with jewels.

Beside her, the unfortunate Lord Allen gave a watery smile to each guest, his disposition no doubt due to the mountain of debt he now found himself in, as a result of his wife's expenditure.

Aunt Agnes steered Henrietta toward their hostess. Henrietta dipped into a curtsey. Lady Allen wrinkled her nose and gave a tight, cold smile.

"Your niece is rather tall, is she not, Lady Agnes?"

"Forgive me," Aunt replied, "but I try my best with her."

"I'm sure you do," came the reply. "Her dress is delightful, but perhaps the color a little too bright? Lady Beatrice Thorpe is almost as tall, but she seems to carry it off rather well. She's wearing a more muted tone, which suits her stature."

"Of course," Aunt said. "But, as you know, Lady Allen, these young people will insist on making their own choices! What can we do?"

Lady Allen didn't reply. She had already turned her attention to the next guests to arrive—Lord and Lady Fairchild, together with their daughter.

"Ah, Lady Irma!" Lady Allen cried. "How delightful to see such a treasure in our midst! I'd quite given up on the prospect of seeing any congenial young ladies here tonight."

Sweet Lord! Henrietta shook her head. What had possessed her to agree to come tonight? Did Aunt not realize that the more Society parties they attended, the more firmly Henrietta's status as a misfit would be established?

Her heart soared when she caught sight of Lavinia together with her chaperone, and she steered Aunt Agnes toward them.

"Dear Edna!" Aunt Agnes cried. "What a pleasure to see you here, and Miss de Grande, of course."

Lavinia dipped into a curtsey, then slipped her arm through Henrietta's.

"Agnes, there's a comfortable sofa beside the fireplace," Lady Edna said. "Shall we claim it before it gets too busy? My legs are a little painful today."

"Shall I escort you over there, Aunt Edna?" Lavinia asked.

"No, no, Lavinia, dear," came the reply. "I'm sure you young ladies have much to talk about. You must put yourselves forward if you're to fill your dance cards. Why don't you go and speak to the Fairchild girl?"

"Or Lady Beatrice Thorpe," Aunt Agnes suggested. "I believe she's coming tonight. I'm sure she dances beautifully."

"She sounds quite the paragon," Lavinia said, rolling her eyes. Henrietta suppressed a giggle, and Aunt Agnes gave her a sharp look.

Once free of their chaperones, Henrietta and Lavinia took a turn about the ballroom.

"I can't see Eleanor," Henrietta said. "I hope she's here to-night."

"Her sister's over there," Lavinia said, pointing toward the window, "using her charms on the Duke of Dunton."

"If she smiled any wider, her face would split."

"It's likely to split anyway, given that she spends the rest of the time scowling," Lavinia said. "Surely a man of sense would recognize her smiles for what they are—a desperate ploy to be noticed."

"I suspect most dukes are lacking in sense," Henrietta said. "All that idle languishing in their estates and aristocratic disdain for others would addle anybody's brain."

"Dunton has a reputation for wanting the best of everything," Lavinia said. "He boasted only the other day about his collection of Gainsboroughs."

"Perhaps he wishes to add Juliette Howard to his collection, given that her looks are her only virtue."

As they approached the couple, the duke bowed and kissed Miss Howard's hand, then he set off toward the punchbowl.

Juliette looked up, and her smile disappeared.

"Miss Redford and Miss de Grande," she said. "I wouldn't have thought tonight's ball would be to your tastes. All credit to Lady Allen and her generosity toward you, but there's something a little undignified in accepting an invitation which was granted out of *pity*, don't you think?"

Henrietta ignored the slight. "Is Eleanor here tonight?" she asked.

"She was indulging in one of her tantrums," Juliette said, "and Mama felt it best she remain at home."

"Poor Eleanor!" Lavinia cried. "Has the doctor been summoned?"

"For what purpose?" Juliette asked. "A childish fit of pique is no occasion for wasting a doctor's time."

"Miss Howard." A thin, nasal voice spoke, and Dunton appeared at Juliette's elbow, holding two glasses of punch. He handed one to her, then stared pointedly at Henrietta and Lavinia. They curtseyed in unison. Henrietta wrinkled her nose at a peculiar odor which had thickened in the air.

"My friends were just leaving," Juliette said.

Dunton gave a grunt and drained his glass.

"Your Grace." Henrietta curtseyed once more, then steered her friend away.

"What the devil was that awful smell?" Lavinia whispered.

"Rotten cabbage?" Henrietta suggested.

"Or six-week-old unwashed breeches," Lavinia said with a giggle. "His Grace's valet deserves a medal for bravery. How can Juliette Howard bear his company?"

"Because she believes that a dukedom is adequate compensation for an assault on her sense of smell."

A gentleman approached and bowed to Lavinia, offering his elbow. "Miss de Grande, I believe we're engaged for the first dance."

"Viscount Marlow." Lavinia flushed and took the proffered arm.

Henrietta retreated to a chair on the edge of the room. Eager footsteps approached from behind, and she whirled round as a hand tapped her shoulder.

"It *is* you! You do scrub up well. I say, Phil, it's Henry!"

Johnny stood before her, a broad grin on his face, ignoring the ripple of tutting at his outburst. Henrietta caught sight of Aunt Agnes's scowl from across the room.

"Hush!" she hissed. "You're making a fool of yourself and of me."

"Oh, don't be such a bore!" he laughed. "Phil! Come over here. I told you Henry would be here tonight." He waved frantically, almost knocking the feathers out of Henrietta's hair. She glanced across the room to where Phillip stood, and her heart sank.

Standing on either side of him were Lady Beatrice Thorpe— and Giles Thorpe. Lady Beatrice had eyes for none but Phillip, but as for Giles…

He looked up and stared at Henrietta. Even from the other side of the room, she could see the disdain in his blue gaze.

Why was it, that the moment she was made to feel like a fool, it happened when *he* was watching?

Phillip bowed to Lady Beatrice, then walked toward Henrietta. Lady Beatrice stared after him, admiration in her expression.

But Giles Thorpe's gaze remained fixed on Henrietta, and she found her cheeks warming at his frank appraisal.

Perhaps Johnny had knocked her feather askew, and he'd found something to criticize—or rather, something *more* to criticize.

A nudge at her arm claimed her attention. "Henry," Johnny hissed, "we've got something simply marvelous!"

"Which is?"

He pulled a vial out of his pocket. "Great Aunt Fanny's dietary tonic."

Henrietta took the vial and read the label.

No more than one spoonful to be taken twice a day after meals.
Signed, Dr. Saint John Odgers.

"What is it?" she asked.

"It aids digestion."

Johnny snickered like an irreverent schoolboy.

"Control yourself, you fool!" she hissed.

"Great Aunt Fanny has difficulty digesting her meals," he said. "Dr. Odgers prescribed her this, to…to…" He broke off with a snort. "It speeds up the process. One spoonful has her running to the privy. Imagine what a whole bottle would do?"

"You don't mean…"

Mischief shone in his eyes. "I *do*. Father is always lecturing us on the evils of liquor, yet he's never without a bottle in his hand." He nodded toward the punchbowl. "What better way to teach everyone a lesson than have them reap the consequences?"

"You'll never get away with it," Henrietta said. "Your guilt is written all over your face. You'll not manage anything without disintegrating into laughter."

"I don't intend on doing it myself," he said. "Father would thrash me."

"Who, then?"

Phillip joined them. "Have you persuaded her yet?"

"I was just about to," Johnny said.

Henrietta shook her head. "Oh, no—you must be out of your wits!"

"Are you too chicken?"

She glanced toward the punchbowl, where Dunton now stood, together with Juliette Howard. The temptation to punish Juliette for her spite was too much.

"Oh, go on, Henry!" Phillip said. "We'll do anything you want if you do."

"Such as?"

"I'll bet you've not had occasion to practice swordplay since you came to London," he said. "We can practice together like we used to, under the guise of going for an elegant little stroll in the park. Your stuffy old aunt would be none the wiser."

The thought of escaping Aunt's clutches for a session of swordplay was tempting.

"How often?" she asked.

"Once a fortnight."

She shook her head. "I'll get into trouble if I'm caught. You'll have to make it worth my while. Twice a week."

"Once."

"Done," she said. "Shake on it."

"Don't you trust me?" Phillip asked.

She rolled her eyes. "Surprisingly enough, I don't."

Johnny let out a laugh. "You're right not to trust him. Phil's turned into a complete rogue."

"He always was," Henrietta said. She slipped the vial into her reticule.

"So, when will you do it?" Phillip asked.

A deep voice spoke from behind. "Do what?"

Henrietta drew in a sharp breath and turned to face the newcomer. Giles Thorpe stood before her, Lady Beatrice on his arm. Henrietta looked away, lest his piercing gaze penetrated her thoughts.

"Phillip was inquiring as to when I would be dancing tonight," she said.

Lady Beatrice's eyes narrowed, and she glanced from Henrietta to Phillip, then back again, hostility in her expression.

"I'm afraid I'm engaged for this next dance," Henrietta said. "Now, if you'll excuse me, I must find my partner before the music begins."

She dipped into a curtsey and made her way toward the punchbowl, weaving among the couples who were lining up for the dance. She glanced back to see Phillip leading Lady Beatrice onto the floor, the young woman looking up at him adoringly.

So, that explained her hostility. The girl was *jealous*. Perhaps she wasn't completely perfect, after all.

About halfway through the dance, Henrietta seized her chance. The dancers were occupied with their steps, the chaperones were indulging in gossip, and many of the men had retired to the games room. The servants, enjoying a brief period of respite while their masters were otherwise occupied, chatted among themselves.

Henrietta pulled the vial from her reticule.

Just a few drops…

She uncorked the bottle and held it over the punchbowl, then her hand slipped, and the contents emptied into the bright red liquid.

Damnation!

She glanced up, but no one's eyes were on her. Slipping the empty bottle back into her reticule, she gave a sigh of relief and moved away from the scene of her crime.

"Indulging in dishonesty, I see?"

Her skin tightened at the sound of Lord Thorpe's voice, and she turned to face him. He stared at her, a knowing expression in his eyes, and she braced herself for a very public admonishment.

"Spying on me, were you?" she challenged.

"Don't flatter yourself," he said. "I merely noticed that you weren't dancing, though you'd said you were engaged for this dance."

"I was mistaken."

"Are you engaged for the next dance?"

"No."

"Then permit me the pleasure of dancing with you."

She shook her head and stepped back, but he caught her hand, and long, lean fingers curled round her wrist.

"I insist."

His voice reverberated through her bones, the tone of possession sending a secret thrill through her. She met his stare with defiance, but her resolve crumbled at the look in his eyes, the raw hunger which caused a secret, wicked thrill to course through her.

She opened her mouth to respond, but the words stuck in her throat. His nostrils flared, and a sparkle of need glowered in his eyes—like silver stars in a deep abyss, drawing her in, tempting her into ruination with the promise of paradise...

Then she realized she'd stopped breathing. He released her, and she inhaled, fanning the heat from her cheeks.

"Good," he said, the corner of his mouth curling into a wry smile. "Until the next dance."

He issued a deep bow, then disappeared among the crowd. She stumbled toward an empty chair and sat, before her legs crumpled beneath her.

As the dance concluded, the guests milled about the room. Phillip seemed occupied with Lady Beatrice, but Johnny looked over in her direction and raised his eyebrows in question.

She nodded, and he grinned. Several guests had lined up beside the punchbowl and were helping themselves liberally—though none as liberally as Dunton, who must have drunk two glasses for every one he handed to Miss Howard.

How long did the potion need to take effect? Phillip had implied that it worked almost immediately, but perhaps, diluted by the punch, it would take some hours—preferably when the victims were safely at home.

The musicians tuned their instruments for the next dance. Henrietta spotted Phillip trying to partner Lady Beatrice again, and she caught sight of Johnny, trying to ingratiate himself with Lady Irma Fairchild and being firmly snubbed.

Dunton helped himself to another glass of punch and drained it, and a sliver of apprehension rippled through Henrietta. He must have consumed at least five glasses.

What have I done?

Lavinia appeared by her side.

"I'm thirsty, Hen," she said. "Shall we have a drink? How about a glass of punch, or perhaps some champagne? I'm sure I saw a footman carrying a tray of glasses earlier."

"Don't drink the punch," Henrietta said.

"Why not?"

Henrietta opened her mouth to reply, then caught sight of Lord Thorpe approaching her, a determined look in his eyes.

"I'll tell you later," she whispered.

"Miss Redford—my dance." He bowed and held out his hand, and she slipped her hand into his, ignoring the thrill at the touch of his skin against hers. He led her to the dancefloor, and they stood facing each other while the rest of the couples lined up.

Then the dance began.

Her partner moved with the grace of a powerful animal—which was to be expected. He'd always had a ruthless air, with a hint of savagery beneath the genteel exterior—a savagery which caused a frisson of excitement to course through her veins.

His body vibrated with barely restrained power. But, somehow, the anticipation of having that power unleashed a greater need than she could have imagined. He danced in silence, and the murmuring of the other couples enjoying a more congenial conversation faded into the distance, until nothing existed in the world except him.

Then he broke the silence.

"Tell me, Miss Redford, why is it that you always look furtive when I approach? Do I unsettle you?"

Yes.

"No."

"Or are you perhaps indulging in something underhand?"

Yes.

"Of course not."

His mouth curled into a smile as if he could read her mind. "From my experience of you, I've come to realize that such a swift denial is indicative of some devilry afoot."

She averted her gaze, painfully aware of the heat blooming in her cheeks—both at the way his tongue curled round the word *experience* and at the knowing gaze he fixed on her.

"I intend to find out what it is," he said.

"So you can assert your moral superiority?"

For the next few steps, they were separated by the dance, but his gaze remained fixed on her, and her stomach twisted in apprehension. Was he about to reveal her trick and give her a public scolding?

Heavens! If Aunt Agnes discovered what she'd done, she'd be in for a thrashing.

When they rejoined, he took her hand and caressed her wrist with his thumb.

"You must admit that you lack a sense of propriety," he said.

The arrogance in his tone needled at her. "Morals and propriety are not the same thing," she said.

"Are they not?"

"Propriety is the convention with which we must all abide in order to satisfy the sensibilities of the weak minded who value tradition, elegance, and particular manners," she said. "Whereas morals, *true* morals, are the code by which we live our lives in order to restore the balance of fairness in the world. In many cases, the two are mutually exclusive."

"Are they?"

"Yes," she said, "but those of us who understand the difference are labeled as misfits."

He fell silent, and the dance continued. She caught him glancing across at his cousin, a fatherly concern in his expression—though perhaps he was merely comparing the two of them and finding Henrietta wanting—then he resumed his gaze on her.

"You find my conversation shocking," she said.

"I wouldn't say that," he replied, "though it's not the kind of conversation one generally indulges in on a dancefloor. Perhaps we could continue it later, over a glass of punch. Have you had some?"

"No."

"How odd," he said. "I could swear I saw you standing by the punchbowl for some time. I've been told it has a distinctive taste. Do you think I would like it?"

"How would I know?" she retorted.

"How, indeed?"

Her stomach flip-flopped, and he tightened his grip on her hand. "Careful, Miss Redford," he said. "You wouldn't want to slip up, would you? Unless, perhaps, you've already done so."

He inclined his head to one side, and she caught sight of the Duke of Dunton departing the room in a hurry.

"Perhaps he's indisposed," she said.

"I'm sure he is. A digestive complaint, I'll wager."

She stopped in her tracks, and he pulled her close. "Tut tut, Miss Redford. You're forgetting the steps."

The dance concluded, and he tightened his hold on her, then steered her off the dance floor.

A spark of need ignited in her blood, and he whirled her round, his eyes darkening as he continued to stare at her. Then he dipped his head, bringing his mouth closer to hers, and his warm breath caressed her skin. She inhaled the scent of woody male spices and clung to his sleeve.

He had only to move his mouth a fraction in order to kiss her. She parted her lips in anticipation, and drank in the sight of him— the strong nose, firm jaw, and those beautiful eyes, which she would willingly drown in.

Then he gave a huff of derision and pushed her away.

"Stay away from my cousin," he said.

"I beg your pardon?"

"Your aunt has been plaguing my mother, insisting that the two of you should be friends."

"Not at my request, I assure you," she said, "I can think of nothing worse…"

"Be very careful what you say," he hissed, the fire in his eyes turning into ice. "Beatrice is the model of propriety, but she's suffered loss in her life. She's an impressionable young woman and is in danger of being led astray by the wrong sort."

"You mean urchins like myself?"

His eyes widened.

"People talk," she continued, "even the ladies you seek to court. Given that you set yourself up to be the epitome of propriety, I'm disappointed to learn that you have been referring to me as a *grubby little urchin* to your acquaintances."

"And I'm disappointed to see that you think nothing of poisoning the company at a Society party. Do you have any idea how dangerous that was?"

She glanced toward the punchbowl.

"You needn't worry," he said. "I instructed the servants to dispose of it. As far as I know, only Dunton had a glass before I was able to repair the damage you'd done. Miss Howard almost drank a glass, but I managed to persuade her to return it. Now—show me the bottle."

"But…"

His eyes darkened. "Need I repeat myself?"

Trembling, she pulled the vial from her reticule, and he snatched it from her. As he read the label, his expression changed, and a glimmer of mirth shone in his eyes. For a moment, she thought he was going to laugh. Then he cleared his throat and pocketed the vial.

"Give that back," she said.

He shook his head. "I'll keep it as surety against further pranks. If anyone knew what you've done, you'd be ruined—and I've a good mind to tell them. Count yourself lucky that Juliette Howard didn't drink any."

Henrietta caught her breath at the pang of jealousy. Why did he have to find that odious woman so alluring?

"Do you really think you have a chance with Juliette Howard when she's trotting after the Duke of Dunton?" she taunted. "I wouldn't be surprised if she's already given herself to him."

His face darkened. "How dare you cast such aspersions against a respectable young lady."

"Respectable!" she scoffed. "I heard that she's been indulging in secret trysts with the duke in the bushes. How does it feel to have been usurped by a man of higher rank? Has she broken your heart?"

But, if she wanted to hurt him as much as he'd hurt her, she failed. He merely shrugged.

"What care have I about what a woman does?" he replied. "As for my heart, I think you'll find I'm not in possession of one."

Her gut twisted at the coldness in his voice, and moisture stung her eyes. She blinked back tears and looked away.

"In *that*, if nothing else, we are in complete agreement," she said. "Rest assured that I'll not attempt to taint the paragon that is Lady Beatrice with my wickedness."

She dipped into a curtsey, then fled before the shame at her folly and shock at his hatred of her spilled over into tears.

Why was it that each time she encountered him, her merriment turned to despair? But it wasn't because she hated him. It was because every time she sought to needle him, she only ever managed to hurt herself.

BLOODY HELL, WHY did he always end up insulting her?

Though Miss Redford turned away from him quickly, he could see that her cheeks were flushed, her eyes glistening with moisture.

But he felt no sense of victory. He preferred her feistiness and propensity to challenge him at every turn.

What had happened to the fire in her belly?

Dunton appeared in the distance, clutching his stomach, and Giles suppressed a chuckle. Wicked it might have been, but he couldn't help but laugh at the notion of that fat lecher running to the privy after swallowing a dose of Great Aunt Fanny's digestive tonic.

Miss Redford stopped halfway across the ballroom as the younger Meredith twin accosted her. He placed his hand on her arm, and she smiled. Giles suppressed a pang of jealousy. Why did she never smile like that at *him*?

The music struck up once more, signaling the start of the next dance. Would she dance with that ridiculous young pup? Meredith gestured toward the dance floor, but she shook her head, then pushed past him to join Miss de Grande at the edge of the room.

Giles found himself smiling at her refusal to dance with another man.

No, not a man. A mere boy.

A *man* would not have taken no for an answer. He would have steered her onto the dance floor, taken control, and met that fiery resistance with resolve...

And she would have loved it.

The older Meredith twin was less of a wet neckerchief than his younger brother. Giles saw him steering Beatrice across the dancefloor, the two of them chatting animatedly, and he smiled. It was good to see Beatrice happy again, and Phillip Meredith seemed a respectable young man, having shed the foolish antics of his youth.

Unlike his brother and Miss Redford. Perhaps that was because Phillip was the heir, the future Lord Meredith, and therefore aware of his responsibilities.

And there was much to be said for the Meredith estate being only two miles from Thorpe Hall. Giles couldn't deny the appeal of the prospect of his young cousin settling close enough for him to keep an eye on her. He'd grown fond of her. She had arrived at Thorpe Hall a traumatized young girl, devastated by her parents' deaths. But over the past two years, she'd blossomed into a lovely young woman, and both he and Mother would miss her when she married.

"Ahem."

He turned to see Lady Irma Fairchild standing before him, together with her mother, an expectant expression in her eyes.

"Lady Fairchild and Lady Irma." He bowed. "A pleasure."

"I believe you belong to my daughter, Lord Thorpe."

Lady Fairchild tilted her head to one side, an expectant expression in her eyes.

"For this dance, at least," she added. "Isn't that right, daughter?"

Irma nodded and gave Giles a smile.

Oh Lord. He'd placed his name on her dance card.

But, as he led her onto the dancefloor, he counted his blessings. Lady Irma might not set his senses ablaze, but she would be a suitable wife. And, given her continual deference to her own mother, she was likely to honor her vow of obedience.

Perhaps he should begin courting her if only to drive the thought of another from his mind.

CHAPTER SEVENTEEN

Henrietta relaxed back against the tree trunk and opened her book. She flicked through the pages until she arrived at the first plate, then traced an outline of the image with her fingertips—a man, holding a foil, lunging toward his opponent.

Perfect. Monsieur Labbat had been an authority on fencing, and though Henrietta's French was passable, she'd been delighted when Mr. Godleigh had managed to procure the English translation of Labbat's work. As soon as Aunt retired for her afternoon nap today, Henrietta could get to work on perfecting her lunges—even if her opponent was only a tree in Papa's garden.

There wasn't a single human voice to be heard in Hyde Park this morning. London might be full of noise and clatter but here, in the park, there existed a little oasis in the desert, a piece of the countryside where she could imagine she was still at home, taking sanctuary in her favorite tree.

The occasional distant voice echoed over the air. London was waking up. Soon, the sounds of carriage wheels rattling over cobbles would shatter the silence, together with the hurried footsteps of servants scurrying about their business, laying fires, and preparing breakfast for their masters and mistresses.

But the hordes of visitors who assaulted the silence with their vacuous gossip and idle chatter, wouldn't be here for hours yet.

There were, of course, exceptions. Nursemaids and governesses, tasked with keeping exuberant children amused by showing them the sights of the park and, more importantly, keeping them out of their parents' way.

A low voice spoke close by.

"You're such a beautiful creature, the prettiest girl in London."

Henrietta suppressed a snort. A young man seeking to flatter his quarry, ought to use more imaginative language than *that*.

Whoever they were, they were too close to Henrietta for comfort. She closed her book and peered through the bushes—the very same rhododendrons that she'd squeezed through, right before bumping into…

"Giles."

Her heart gave a jolt at the breathless female voice, uttering his name. To her shame, a pang of jealousy needled at her.

Was Lord Thorpe engaging in a tryst in the park? Surely not with the prim Juliette Howard—her chaperone would never allow it. Another woman, perhaps? Lady Elizabeth Grey was rumored to be his mistress.

Henrietta approached the bush and caught a glimpse of the hem of a pale skirt.

"Kiss me," the man's voice said.

"No!" the female voice replied. "Giles…he wouldn't approve."

"But I love you. May I call on you tomorrow?"

The male voice sounded familiar, but it wasn't Lord Thorpe.

"I'll ask my cousin," the female voice said.

"He's not your father,"

"He's my guardian. He wants what's best for me."

"Shall I walk you home?"

"I don't think so."

"I understand, my darling. You're right. I must court you properly. I shall see you anon."

With a rustle of leaves, a male form appeared. Henrietta caught sight of a dark blue jacket through the bushes.

At least the man, whoever he was, had respected the young woman's reluctance, even though his voice had taken on a note of petulance.

Henrietta waited until the footsteps faded, then she retraced her steps and emerged onto the path.

"Who are *you?*" A voice called out. Henrietta froze, then turned to face the owner of the voice.

"It's you!"

Oh no…

That's *all* she needed.

It was Lady Beatrice Thorpe.

"What are you doing here, unchaperoned, Lady Beatrice?" Henrietta asked.

Lady Beatrice colored. "What are *you* doing, Miss Redford?"

"I asked first," Henrietta said.

"I went for a walk."

"So did I," Henrietta said, "but *I* was alone."

"Isn't that dangerous?"

"Far less dangerous than fraternizing with a man and risking your reputation."

Lady Beatrice drew in a sharp breath, then glanced away, her eyes bright with tears. In the dawn light, she looked completely different from the haughty creature Henrietta had taken an instant dislike to. Instead, she looked like a vulnerable, naïve young woman.

"Does your guardian know you're here?"

Beatrice's eyes widened. "Please, don't tell him!"

Henrietta folded her arms. "At least you recognize the fault in your behavior," she said. "You do know that a young woman in your position shouldn't be wandering about London unchaperoned?"

"*You're* unchaperoned."

"I'm different from you."

"How?"

"For one, I'm older," Henrietta said. "You're how old—

sixteen?"

"Seventeen," Lady Beatrice said, her tone petulant. "Why would you want to come to the park alone?"

"None of your business," Henrietta said. "I'm going home, and I suggest you do the same before you're discovered."

She set off toward the park gates. Though she increased her speed until she'd almost broken into a run, Lady Beatrice followed, keeping pace with her.

Infuriating girl!

"What do you want, Lady Beatrice?" Henrietta asked.

"I want to know how you and I are different."

Henrietta stifled a laugh. "Are you serious, Little Miss Perfect?"

A hand caught her sleeve, and she stopped and turned. Beatrice's expression was full of hurt, and tears shone in her eyes.

"Why don't you like me?"

"I have no opinion on you at all," Henrietta said.

"But you called me Little Miss…"

Henrietta raised her hand. "Forgive me. I spoke out of turn."

"Then, tell me why we're different. Why do you think you can wander about unchaperoned, but I can't?"

"Two reasons," Henrietta said. "I've spent a lifetime climbing trees, playing with a sword, and generally behaving in a manner which would lead to ruination. As a result, I know how not to get caught."

Lady Beatrice's eyes widened. "Climbing trees? How marvelous! Have you climbed the trees in the park?"

"No," Henrietta said. "Even *I'm* not foolish enough to risk climbing trees in London."

"But in the country?"

"The country's another matter," Henrietta said. "But we're not in the country, are we? We're in London, where we must all behave. Woe betides a woman who wishes to indulge in anything remotely adventurous."

"I long for adventure," Lady Beatrice said with a sigh.

"I doubt that," Henrietta said. "You're what a young lady should be—everything I'm not."

"What do you mean?"

"You're beautiful, elegant, and destined to make a great match. Your guardian expects you to behave as a young lady ought and not be subjected to undesirable influences."

"Is that why he's told me to stay away from you?"

Ignoring the pain elicited by Lady Beatrice's words, Henrietta nodded. "I dare say he's told you how undesirable I am."

"Actually, I think he's a little afraid of you," Lady Beatrice said. "He has a particular look in his eyes when he speaks about you."

The temptation to ask was too great to resist.

"Does he speak of me often?"

"Oh yes! That is, Aunt speaks of you, so I suppose he has to if he wants to join the conversation."

Henrietta smiled. "Dear Lady Thorpe!" she said. "Is she well?"

"Very, but she's often too tired to accompany me, so I'm stuck inside. Not that I mean to criticize her—she'd accompany me if she could—but it would be unfair to burden her."

"Don't you have friends to accompany you?"

Lady Beatrice shook her head. "None that I like. Any lady Giles brings home is always telling me to behave appropriately, not to spill my tea, not to fidget in my seat, or scratch my nose, and..."

A ripple of mirth erupted inside Henrietta, and she burst out laughing.

Lady Beatrice stopped, hurt in her expression.

Henrietta took her hand. "I'm sorry, I meant no offense. It's only that you're describing what everyone used to say about *me* when I was a child. Including your guardian."

"Really?"

Henrietta nodded. "My Aunt Agnes quite despairs of me. As for Papa...he has given me as much freedom as he can in this world."

"That's what *I* want. Freedom."

"Freedom doesn't last forever," Henrietta said. "It's one of the indulgences of childhood that we must all shed eventually."

"So, what do you do?"

"I enjoy it while I can."

"Can't I do the same?"

"You're destined for greater things, Lady Beatrice," Henrietta said.

"Can you call me Beatrice? Then perhaps…" she hesitated, "…perhaps I may be permitted to call you Henrietta?"

"Why?" Henrietta asked.

Lady Beatrice gave her a shy smile. "Because I'd like you for a friend—unless you don't want to, of course."

"Why me?"

"Because you're different. You're free. And I find that I like you…" she hesitated again, then added in a whisper, "…even if you don't like me."

"You barely know me," Henrietta said.

"You're adventurous, and you're not constrained by what's expected of you. I find that exciting."

"It lands me in trouble," Henrietta said. "Your cousin has threatened to have me thrashed."

"Oh, never mind Giles! He wouldn't thrash someone he admires as much as he does you," Beatrice said.

"He doesn't admire me," Henrietta said.

Beatrice sighed. "I wish I had someone to admire me as much."

"Like the young man you were with earlier?"

Beatrice's expression changed into one of horror. "Please don't tell my cousin. He'll be ever so angry!"

"And rightly so," Henrietta said. "There's a difference between indulging in a little freedom and placing yourself at the mercy of a man."

"We didn't do anything," Beatrice said. "I'm not sure if I like him, anyway."

"Then, you must promise not to meet him again unchaper-oned," Henrietta said. "It's a sad fact of the world we live in that a man may do what he likes without retribution, but a young woman, such as yourself, will suffer for it for the rest of her life if her reputation is ruined."

"I meant no harm."

"It matters not. You should count yourself lucky that no one else saw you."

"You won't tell?"

"No, Beatrice," Henrietta said.

Her companion's eyes lit up with hope, and Henrietta linked her arm through hers.

"Then I'll promise not to venture out again, Miss Redford."

"Call me Henrietta."

Beatrice's eyes glowed with delight. "Aunt will be so pleased we're friends, even if Giles thinks you're an unsuitable compan-ion."

Giles…

Why couldn't he leave her alone? No doubt his stuffy manner was stifling his cousin. All young women, especially those with minds of their own, needed a little freedom.

A wicked voice whispered in her mind of the prospect of turning Lady Beatrice into a hellion.

"Do you really know how to climb trees?" Beatrice asked.

"I did," Henrietta said. "I've been climbing trees all my life." She held up her book. "I can also fight with a sword."

Beatrice glanced at the title *"The Art of Fencing*—how wonder-ful! Could you teach me?"

"Your cousin wouldn't approve."

"He needn't be told. What's the harm in letting me have a little fun?"

Beatrice's expression had changed from the aloof debutante into an eager young woman. Maybe Eleanor was right—Beatrice was merely shy, which gave her an awkward demeanor such that those incapable of looking deeper mistook her shyness for haughtiness.

Ashamed at her own judgment, Henrietta squeezed her new friend's hand. "There's no harm in it at all," she said.

"Then we'll be adventurers together," Beatrice said. "Are you perhaps attending Lady Caldicott's house party next month? It's in the country. Perhaps you could show me how to climb the trees there."

"My Aunt Agnes is taking me," Henrietta said. "Papa is unable to leave his business, but he's insisted I go and has even let me take his horse for the hunt. Do you ride?"

"A little," Beatrice said, "but not well enough to take part in a hunt. Your papa is very kind to let you take his horse."

Henrietta smiled. "Papa is kind, and he doesn't mind having a hellion for a daughter."

"And he's in business, you say? How exciting! What does he do?"

"He makes furniture, or rather, he employs others to do so," Henrietta said. "Many houses in London have his pieces. The marquetry work is exquisite, and he designs much of it himself."

"How wonderful to be able to make something and to earn an income."

"You have your fortune," Henrietta said, "and therefore no need to earn a living."

"That doesn't mean that I don't want control over my destiny."

Henrietta slipped her arm back through Beatrice's, and they resumed walking. By the time they reached the park gates, the sun had risen above the tree line, illuminating the landscape, picking out dewdrops that glistened like tiny diamonds in the grass.

A baker's boy scuttled past carrying a basket, and Henrietta caught the aroma of freshly baked bread. The park was beginning to come alive. A lone horseman rode by, and a couple stood at the edge of the Serpentine, deep in conversation.

"I didn't think there'd be so many people about," Beatrice said. "Giles will be angry if I'm seen."

"He has a point," Henrietta said. "You shouldn't have gone wandering alone. Shall I walk back with you? Then, if you're seen, you can say, truthfully, that you had a chaperone."

"You don't mind?"

"No, Beatrice. It's a pleasure to help a friend."

Beatrice's face broke into a smile, and she tightened her hold on Henrietta's arm. "Aunt will be so pleased I have a friend!"

Arm in arm, they exited the park.

Today had taught Henrietta a lesson.

That first impressions could be wrong.

CHAPTER EIGHTEEN

GILES GLANCED UP from his paper as Mother entered the breakfast room accompanied by her maid, who steered her toward her chair, sat her down, and helped her to a plateful of eggs.

"Where's Beatrice?" he asked.

"She must still be asleep," Mother replied. "Leave her be."

"No." He gestured toward the maid. "Annie, fetch Lady Beatrice. If she's not up yet, send Kitty in to help her dress."

"Yes, your lordship." The maid bobbed a curtsey and exited the room.

"You're too harsh on that child, Giles." Mother picked up her fork and took a bite of her eggs. "These are perfect," she said. "Just how I like them."

He eyed her with suspicion. Mother was all too apt to change the subject when he was discussing Beatrice and her manners.

"I think Beatrice needs…"

"In fact," she interrupted, "this is how I remember the eggs were cooked when I was younger. My mama insisted on employing a French chef."

"Mother…"

"I never could abide overcooked eggs," she continued. "Eggs need to be treated with care. Overcooking them spoils them intolerably, forcing them into rigid unpalatable shapes, devoid of any character or taste. They need to be treated with a delicate hand."

She glanced over in his direction, her short-sighted eyes clear in the morning sunlight.

He set his paper aside. "All right, Mother, you've made your point."

She raised her eyebrows in an innocent gesture—momentarily reminding him of another woman who'd try to appear innocent—a hellion who was always up to mischief.

"My dear boy, I'm merely remarking on the excellence of my breakfast."

"Yes," he said, "and you were, no doubt, going to follow up with a comparison between eggs and young ladies, saying that young ladies should also be treated with a delicate hand and given free rein to preserve their individuality."

She had the grace to blush.

"Tea?" he asked.

She nodded, and he reached for the teapot and filled her cup.

"I only want Beatrice to learn the benefits of discipline," he said.

"Yes, but must you be so regimental about it? She's not enlisted in the militia."

"She must understand her boundaries."

"Your father and I gave *you* free rein."

"A young woman is in greater danger of ruination from her behavior than a young man," he said, "Like it or not, that's the way of the world. Beatrice has a title and a considerable dowry, which means that she's prey to all sorts of unscrupulous men who seek to take advantage of both."

She shook her head. "You make it sound like the world outside is a battlefield."

"In some ways, it is."

Hurried footsteps approached.

Annie opened the door and entered the room, together with Beatrice's maid. Giles's stomach tightened at the distress in her face.

"What's the matter, Kitty? Has your mistress been taken ill?"

"She's not in her room, your lordship. Her bed's been slept in, but she's dressed herself."

"She must be around somewhere," Mother said. "Try the garden."

"She's nowhere to be found," Kitty said.

Giles let out a sigh. "Cursed girl. She must be playing a trick."

"Beatrice wouldn't be so foolish," Mother said.

"Then, where is she?"

A ripple of fear threaded through him. What if she'd run off with a man—or been abducted?

He leaped to his feet, knocking his teacup over, which fell to the floor, shattering on impact.

"Giles!" Mother cried.

At that moment, the front door slammed, and he heard voices.

He sprinted to the door, pushing Kitty aside.

Beatrice stood in the hallway, an animated expression in her eyes. She looked the happiest he'd seen her since the day she'd arrived at Thorpe Hall, a broken-hearted orphan of fifteen.

Her companion stood beside her, face flushed, eyes bright, and her hair in a tangle, unruly ringlets hanging on either side of her face. Her skin glowed with good health and exercise, and she radiated a vitality so potent that his breath caught in his throat at the sight of her.

She looked like a wild, pagan goddess. His gaze wandered over her body—the delectable curves of her youthful form, and the firm, ripe breasts which heaved against the muslin of her gown.

He drew in a sharp breath as a surge of heat raged through his blood, and he found himself hardening in his breeches.

It was Henrietta Redford.

Fighting to control the primal need to take her in the hallway, he fisted his hands, digging the nails into his palms, using the sharp sting to regain his senses.

"Where the devil have you been!" he roared.

Beatrice's eyes widened, and she took a step back. She glanced at Miss Redford, who took her hand in a gesture of comfort.

"I-I've been in the park," Beatrice said. "Forgive me, I went for a walk, and…"

"On your own? You little fool!" He advanced on her, and tears pooled in her eyes, which shimmered with terror.

"How many times have I…" he began, but Miss Redford darted forward, shielding Beatrice with her body, and raised her hand.

"Stop!" she cried. "It was *my* doing. I invited Beatrice to take a walk before breakfast. I saw no harm in it. Isn't that right, Beatrice?"

Beatrice hesitated, then nodded.

He held out his hand. "Come here, Beatrice."

Beatrice glanced at Miss Redford, who nodded encouragement, then she approached him.

"Go and join your aunt for breakfast," he said. "I'll deal with you later."

"Giles, Miss Redford didn't…"

"Now."

She slipped past him into the breakfast room.

"Don't punish her," Miss Redford said.

"How dare you tell me what I can and cannot do!" he cried. "I'll deal with my cousin as I see fit."

"But *I'm* to blame."

"You think I don't know that?" he replied. "You're trouble. Ruin your own life with your escapades if you wish. Your reputation matters not. But leave Beatrice out of it. She's suffered enough in her life."

"And, I suppose, an association with me would be further torment?" she cried, her eyes flashing with anger.

"For once in my life," he said, "I find I'm in agreement with you."

The anger in her expression disappeared and was replaced by resignation.

She inclined her head, then retreated toward the door.

"Wait!" he cried. "At least let me send for the carriage to take you home."

"I can walk," she said. "After all, as you so eloquently put it, my reputation matters not. Please, give my regards to your mother."

She gestured toward the door. The footman opened it with a bow, and she thanked him with a brilliant smile. Then she turned her back on Giles and slipped outside.

When he returned to the breakfast room, Beatrice and Mother were chatting animatedly while they ate, as if nothing untoward had happened.

He slid into his seat. Beatrice cast a nervous glance in his direction, then resumed eating.

"Well?" he asked. "Do you have nothing to say?"

"I'm sorry," she said, her mouth full.

"Is that it?"

"Leave her be, Giles," Mother said. "You've already admonished her."

"Not nearly enough."

"I may have poor sight, Giles, but my hearing is as good as ever. I think *you* should be the one apologizing."

"To Beatrice?"

"And to Miss Redford. Did you have to insult that charming young woman quite so dreadfully?"

"Charming!" he scoffed. "She's the devil in female form."

"Giles!" Beatrice cried. "She's my friend."

"She's not your friend, Beatrice!"

"Yes, she is. She's coming to Lady Caldicott's house party, and we're going to…"

"You're going to do nothing with her, do you hear me?" he roared.

"Cousin…"

"No," he interrupted. "I'm your guardian, which means I'm responsible for your welfare. If you don't promise that you'll stay away from Miss Redford, I'll have you remain here instead of going to Caldicott Abbey. I won't have you running wild, encouraged by that hellion."

Beatrice pushed her plate aside, and her fork fell to the floor with a clatter. "Actually, it was Miss Redford who told me how inappropriate it was to wander about unchaperoned."

He let out a snort of derision. "What a pity she doesn't follow her own advice. She wanders about like a wild thing."

"Why shouldn't she?" Beatrice cried. "Everyone, most of all you, thinks the worst of her. So, she might as well indulge in the sins that the world accuses her of committing. I don't understand why you hate her so much!"

She flinched at the ferocity of her tone, then reached for Mother's hand. "Forgive me, Aunt."

"It's not your fault, Beatrice," Mother said.

Giles reached for his teacup, but his hand shook so much, it rattled on the saucer, and he set it down.

Bloody women—always siding with each other instead of listening to reason!

"Giles, darling," Mother said, "we all know you want what's best for Beatrice, but you must let her choose her own friends. She'll only fight against you all the more if you restrict her too much."

"That's exactly what Henrietta says," Beatrice said. "Is that why you hate her?"

"I don't *hate* anyone."

"But you dislike her," Mother said. "What is it about her you find so abhorrent?"

Unable to reply, he rose to his feet. "I'll let you two ladies enjoy your breakfast in peace," he said. "If anyone wants me, I'll be in my study."

He swept his chair aside, then exited the breakfast room. Mother might have poor eyesight, but her insight seemed to have developed to compensate, and the expression in her eyes when she looked at him was unsettling....

...almost as if she understood the true reason for his anger—the fact that he struggled to control his desire every time he thought of Miss Redford.

CHAPTER NINETEEN

"**C**OME ALONG, *MES amis*—time ticks!"

Henrietta entered the high-ceilinged great hall of Caldicott Abbey just in time to catch sight of Lady Caldicott standing at the top of the main staircase, making an announcement as if she heralded the arrival of royalty. Resplendent in a dark crimson riding habit, Lady Caldicott was every bit the grand hostess, and her French ancestry gave her an exotic air.

Lady Caldicott descended the grand staircase in a slow, deliberate fashion as if she savored each step. Henrietta glanced at the other guests mingling around the hallway. Each and every one of them stared at their hostess—the men mostly open mouthed, admiration in their eyes. As for the women—half of them watched her with admiration, the other half with envy.

Or spite, in the case of one woman.

Juliette Howard stood across the hallway, arm in arm with Lady Irma Fairchild, the expression on her face sour enough to curdle milk.

How was it that someone as delightful as Eleanor Howard had such an unpleasant sister? Juliette had, yesterday evening before dinner, singled Henrietta out to tell her that Eleanor had "yet again, indulged in a tantrum" and had been forbidden to attend the house party.

And now Lavinia had disappeared, there was no congenial company to be had today, given that Lord Thorpe had also taken

Henrietta to one side last night and warned her to steer clear of Beatrice.

Why did everyone feel the need to pull her into alcoves to admonish or insult her?

She smiled to herself. Today, during the hunt, she would give them all another reason to admonish her. She had no intention of riding alongside the other women or cantering at the ladylike pace expected of her. As soon as they were out in the open, she'd be off, and nobody could stop her. Papa's gelding was capable of clearing even the tallest hedges.

If only she could have worn her breeches today, rather than the cumbersome riding habit that had arrived from the modiste shortly before they'd left for Caldicott Abbey. But on hearing her suggest it after dinner last night, Aunt Agnes had smacked Henrietta with her fan in front of the other guests, much to the obvious delight of Lady Irma Fairchild. Henrietta's arm still smarted where Aunt's fan had struck it.

There was no chance of her leading Beatrice astray today, for Beatrice wasn't among the riding party. Henrietta caught sight of Lord Thorpe, standing in a corner together with Viscount Marlow. But, unlike the rest of the party, he wasn't staring at their hostess.

He was looking directly at her.

His eyes sparkled, and the ghost of a smile played on his lips. Then, as if recalling himself, he frowned and looked away.

Lady Caldicott reached the foot of the stairs and swept her way toward the main doors, and the guests followed. Henrietta stayed at the rear of the party, and as they followed the path toward the stables, Lord Thorpe glanced over his shoulder and met her gaze briefly, before resuming his attention on the path ahead.

THE HOUNDS VIBRATED with pent-up energy, baying in eagerness, tails wagging stiffly. The buzz of conversation filled the air, together with the echo of hoofbeats on the stones as the grooms led the horses into the cobbled stable yard.

Henrietta approached her mount, which stood a full hand taller than the dainty mares provided for the rest of the ladies. In her view, riding was a pursuit to be indulged in for the sake of enjoyment. Tradition might dictate that women rode sidesaddle but, in all likelihood, it was yet another mechanism by which men ensured that women were kept subjugated. Side-saddles were damned uncomfortable, and it was almost impossible to ride at speed without falling off. Riding astride in breeches would have been far more practical.

Refusing the mounting block, she lifted her foot into the stirrup, grasped the pommel of the saddle, and launched herself upward, sliding into position.

"Did you see that, Irma?" a nasal voice cut through the air. "She's like a wild animal, incapable of mounting like a lady! I wonder at our hostess allowing such savagery."

"Lady Caldicott's half French," a softer voice replied. "They're a little more liberal, are they not?"

"Heaven preserve us from the liberal attitude which impels peasants to cut off the heads of their betters."

Henrietta turned her mount in a tight circle to see Juliette Howard and Lady Irma, sitting on identical mounts, and wearing identical riding habits, adorned in a military fashion, as if they were about to engage in battle.

The fox wasn't the only creature being hunted this morning.

And, as if on cue, their quarry appeared, astride an enormous black stallion. His jacket fitted his body to perfection, and the material of his breeches stretched across broad, muscular thighs.

He drew the animal to a halt, and the sneers turned into smiles of admiration.

"Oh, Lord Thorpe, there you are! We're so eager to see you ride, are we not, Irma?"

Henrietta suppressed a giggle, and he glanced in her direction. Then she urged her mount on and rode out of the courtyard to join the rest of the party.

The master of the hunt blew his horn, and the party set off.

It wasn't long before the hounds caught the scent of their quarry, and the riders cantered across the fields in pursuit.

Henrietta's chance had come. She steered away from the main party, skirting round the hedge at the perimeter of the field.

The hounds disappeared into a thicket, and the party followed, but Henrietta continued her path alongside the hedge. Before she could urge her mount into a full gallop, a voice cried out.

"Miss Redford!"

Lord Thorpe was in pursuit.

She slowed her horse to a trot, and he drew alongside.

"What do you want?" she asked.

"I was hoping to have a word with you."

"You've already made it clear you want me to stay away from Beatrice," she said. "There's no need to tell me again."

"It's not about that," he said. "Something's been stolen from our host. A Medieval sword."

"And?"

"Viscount Marlow told me this morning. Lord Caldicott is most upset."

"And you want my help in finding it?"

He arched an eyebrow, and the realization hit her.

"You think *I* stole it?" She shook her head. "How dare you! Just because I'm not some ninny who prefers to stitch cushions indoors, you think I'm a thief? What the devil would I want with a sword?"

"You indulge in sword fighting," he said. "You have a sword of your own."

"So, why would I want another?" she asked. "Besides, I fight with a foil, which is entirely different to a Medieval sword."

He narrowed his eyes, uncertainty in his expression. "I never meant to accuse…"

"Oh, save your breath!" she cried. "What have I ever done to make you hate me so much?"

He flinched and shook his head. "Miss Redford, I don't…"

She held up her hand, brandishing the crop. "No," she said. "Don't bother to answer. In fact, don't bother to speak to me at all."

"I…"

"You asked me to stay away from your cousin," she snarled, anger boiling inside her. "Now, I'm asking you to stay away from me."

She urged her mount on, then set off across the field.

He shouted after her, but she ignored him.

Arrogant swine! Tears of anger clouded her vision, and she wiped them with the back of her hand. Then, releasing her pent-up fury, she leaned forward in the saddle, and spurred her mount into a full gallop, letting the air cool her cheeks.

"Miss Redford!"

The deep rumble of hoofbeats reverberated in the ground as he pursued her, matching her speed. She glanced back to see him following, his horse's hooves throwing clods of earth into the air, puffs of breath forming around the animal's nostrils.

"Go back to your admirers!" she yelled. "Leave me alone!"

She turned back and forged ahead, toward a thick beech hedge at the far end of the field. The urge to release the tension and fly to freedom overwhelmed her, and she increased her horse's pace, gauging the distance to the hedge, before preparing to jump.

"Henrietta!" a voice cried, filled with panic, but she ignored it.

"Come on, boy…" she breathed. "One, two, three, *lift!*"

The animal launched into the air. She dipped forward, clutching the reins, and gripped the animal's flank with her thighs as they sailed over the hedge. She leaned back as her mount cleared the hedge and landed on the other side.

She drew in a deep breath, indulging in the exhilaration of the maneuver.

Let him try and catch her now!

A cry of panic tore through the air, followed by a deep, male scream.

Henrietta reined in her horse, and the animal reared, almost unseating her. She turned and looked back, shielding her eyes against the sunlight.

Standing beside the hedge was a horse.

A riderless horse.

She followed the line of the hedge with her gaze, and icy fingers clawed at her heart.

A man lay on the ground at the base of the hedge, where she'd jumped over it just moments before.

And he wasn't moving.

"Lord Thorpe! Are you hurt?"

He lay still, and a wave of panic rippled through her.

"Giles!" She let out a scream and spurred her mount toward him, then dismounted as she reached the hedge.

He lay on his back, legs and arms twisted, his face ashen. His eyes were closed, mouth open, as if in a scream, showing white, even teeth.

"No…"

Tears clouding her vision, she crouched beside him, then loosened his collar, and felt his neck, until she found a pulse that beat to a steady rhythm against her fingertips.

"Oh, thank heaven!"

She ran her hands along his arms and legs, checking for breaks. The bones seemed sound, so why hadn't he woken? Then she felt it—a gash on the side of his head. She lifted her hand, and her fingers were sticky with blood. Fumbling at her collar, she pulled off her necktie and pressed it against the wound, then wrapped it around his head, securing the makeshift bandage with a knot.

"Oh, Giles!" she cried. "Why did you have to follow me? The last thing I wanted was to see you hurt."

She placed her palm against his cheek and caressed it. His skin was cold, and a shiver of fear rippled through her. What if he didn't wake?

Moisture stung her eyes, and she blinked. A fat tear splashed onto his cheek, and she wiped it away.

"Giles, my love, come back to me."

But he didn't respond.

Another tear fell, followed by another. Then she wiped them away, cursing herself for being such a fool. Crying over him wouldn't serve any purpose.

She grasped his hand and lifted it to her lips.

"Stay here, my love," she whispered. "I'll get help."

Closing her eyes, she kissed his hand and held it against her cheek.

"What the devil are you doing?" a voice spoke.

She lifted her head to find clear blue eyes staring straight at her.

"Oh, thank goodness!"

She placed her hand on his cheek and lowered her mouth to his. A hand fisted her hair and pulled her close, and he slipped his tongue between her lips, stroking her mouth. A deep groan erupted from his chest, and he deepened the kiss, devouring her with hungry, insistent lips.

Then he pulled free and stared at her, his eyes dark with desire, the pupils fully dilated until they were almost black.

She moved forward to kiss him again, and he froze, casting his gaze about.

"What happened?"

"You fell off your horse, jumping the hedge."

The passion in his eyes dissolved, replaced by the original fury.

"I was following *you*, if I recall."

"Are you in pain?"

He shook his head.

She rose to her feet and took his hand.

"We need to get you back to the house and send for a doctor," she said. "Can you stand?"

He snatched his hand free. "Of course I can bloody stand!"

He struggled to his feet and lost his balance, but she caught his arm before he fell.

"You *are* hurt," she said.

"It's just a sprain." He limped toward the horses, which stood patiently waiting, but when he placed his foot in the stirrup and tried to mount, he gave a yelp of pain and let out a curse.

"Shit!"

"Let me help," she said. "I can push you up."

"Don't be ridiculous," he said. "It would be most improper."

"Do you *want* to walk all the way back?" she asked. "There's nobody to see us, and besides, as you've said on many occasions, I have no reputation to ruin. I can mount by myself, but you can't." She placed a gentle hand on his arm. "Please—Giles—can't we declare a truce, just for a moment?"

His eyes widened at her use of his name.

"I'll not tell anyone," she said, "and I promise to give you leave to hate me again as soon as you've returned to the house."

He let out a sigh. "Very well. Push me up when I say."

He placed a foot into the stirrup and grasped the reins. She placed her hands on him, ignoring the frisson of desire at the feel of his warmth through the material of his breeches. He drew in a sharp breath and closed his eyes.

"Giles?"

He exhaled, slowly, then opened his eyes. "On the count of three," he said. "One…two…three!"

She pushed up, and he pulled on the reins and swung his body over the saddle, then she stepped back, shielding her eyes against the sun as he stared down at her.

His eyes seemed to glow, and an uncomfortable heat pooled in her center.

"Aren't you going to thank me?" she asked.

"What for?" he replied. "If it wasn't for you, I wouldn't have fallen."

The arrogance hadn't taken long to return.

"I'm not to blame for your poor horsemanship," she retorted.

She approached her horse, took the reins, and mounted in a swift, smooth gesture.

"The problem with you, Miss Redford," he said, "is that you're too damned good. Only when you've failed will you understand humility."

He gathered the reins and turned his mount in a circle.

"By the way," he said. "You're wrong."

"About what?"

"I don't hate you. I never have."

He squeezed his horse's flanks and set off, not even bothering to look back.

"You may not hate me," she whispered, watching him disappear, "but you don't love me either."

CHAPTER TWENTY

G ILES LAY IN bed, watching the flickering light from the candle dancing across the ceiling.

Try as he might, sleep eluded him. He'd returned from the stables ahead of the rest of the hunting party and his valet, other than arching an eyebrow, had said nothing about the state of his clothes. The man had merely prepared a hot bath and engaged in idle chatter about whether velvet jackets were to be preferred in the winter months over flannel ones, before selecting a fresh suit for dinner.

Guilt had gnawed at his conscience over the way he'd abandoned Miss Redford in the field. And he was ashamed—ashamed of his poor horsemanship, his behavior—and the way he relished the feel of her lips on his as she'd initiated their kiss.

He closed his eyes, reimagining the feel of her body against his, soft and pliant, liquid brown eyes filled with desire, and those whispered words…

Giles, my love. Come back to me.

Had he imagined them?

He opened his eyes, rolled onto his side, and winced. A bruise had formed on his side where he'd fallen, and his head still throbbed.

He reached out to the table beside the bed and picked up the bloodstained neckerchief.

Her neckerchief, which she'd bound his head with. His valet had offered to clean it, but Giles had refused. When he held it to his nose and inhaled, he could still detect a soft scent of roses and fresh air.

The scent of her.

It was a piece of her he could treasure, out of sight, when the world wasn't watching.

A piece of her that nobody could take away.

Fisting the necktie in his hand, he closed his eyes and drifted into sleep, dreaming of warm chocolate-brown eyes and whispered words of love.

THE FOLLOWING DAY, while the rest of the men went out shooting, Giles pleaded a sprained ankle, which was, at least, not a falsehood.

Miss Redford had disappeared. Given her distaste for feminine pursuits, she'd most likely tagged along with the men, and would return brandishing a brace of pheasant, hair in disarray, like a wild huntress from ancient Greece.

Pall-mall with the ladies held no attraction for him and, leaving Beatrice in the care of Lady Caldicott, where at least he could be assured she was free from Miss Redford's influence, he chose to explore the abbey grounds. The Caldicotts had more liberal ideas about aesthetics than most, and much of the grounds had been left to nature. Ivy smothered the walls, and many of the tree-lined paths were overgrown such that the branches formed a tunnel through which the sun strained to penetrate, casting mottled patterns on the pathway.

He could almost imagine a host of faeries or wood nymphs residing in the gardens—ethereal creatures which tended to the ancient spirits, whispering to themselves in the breeze.

Did they watch him—the intruder in their realm?

The whispers turned to laughter, a laugh so full of life that he couldn't help smiling. Unlike the elegant, restrained chatter of the ladies over luncheon, the laughter was wild and untamed, and he found himself drawn to it. The path opened out into a meadow, which sloped downward in a gentle incline toward a copse. Long grasses swayed in the breeze, punctuated by the occasional bright flower which shimmered in the sunlight.

Then he saw her.

Running through the grass, arms in the air, trailing a fringed shawl behind her, hair loose…

Had he not known it was Miss Redford, he'd have believed she was a nymph in human form. She seemed to float through the grass.

"Hen, wait up! You're going too fast!"

Another young woman ran behind her, picking her way through the grasses in measured steps, and he recognized Miss de Grande. He couldn't help but smile to himself. Both young women were at the house party with their chaperones—two aged, rotund aunts, who were, even now, absorbed in their game of pall-mall, mallets in hand, oblivious to the antics of their charges. He could just imagine their chaperones' voices, rising in pitch in admonishment. Then he checked himself. *He'd* admonish Beatrice if he caught her running about like some farm girl. But he couldn't deny the allure of seeing an athletic, female form, full of vibrancy, indulging in the simple pleasure of running through the countryside.

He froze as a shriek echoed across the landscape. Miss Redford tripped and fell forward, disappearing into the long grass.

"Henrietta!" Miss de Grande cried out and picked up the pace. Giles set off in pursuit, his heart racing, wincing at the pain in his ankle.

Then, a head and shoulders appeared as she sat up.

"Hen, are you all right?" Miss de Grande cried.

A deep, hearty laughter echoed across the meadow. Miss Redford emerged from the grass as her friend reached her, then she threw back her head, body shaking with mirth.

"Henry!" Miss de Grande cried. "Look at your dress! Your Aunt Agnes will have a fit."

"So, what's new?"

More laughter.

"You're a bad girl, Henrietta, do you know that?"

She linked her arm through her friend's. "Yes, but that's why you and Ellie like me, even if nobody else does."

"I thought the Thorpe girl was your friend," Miss de Grande said.

"Ah, but the poor creature suffers the disapproval of her guardian—an insufferable man who loathes the idea of anyone having any fun and is resolved to hate me."

They continued along the meadow, their backs to him, their voices fading as they skipped toward the copse.

Giles retreated to the path, his cheeks warming with shame.

Is that what she thought of him? She'd said it to his face plenty of times, but hearing her say it to someone else somehow made it more real.

Had he been too hard on Beatrice by forbidding her to go near Miss Redford, when he himself was drawn to her? Henrietta Redford was the wild fruit which he'd forbidden himself to taste.

But forbidden fruit was always the sweetest.

Unladylike she might be, ignoring propriety and social convention, but her lust for life and her kindness was unlike anything he'd seen in a woman. Who else would have crouched in the mud and tended to him after he'd fallen from his horse? Most ladies would have either wrinkled their noses at the thought of stepping in the mud or fainted at the sight of him.

But not *her*. With no thought for herself, she had helped him onto his horse, tended to his wound…

…and kissed him.

And now, watching her skip through the meadow with her friend, he felt like a voyeur, an adolescent schoolboy indulging in his first crush by watching her unobserved.

But it was no mere infatuation. A powerful connection existed between them, as if she were a siren, and he the sailor, adrift, drawing closer until the point of no return, where he dashed himself against the rocks and met destruction.

He turned and limped back along the path. The surrounding trees whispered in the breeze as if the wood nymphs understood his weakness and mocked him.

His weakness was—and always had been—*her*.

By the time he returned to the house, tea was being served. The men had returned from their shoot, regaling each other with tales of how many birds they had bagged. Giles smiled to himself at the one-upmanship of his companions, where each one outdid the other, imagining that the number of birds he'd shot was in direct proportion to his male prowess.

A hand tugged at his sleeve, and he turned to see Juliette Howard, holding out a teacup.

"Tea?"

"Thank you." He took the cup and sipped it.

Ugh. How much sugar was in there?

"Is it to your taste?"

He swallowed, then nodded.

"I knew you were a man after my own heart," she said. "Tea is such an unpalatable drink without sugar. I cannot drink it if it has less than three spoonsful. Irma and I were wondering whether you felt the same. I'm happy to be proved right. Would you care for a biscuit?"

"To take away the taste of the tea?"

She frowned as if trying to make out whether he'd just insulted her, then the smile returned.

"I was disappointed to learn that you weren't with the shooting party today, Lord Thorpe."

"I'm sorry to disappoint you, Miss Howard."

"I told Irma that you were sure to bag the most birds today, at least more than Viscount Marlow. But *he* didn't attend the shoot, either."

"Then it seems as if we've both been a disappointment."

"I wouldn't say that," she said, giving him a smile that he presumed was intended to be alluring, and—*sweet lord*—fluttering her eyelashes.

Did women really think that rapid blinking encouraged a man to find them more attractive? He couldn't deny that Miss Howard was the most beautiful woman in the room, but physical beauty needed to be tempered with a beauty of character—and of that, she had none.

He crossed the room, moving toward the window through which he could see a handful of ladies still playing pall-mall. Undeterred, she followed.

"How many birds would you have bagged today do you think?" she asked.

"None, probably," he said. "I'm a terrible shot."

She gave a ladylike titter that set his teeth on edge. "I can't believe that."

"I've never been fond of shooting."

"Don't say you're one of these liberals who wages war on hunting?"

"On the contrary," he said. "But a gunman bags his quarry from a safe distance. He doesn't have to watch while his victim's lifeblood drains away. I prefer to look my prey in the eye."

Her eyes widened, and she paled.

"I-I believe…" she hesitated, "…Lady Caldicott wanted to speak with me." She dipped into a curtsey and fled.

His conscience pricked at him. How could he have said something so shocking? But it had achieved the desired effect. There was something to be said for a lack of propriety if it rid oneself of the company of undesirables.

There was something to be said for behaving a little badly, after all.

Setting his teacup and its disgusting brown contents aside, he went in search of Beatrice.

The pall-mall match was still in full swing. Mother sat wrapped in a shawl, together with Lady Agnes Redford, but there was no sign of his cousin, so he made his way back inside.

Hurried footsteps approached.

"Lord Thorpe! Sir!"

He turned to see Beatrice's maid running toward him, her features creased with distress.

"Kitty!" he cried. "What the devil's the matter?"

"It's Miss Beatrice!" she cried. "She's in trouble. Come quickly!"

"Is she hurt?"

"Not yet."

She set off toward the gardens, and he limped after her.

Not yet? Dear God, what had happened?

CHAPTER TWENTY-ONE

"HEAVENS, I'M HUNGRY! I don't know if I'll last until dinner. I hope we've not missed tea."

Henrietta glanced at the sun, which was already low on the horizon. "I suspect we've missed it, Lavinia."

"You'll have to change your gown," her friend said. "The hem is soaked."

"No more than yours."

"You shouldn't have pushed me in the water, then."

"I didn't—you just slipped!" Henrietta laughed. "In any case, it wouldn't matter whether I changed my gown or not. Half the company will disapprove of me whatever I wear."

"Such as Lord Thorpe?" Lavinia suggested.

Henrietta slipped her arm through her friend's, and they retraced their steps toward the abbey, where the turrets were visible above the trees.

"What have you done to incur his dislike?" Lavinia asked.

"What have I *not* done!" Henrietta laughed. "He even accused me of theft, can you believe it?"

Lavinia tripped and stumbled against her.

"Careful!" Henrietta tugged at her friend's arm.

"Are you all right, Lavinia?"

"Y-yes," came the reply. "Theft, you say?"

"That's right—a sword or something," Henrietta said. "As if I'd want to steal a sword when I have plenty at home!"

Lavinia drew in a sharp breath. "Perhaps Lord Caldicott's mislaid it and has forgotten where it is," she said. "Doddery old fool, he's older than Papa. Lady Caldicott must be twenty years younger than him, at least. I can't think what induced her to marry him."

"Other than his title, estate, and fortune?" Henrietta said. "'Tis a veritable mystery, indeed."

Lavinia let out a laugh, and the tension in her voice disappeared.

"Come on!" she cried. "I'll race you to the top of the field."

She set off, a spring in her step.

"Hey, that's not fair!" Henrietta cried. "I wasn't ready!"

"Catch me, then!"

Lifting her skirts, she set off after her friend, catching up with her just as they reached the path.

"I declare that a draw," Lavinia said.

"Only because you had a head start." Henrietta wiped her brow. "I'm all sweaty. Aunt will have a fit if she sees me like this."

A high-pitched scream echoed through the air.

Lavinia clutched Henrietta's hand. "Good Lord, what was that?"

"It sounded like a woman," Henrietta said. "Perhaps Aunt Agnes has seen the mud on my riding habit from yesterday."

Another scream rang out, and her blood froze. It was a scream of pure terror.

"Help me!"

"It's coming from the other end of the path," Henrietta said. "Come on!"

They set off in the direction of the screams.

"I can't see anything," Lavinia said. "Can you?"

Another scream rang out, which sounded as if it were coming from above.

Henrietta looked up and saw the source of the scream.

A young woman was hanging from a branch, halfway up a fir tree. Legs flailing in the air, she was trying to get a purchase on the trunk with her feet, but the jerky movements in her body spoke of panic.

And panic was never a good thing. Panic often led to tragedy.

A male voice roared out. "Beatrice!"

"Sweet Lord, it's the Thorpe girl!" Lavinia cried. "What the devil is she doing up there?"

"Putting her life in danger," Henrietta replied, "to say nothing of her reputation."

They sprinted toward the tree, where Lord Thorpe stood at the base, staring up into the canopy. Beside him stood a maidservant, her body shaking with sobs.

"Lord Thorpe!" Henrietta cried. "What's happened?"

He glanced toward her. "As if you don't know!" he cried, his voice strained with panic. "Did you persuade her into it?"

"Of course not!"

"Help! I don't want to die!" Beatrice cried. She kicked out with her legs, trying to gain a purchase on the tree trunk.

"You should have thought of that before you played the fool!" Lord Thorpe replied.

"That's not helping," Henrietta hissed. "She's panicking. If she doesn't calm down, she'll fall."

She tipped her head up. "Beatrice!" she called out. "Beatrice, it's Henrietta."

"Henrietta! Help me!"

"I will, Beatrice, but I want you to do something for me first. Do you think you can?"

"I-I'll try."

"Take a deep breath in and count to three, then breathe out and count to five. I want you to do that four times."

"A-all right."

"What good will that do?" Lord Thorpe snapped.

"Considerably more good than your admonishments," Henrietta retorted.

"She shouldn't have climbed up in the first place! If she's seen, she'll be ruined!"

"I agree," Henrietta said, "but don't you think it's better to tell her that once she's safely down? Have you sent for help?"

"I tried to help her, but…"

Henrietta turned to her friend. "Lavinia, go and find the gardener. Tell him to bring a ladder and some rope." She glanced at Lord Thorpe, then resumed her attention on her friend. "Try to swear him to secrecy if you can. Nobody must find out what Beatrice has done."

Lavinia nodded and sprinted off.

Henrietta looked up. To her relief, Beatrice had stopped kicking.

"That's good, Beatrice," she said. "Keep breathing for me and stay still. Help is on the way."

Her gaze wandered up the tree. It was easy to see what had happened. The remnants of a branch stuck out from the trunk just beneath Beatrice's feet. It must have snapped under her weight.

"Can you hang on until help arrives?" Henrietta called up.

"I c-can't," came the reply. "I'm slipping!"

"Dear God, she's going to die!" the maid cried.

"For heaven's sake, Kitty!" Lord Thorpe roared. "Keep your thoughts to yourself!"

More sobs echoed from above as Beatrice began to panic again.

There was nothing for it—and no time to wait.

"Hold on!" Henrietta cried. "I'm coming."

She approached the trunk, and a hand caught her sleeve.

"Do you want to risk your neck as well?" Lord Thorpe cried. "I've already tried."

A number of the lower branches had broken off. He must have attempted to climb after her, but the branches had given way beneath him.

She placed her hand over his, and he met her gaze. Though his voice had been full of anger, it was anger born of fear. A deep-seated terror darkened his expression.

"She's already lost her parents," he said. "She can't lose her life…"

"That won't happen," she interrupted. "I've been climbing trees all my life. I'll get her down safely. Trust me. I'm her friend—and it's what friends do."

He opened his mouth to protest, then glanced up and nodded.

"Give me a hand up," she said, "so I can reach the higher branches…" She gave a smile of reassurance. "Imagine I needed help mounting a horse." She spotted a sturdy-looking branch about eight feet from the ground. "Over here."

He moved to where she indicated, then locked his hands together and bent down. Placing a steadying hand on his shoulder, she placed a foot in the makeshift stirrup and launched herself upward, catching hold of the branch and curling her fingers round it. It gave a creak but held firm. Then she placed her legs on either side of the trunk and gripped with her knees and toes to gain a purchase.

"Henrietta, be careful."

She glanced over her shoulder to find him staring directly at her.

"Keep talking to Beatrice while I climb up," she said. "And be kind—if not for my sake, then for hers."

His lips curled into a smile, then he nodded and called up. "Henrietta's coming, Beatrice. Be brave and hold on."

Henrietta pulled herself up with her arms, shuffling her knees upward. After a few maneuvers, she was able to reach another branch. Then, she hauled herself up until she drew level with Beatrice.

"Oh, Henrietta!" the girl cried. "You must help me. I can't climb down."

"Yes, you can," Henrietta said. Where the branch had snapped, there was room for a toehold.

"Keep a firm hold of the branch and move your right leg slowly toward the trunk."

Beatrice complied, and Henrietta nodded with approval. "That's it. Now, stretch out just a little, and point your toe toward the trunk."

Beatrice moved her foot and placed her toe on the stub. "It doesn't feel safe."

Henrietta shuffled further up, squeezing her knees against the trunk. Then, gripping a branch with her right hand, she held out her left.

"Beatrice, I want you to take my hand. Then you'll be able to reach the next branch with your left foot."

Beatrice's eyes widened with terror. "No—I can't do that!" she sobbed. "I'll fall!"

"Listen to Miss Redford, Beatrice!" Lord Thorpe cried from below. "Trust her."

"Would *you* trust her, Giles?" Beatrice cried.

"Yes," he said. "I would trust her with my life."

Henrietta glanced down and saw him staring up, intensity in his blue gaze. Was he merely reassuring the terrified young woman?

Or did he speak from the heart?

Beatrice gave her a watery smile. "If Giles trusts you, then it must be serious."

"What matters more is whether *you* trust me," Henrietta said.

Beatrice reached out and took Henrietta's hand.

"I'm slipping!"

"Reach out with your left foot," Henrietta said. "There's a branch just beneath it."

Moments later, Beatrice was standing on the branch, sobbing with relief. "I thought I was going to fall!"

"It's not over yet," Henrietta said. "You must lower yourself onto the next branch."

She continued issuing instructions until Beatrice was almost at the bottom.

Lord Thorpe held his arms out. "Jump, Beatrice, and I'll catch you."

Beatrice slipped off the branch, and he caught her in his arms.

"Oh, Beatrice!" he cried. "I was so worried."

She wriggled free and looked up through the branches at Henrietta, her expression bright with excitement, her earlier terror forgotten.

"It was much easier going up than coming down," she said.

"Climbing down is always more treacherous than climbing up," Henrietta replied, lowering herself onto the branch, "mainly because you can't see where you're going."

"I'll remember that next time."

"There won't be a next time," Lord Thorpe said. "What on earth possessed you, Beatrice?"

"Henrietta's told me about the tree she used to climb at Thorpe Hall. I thought I'd give it a try. I'd have made it to the top if that branch hadn't snapped."

"I knew it," he growled. "I bloody *knew* it!" He glared up at Henrietta. "It was your doing, wasn't it? Didn't I tell you to leave Beatrice alone?"

"If I'd left her alone, she would have fallen out of the tree," Henrietta retorted.

"She was only up the damn tree because of you," he snapped. "Come on, Beatrice, we need to get you inside. Grubbing about with urchins will result in your ruination. I knew I shouldn't have brought you here. I'm taking you back to London this instant. You can explain to your aunt why our excursion has been cut short."

He took her hand and strode off.

She glanced over her shoulder. "What about Henrietta?"

"She can look after herself," he said. "*You're* my only concern."

"Go," Henrietta said, "I'll be fine."

Beatrice nodded and let her cousin lead her away.

Horrid man! Just when she thought a kind heart lived beneath that arrogant exterior, the adversary resurfaced—the man who was always determined to think the worst of her.

"The devil take you, Lord Thorpe," she muttered, sliding off the branch, reaching for a foothold. But she missed the hold, and her ankle slipped against the tree trunk. Then she fell to the ground, her leg twisting sideways on impact.

For a moment she lay in the undergrowth at the base of the tree, her eyes shifting in and out of focus.

Then she tried to stand and let out a curse.

A sickening pain tore through her left leg, and she fell back, taking a deep breath to stem the rising tide of nausea. The world seemed to tip sideways, pulsing in and out.

Sweet Lord, surely, she wasn't going to faint like a ninny?

She lay on the ground, focusing on her breathing until the pain receded. Then she sat up and drew back the folds of her skirt to inspect the leg. It looked uninjured, but as she brushed her hands over the front of the leg, below the knee, she yelped at a spike of pain. Using the tree as a prop, she stood more carefully this time and tested her weight on her left foot.

Ouch!

She cast her gaze about for a stick to use as a prop. But there was nothing sturdy enough. She hopped across the path, toward the wall on the opposite side then, placing her hands against the bricks, she began to move along the path—bending her left leg, hopping on her right—stopping after every few steps to regain her breath.

At this rate, she wouldn't be back in time for dinner, let alone tea.

About halfway along the path, a voice cried out, and she looked up to see two silhouettes. One, presumably the gardener, carried a coil of rope and a ladder.

"Hen!" Lavinia's voice cried out. "What the devil are you doing?"

"Walking back to the house," Henrietta said.

"Have you abandoned Lord Thorpe and his ward?"

"He abandoned me."

As Lavinia drew close, she let out a cry. "Dear Lord, you're injured!" She turned to her companion. "I say, come here."

"Right you are, Miss." The gardener put the ladder down and approached Henrietta.

"It's my leg," Henrietta said. "I can't put any weight on it. I don't think it's broken. With luck, it's just a sprain."

"A sprain can be right nasty," the gardener said. "Worse than a break, sometimes."

"Miss Redford cannot walk back," Lavinia said. "You'll carry her, won't you, Mr. Brown? And fetch a doctor?"

"No doctor!" Henrietta cried. "We can't let anyone find out what's happened—for Beatrice's sake. My leg just needs a bandage. But, please, don't carry me through the front doors. I have no wish to be seen."

"Aye, Miss," the gardener said. "I'll take ye through the kitchens."

"Good," Henrietta said. "Aunt Agnes will be angry enough as it is. I've a huge tear in my skirt."

"*I'm* angrier than your aunt," Lavinia said. "I won't be satisfied until Lord Thorpe's had a piece of my mind."

The gardener swept Henrietta up into his arms and set off for the house. Once inside, Lavinia took charge and helped Henrietta to dress, binding her leg until she could bear putting her weight on it without flinching. With luck, the rest of the party, including Aunt Agnes, would be none the wiser at dinner.

Except Lord Thorpe. Henrietta found herself smiling at the notion of her friend giving him a scolding.

But she was denied the satisfaction. By the time they arrived in the drawing room where sherry was being served, their hostess informed them that Lord Thorpe, together with his mother and cousin, had already left for London.

CHAPTER TWENTY-TWO

"Would you care for some tea, Beatrice?" Giles asked, picking up the teapot.

"Not particularly. I'm going to see how Aunt's doing."

"She's resting. I doubt she'll want to be disturbed."

"She won't mind *my* company." Beatrice rose to her feet and exited the room without so much as a nod.

Being a guardian was worse than being a parent. At least parents had years to acclimatize themselves to the role. They also had the benefit of a child's early years when they were wide-eyed with wonder at the world and always looking for joy in everything.

Unlike the sullen teenager he'd been landed with.

From the moment they'd left Caldicott Abbey, Beatrice had entered into a sulk. Today marked the third day of its duration, and, like the blizzard of two winters ago, the storm didn't look like easing any time soon.

He was determined not to give her the satisfaction of asking what the matter was.

But, when Mother had asked, Beatrice had bestowed a sweet smile on her aunt and said she had a headache. The real reason for her temper—Giles's admonishment and his abandonment of Miss Redford—she'd kept to herself.

Which only went to prove that Beatrice had more honor in her little finger than he had in his whole body.

He'd been so beset with anger that he'd lost all reason. Together with his frustration and an overwhelming sense of inadequacy, it made for a potent cocktail.

No man of his standing liked to be overshadowed or belittled. But, when he'd seen Miss Redford effortlessly climb that tree and rescue Beatrice—something he'd failed miserably at—and, with little to no fear, his male pride had been bruised beyond repair.

How she must scorn him!

Since his return to London, he'd steered clear of Hyde Park, her usual haunt. She was, most likely, spoiling for a battle of wits, which he was destined to lose.

You're a coward.

He jumped at the sound of knocking on the main doors, followed by voices—the footman and a woman's.

Sweet heaven, was she bringing the fight to him?

He sat, motionless in his seat. The parlor door opened, and the footman appeared, brandishing a silver salver containing a single card.

"You have a visitor, my lord. Shall I say you're not at home?"

Giles picked up the card and read the inscription.

Lady Elizabeth Grey

His relief at the caller not being his adversary overshadowed any sense of propriety at his former mistress visiting him in broad daylight.

"Show her in," he said, rising to his feet.

Moments later, Lady Betty appeared in the doorway, resplendent in dark purple silk. He bowed over her hand and kissed it.

"To what do I owe the honor?"

"Giles, darling, can I not call on an old friend?"

He caught the faint scent of expensive perfume—one which he himself had ordered for her from Paris.

"Betty," he said, "you do remember we agreed that…"

She let out a laugh. "Darling, how transparent you are! But

you need not have any concerns in *that* quarter. I have no intention of resuming our little liaison, that's not why I'm here. One must never look back, only forward. Dear Jimmy has offered to take me for a ride in his barouche this afternoon, before taking me to the opera."

"Jimmy?"

"Lord James Russell."

"That old stick-in-the-mud!" he scoffed. "I can't imagine what you see in *him*."

She gave him a saucy smile. "Many of my acquaintances have said the same of *you*."

He shifted uncomfortably in his seat, and she laughed. "Have no fear, darling, I adopt the same line of defense against *your* critics, an exercise which takes up considerably more time."

If she thought that would make him feel any better, she was mistaken.

"Which opera are you seeing?" he asked, eager to change the subject.

She waved her hand dismissively. "Heaven knows, darling! But it's bound to end in several deaths, a deflowering, and involve a hero harboring an unhealthy obsession over his mother."

She glanced about the room, and her gaze fell on the tea tray, set for two.

"Am I intruding?"

"No," he said. "Beatrice and I were about to have tea, then she changed her mind."

She arched an eyebrow. "Is your charge displeased with you?"

How the devil was Betty so perceptive?

Her mouth curled in a smile, and her eyes glittered with merriment." Ah! So, I'm right. I hear you've caused quite a stir."

"Is that why you're here, to lecture me on *my* behavior?"

"After a fashion," she said. "Shall I pour?" He nodded, and she poured two cups, then handed one to him, playing the hostess, as if they were back at her townhouse, indulging in refreshment after a morning of lovemaking.

"What am I rumored to have done?" he asked, sipping his tea.

"I hear you've been most ungallant."

Bloody gossipmongers. Had Lady Fairchild been complaining about his lack of interest in her daughter? Or perhaps Juliette Howard was attempting to shame him into offering his hand by spreading rumors. The lengths some women went to in order to secure a man never ceased to amaze him.

"Lord save me from desperate young ladies and grasping mamas," he muttered.

"Only in *this* instance," she said, "I hear the young lady was courageous, rather than desperate, and there wasn't a grasping mama in sight."

"What the devil are you talking about?"

She sipped her tea, lifting her little finger, then placed her cup on the saucer, in a slow, measured gesture, giving a show of elegance.

"Betty…"

Fluttering her eyelashes, she set the cup aside. "What fine tea!" she exclaimed. "My gain is your cousin's loss. Tell me, how is dear Beatrice?"

"Beatrice is as well as can be expected," he said.

"Especially given her escapade at Caldicott Abbey."

"How did you know…"

"Lord de Grande is an old friend."

"As are half the men in London."

She set her cup aside. "Don't be churlish, darling. It was a long time ago, and poor Dickie's not in the best of health. He never comes to London anymore, he's too ill to travel."

"Then, when did you see him?"

"I didn't," came the reply. "I saw Miss de Grande yesterday in the park with another young woman."

Miss de Grande—Henrietta's friend, who was with her the day Beatrice got herself stuck up the tree.

"The other young woman was in something of a state," Betty continued.

"Oh?" He affected nonchalance, but Betty gave him a sharp look. She'd always been able to read his moods.

"Yes, poor thing," she said. "Her leg was heavily bandaged, and she walked with a stick. Such a shame! I've seen her in the park before. A spirited young woman, though perhaps a little too lively for some."

"How did she hurt herself?" he asked.

She fixed her gaze on him. "She fell and broke her leg."

"In the park?"

"No, darling, at Caldicott Abbey," she said in the manner of a nanny pointing out the obvious to a belligerent toddler. "Shortly after having saved a young woman's life…" she added, "…though I suspect you've worked that out by now."

Oh, shit.

"She told you this herself?"

She shook her head. "*She* said very little, but Miss de Grande had quite a lot to say about you. Apparently, you lost your temper with the young woman, then left her in danger, after which you fled the Abbey, taking Beatrice and Lady Thorpe with you, like a thief in the night."

Put like that, he sounded the very worst of rogues.

"Am I to be the talk of London?" he asked.

She let out a laugh. "Unlikely, given that nobody knows how she broke her leg. And I have no intention of telling them, given the damage it would do to the poor young woman's reputation. No—Miss de Grande confides in me because she considers me a friend."

"But you were merely her father's mistr…"

Betty's eyes took on a glint of steel. "Be very careful what you say, Giles. Dickie was already widowed when he and I were acquainted. Lavinia de Grande is a sensible young woman who considers her papa's happiness over propriety. Why should the two of us not be friends?"

"And…" he hesitated, and shifted position, "…Miss Redford?"

She gave him a lopsided smile. "Ah, so you *do* know her

name. If I didn't know you better, I'd say that you were in love with her."

"Don't be ridiculous!" He looked away.

"Have it your own way," she said, "but when you mentioned her name, you sat back in your chair, folded your arms, and averted your gaze."

He unfolded his arms and reached for his teacup. "What does that signify?"

"That you wish to conceal your feelings—not only from me but from yourself."

She glanced at the clock over the fireplace. "Sadly, I'm unable to tarry here any longer. Jimmy's expecting me." She rose to her feet, and Giles followed suit.

"How come you're so perceptive?" he asked.

"By being observant," she replied, "I understand you well enough to know that you rarely display emotion. You are, to your detriment, a paragon of seemly behavior, even toward those you dislike. Even at your most—*passionate*—you show a degree of moderation in your emotions that might be described as soulless. Therefore, for you to have shown such a lack of restraint, must mean one of two things."

"Which are?"

"That you either harbor hatred for her, or you're experiencing previously unknown feelings that you're too afraid to admit—feelings of love."

She held out her hand, and he took it and brushed his lips against her skin. Then he escorted her out of the parlor, to the main doors where the footman stood waiting.

"Are you attending Lady Olyphant's ball next week?" she asked. "I hope to have the pleasure of seeing your cousin dancing. A young lady in her first Season must attend as many balls as she can."

Whatever anyone said of her, Lady Betty knew enough of propriety not to gossip in front of the servants.

"I believe we are attending," he said. "Would you do me the

honor of dancing the first set?"

"Wouldn't it be improper?"

"What, two good friends—an earl and a respectable widow?" He shook his head. "*I* certainly wouldn't disapprove of being seen on the dancefloor with you."

She let out a laugh. "Coming from a man who's disposed to disapprove of everything, I'll take that as a compliment. But..." she squeezed his hand, "...though you might disapprove of the world, I know you're incapable of hatred. Perhaps it's time to show your mettle. I believe a certain young woman with a broken leg is resting at home today."

She dipped into a curtsey, then the footman showed her out. Giles watched as she descended the front steps and disappeared down the street.

CHAPTER TWENTY-THREE

WHILE BEATRICE STOOD next to him, clutching a posy of wildflowers, Giles knocked on the door to Mr. Redford's townhouse. It swung inward to reveal a footman.

"Is the family at home?" Giles asked.

"Mr. Redford is in the city," came the reply. "Lady Agnes has asked not to be disturbed."

"And…Miss Redford?" Giles offered his card.

The footman took it and met his gaze. "I can inquire, but I believe she's indisposed."

He retreated into the hallway, and Beatrice called after him.

"Tell Henrietta that Beatrice is here to see her!"

Giles gave his cousin a nudge. "Decorum please, Beatrice. You don't shout on the street so the world can hear you."

"You want Henrietta to admit us, don't you?"

"You heard the man. She's unwell."

"Pah! Your lack of perception is astonishing, cousin. I believe *indisposed* means that she's asked her man to assess the callers so that he may turn away the undesirable and admit the favored."

"And?"

"Your calling card will tell her that the first sort of visitor is on her doorstep. I merely wish her to know that there's also one of the second."

"Oh, *favored*, are you?"

The footman returned and glanced at Giles, discomfort in his expression. For a moment, Giles wondered if he would be evicted, and Beatrice invited in. But, at length, the footman ushered them both in, then led them to a parlor at the back of the house.

Miss Redford lay reclined on a chaise longue, her left leg propped up on a footstool. As Giles entered the parlor, she was arranging a shawl over her leg, but not before he caught a glimpse of the bandage which covered almost all of her lower leg. A deep scratch ran across the back of her hand, and he caught the faint scent of herbs.

She glanced up and tried to stand.

Beatrice ran toward her.

"No, don't get up!" she cried. "Oh, Henrietta, why didn't you let me know you'd hurt yourself? Ever since I heard of your accident, I've been so worried. We *both* have."

Miss Redford glanced up and met his gaze. She had every right to call him a cad of the worst degree, and he waited for the tirade.

He looked away, his cheeks warming in shame. When he looked back, her expression had softened. She gave a slight nod and turned to his cousin.

"That's very kind of you, Beatrice," she said. "I am well, as you see."

"But your leg!" Beatrice cried. "And your poor hand! Why is it not bandaged?"

"It's healing better in the open air," Miss Redford replied. "Dr. McIver may not be as revered in certain quarters as that charlatan Dr. Odgers..." she glanced at Giles, "...but I find his modern approach to medicine refreshing. And, though my hand smells like a herb garden, it's healing marvelously.

"And...your leg?"

Miss Redford smiled—a smile that was a little too broad for sincerity. "It's nothing I regard."

"A break, or so we were told," Beatrice said.

"A minor break, and it's already healing."

"I wonder, Beatrice," Giles said, "if you'd be so obliging, might you see if one of the servants can find a vase for your flowers?"

"There's no need," Miss Redford said. "Just ring the bell."

"You don't mind, do you, Beatrice?" Giles gave his cousin a pointed look. She raised her eyebrows, then nodded and slipped out of the parlor.

His chance had come.

He approached Miss Redford and kneeled at her feet, then he took her hand and held it to his breast.

Her eyes widened in shock, and she made to snatch her hand free, but he tightened his grasp.

"Miss Redford," he said. "Permit me to say this while I have the chance—and the courage."

"Lord Thorpe, this is hardly the time…"

"I want to apologize," he interrupted. "That's why I came here, to beg forgiveness for my unseemly and callous behavior at Caldicott Abbey. It's my fault you're injured."

"I doubt that," she said. "I've been climbing all my life. I was bound to fall at some point."

"No, *I'm* to blame," he said. "Almost as soon as I left Caldicott Abbey, I realized my mistake, but I was too proud to return and beg your forgiveness. I hoped I might encounter you after you returned, to express my regrets, but when I heard what had happened…"

"How did you hear?"

"From a good friend, Lady Betty Grey. Do you know her?"

Her expression hardened. "Lady *Elizabeth* has many male friends, I hear. Lavinia and I met her the day we returned to London." Then she sighed. "So, *that's* why you've come, to demand I refrain from gossiping."

"No…"

"I can assure you that you're safe on that count," she said. "I have no wish to endanger Beatrice's reputation. Neither does Lavinia. My friend is usually discreet, but she's fond of Lady

Elizabeth and told her before I could prevent it. Apparently, Lady Elizabeth was *good friends* with Lord de Grande."

"So, I hear," he said.

"I take it Lady Elizabeth's friendship with his lordship was of a similar form to the friendship she enjoyed with you?"

He looked away, lest she see the truth in his eyes.

Then she held out her hand.

"Come, Lord Thorpe," she said, mischief in her eyes. "Let us not quarrel. I seek only to tease. Given your disposition and propensity to frown upon all forms of merriment, I consider it an appropriate punishment for your behavior—if, indeed, punishment is necessary."

"I believe you deem a punishment to be necessary," he said. "After all, don't you regularly berate me for being an arrogant swine?"

Her eyes sparkled with merriment, their rich chocolate color reminding him of warmth and sweetness.

It was the first time she had given him a genuine smile, as if the sun had emerged from a thundercloud, bathing him in warmth and light.

"If Aunt Agnes were to hear of my abusing you thus, she would delight in pointing out my own arrogance," she said. "You are fortunate that she's occupied with Lady Olyphant this afternoon, discussing, no doubt, how a quadrille is to be preferred over a waltz."

"Surely you're not attending Lady Olyphant's ball?"

"Do you think me unworthy of an invitation, Lord Thorpe?"

Oh Lord, why could he never open his mouth without offending her?

"I meant no insult, Miss Redford," he said. "I'm merely thinking of your injury."

"I take it you're going?"

He nodded.

"Don't you recall that you also sustained an injury at Caldicott Abbey?"

Recall it? He'd not stopped thinking about the moment they'd shared after he'd fallen off his horse—the tender words she'd whispered before they kissed. He'd spent every night since, his body hard and ready, imagining what it might be like to make her his and claim her, thoroughly and completely. The brief sight of her leg, even the flash of an ankle, sent a bolt of lust through him, which he struggled to control. In fact, were he to stand at this moment, his desire for her would be plain for all to see, straining against his breeches.

"I'm much recovered," he said. "I sustained a minor sprain and was fortunate enough to have a guardian angel to assist me. Whereas you, my dear Miss Redford, have been unfortunate, both in the severity of your injury and lack of a guardian angel."

He held her hand and caressed her skin with his thumb, his fingertips following the line of the scar. She caught a breath, parted her lips, then she looked away.

"I can take care of myself, Lord Thorpe."

"Then will you listen to my counsel, which is given with your best interests at heart, and consider remaining at home? Balls are noisy, crowded affairs, and dangerous places for a young woman with an injured leg. You risk further injury."

"I wish to go because Eleanor will be there," she said. "She dislikes crowds, and I promised to accompany her so that she might not be overwhelmed."

"Shouldn't you place your own welfare first?"

"I don't intend to dance," she said. "But I value loyalty and friendship over personal comfort."

"That you do," he sighed, regarding her with admiration. "Loyal, brave, and always ready to champion those you love."

The warmth in her gaze intensified, and delicate sparkles of gold glittered in the depths of her eyes. Curling his fingers round her hand, he drew her close, until her soft breath rippled across his skin.

"Careful, my lord," she whispered. "I believe you came dangerously close to making a compliment."

A spark ignited in the depths of her eyes—a spark of passion, as if her soul called out to his—giving him permission to claim what he so desperately wanted.

"Henrietta..."

He lowered his mouth to hers.

With a sigh, she parted her lips, and he slipped his tongue inside, relishing the sweet taste of her—the taste of honey with a hint of spice and the promise of wicked delights. He flicked his tongue across the roof of her mouth, and she leaned toward him with a sigh. Reaching up, he placed his hand on the back of her head, caressing her hair, then pulled her close, teasing, coaxing...

The door opened, and a voice cried out.

"Here it is!"

He drew back and rose to his feet, his body shaking with shame and unmet desire. Miss Redford rearranged the shawl over her leg, making a concerted effort at smoothing the creases in the fabric.

Beatrice stood in the doorway, holding a vase filled with flowers. "Don't they look pretty?" she cried. "Henrietta, where shall I place them?"

"By the window, I think."

Beatrice seemed to notice nothing untoward, but Henrietta's voice was a note higher in pitch than Giles had grown used to, her tone a little breathy. Her cheeks were flushed, a soft bloom giving her a little color, and her chest heaved up and down as if she'd been engaging in exercise, her breasts rising and falling softly against her neckline.

He daren't lower his gaze, for he knew what he'd find—two little peaks, beaded and ready for him to taste.

"Giles, is something the matter?" Beatrice asked.

Shifting his position to hide the bulge in his breeches, he shook his head.

"Forgive me," he said. "I believe I have an errand to run. But, Beatrice, I give you leave to remain here with Miss Redford if you wish it."

"You do?" Beatrice glanced at him, suspicion in her eyes.

"I do," he said. "In fact, you can spend as much time with Miss Redford as you wish, subject to her tolerating your company, of course."

"*Beatrice* can stay as long as she wishes," Miss Redford said, casting him a saucy smile.

"Then I shall take my leave," he said. He bowed and took Miss Redford's hand, lifting it to his lips. "I'll see you at Lady Olyphant's ball. And perhaps, if I may be so bold, you would give me the pleasure of partnering you during one of the dances?"

"But I won't be dancing."

"I wish to sit with you," he said, "in the same manner of a dance partner, in that I shall claim you as my own, for the duration of the dance, at least."

Her eyes widened and, for a moment, he thought she was going to ridicule him. Then she nodded.

"It would be my pleasure."

Pleasure...his blood warmed at the way her tongue curled round the word.

He bowed, then took his leave.

What exquisite pleasures might he find with a woman such as her?

He'd been so determined to look the other way, that he'd missed the obvious.

His perfect partner was not Lady Irma Fairchild or any other primped-up little debutante.

His perfect partner was the tomboy who had been under his nose all along. And, from the connection they'd shared just now, he was sure that she felt the same.

CHAPTER TWENTY-FOUR

"LORD THORPE LOOKS quite at home on the arm of the Merry Widow."

Henrietta glanced up at Lavinia's words. The first dance was in full swing, and she caught a glimpse of Giles, arm in arm with Lady Elizabeth Grey, the woman she'd met in the park with Lavinia, and whom Giles had spoken of with such—*familiarity*.

Eleanor, who sat between Henrietta and Lavinia, lifted her fan and peered over the top to observe them without drawing attention to herself. "They make a pleasant contrast," she said. "He's dark and brooding, and she's blonde and so…*vivacious*." She sighed. "She seems to sparkle wherever she goes, and everyone smiles when she's around. I wish I could be like that."

"What—the center of attention?" Henrietta asked.

Eleanor stiffened. "Good heavens, no, but I wish I could be as comfortable in company as she is. She's happy wherever she goes."

"Lady Betty has the enviable quality of making everyone around her feel loved," Lavinia said. "Papa once said that being the object of her attention was like having the sun shine on him and only him."

Eleanor lowered her fan and sighed. "I'll wager nobody has had to admonish *her* in public for not making friends or not speaking up during a conversation."

Henrietta placed a hand on her friend's arm. Not five minutes earlier, Eleanor's mother had berated her in front of Lady Olyphant for not joining in the idle chatter on arrival—the inane remarks which pass between acquaintances when first meeting. Ignoring Aunt Agnes's admonishments about her injured leg, Henrietta had come to Eleanor's rescue and dragged her across the dance floor to a quiet corner. But not before poor Eleanor's cheeks had turned as red as a raspberry, after which both Henrietta and Lavinia resolved to keep Eleanor under their protection tonight.

"Would you want to be blonde and vivacious, Ellie?" Henrietta asked.

"I suppose not," came the reply, "though I often wonder what it's like."

"It takes a tremendous amount of effort," Lavinia said. "Lady Betty is rumored to be approaching her fifties, therefore must work harder to keep pace with all the debutantes vying for dance partners."

"You don't mind her being here?" Henrietta asked. "On account of your father?"

Lavinia let out a laugh. "They were never in love. Papa was lonely after Mama's passing. Lady Elizabeth made him very happy, and they parted on good terms. He offered for her, did you know that? I should have liked her for a stepmother, but she turned him down."

"Imagine that," Eleanor sighed, "being able to turn down an offer of marriage! I live in fear of receiving an offer, of having to…" She waved her hand, as if trying to articulate her thoughts, then shook her head. "Mama's already angry with me. But at least her mind's on Juliette this Season and her prospects for securing a match. Perhaps she'll leave me be until next Season."

"Isn't that simply deferring the inevitable?" Henrietta asked.

"I suppose it is," Eleanor said. "I live in fear of being an old maid, and I'm so unmarriageable that Mama will force me to accept the first man who asks. Women like Lady Betty, at least, have the power of choice."

"Except perhaps in regards to one man," Lavinia said, her attention focused on the dancers.

Henrietta glanced up as Giles Thorpe and Lady Elizabeth passed them, hand in hand, laughing animatedly and dancing to the music with smooth fluid movements, as if they were made to be together.

Lavinia lowered her voice and leaned toward Henrietta. "Rumor has it that out of all her male friends, the one suitor she wanted was the one who didn't offer for her."

It was plain which *male friend* Lavinia was speaking of.

Swallowing the spike of jealousy, Henrietta shifted in her seat, smoothing the skirt of her gown over her bandaged leg.

As the dance continued, another couple came into sight—Phillip Meredith and Beatrice. Beatrice's attention was focused on her partner. Phillip looked upon Beatrice with hunger in his eyes. Was he falling in love?

It would serve him right if he lost his heart to a young woman, given his boasts about wanting to grow up to be a rake. In fact, it would serve mankind right if every man suffered unrequited love, given the power they had in the world.

The dance concluded, and the partners dispersed while the musicians tuned their instruments for the next set. Lavinia checked her dance card.

"Who has the pleasure of partnering you, Lavinia?" Henrietta asked.

"Viscount Marlow."

"I don't think I know him," Eleanor said.

"He's over there." Lavinia pointed toward the main doors. "The tall fellow standing between Lady Olyphant and the Duke of Whitcombe."

Eleanor drew in a sharp breath. "Whitcombe, did you say?"

"Do you know him?" Lavinia asked.

"N-no," Eleanor stuttered. "Juliette was hoping he'd ask her to dance."

Lavinia let out a laugh. "She has *no* chance! He detests dancing and detests company even more. It's a wonder he's here at all. Oh, he's coming over."

Eleanor leaped to her feet. "Forgive me," she said, "I'm in need of fresh air."

"Eleanor, what's the...?" Henrietta began, but before she finished, Eleanor was already halfway to the terrace doors.

Viscount Marlow approached them. "I believe it's my turn to claim you for the quadrille, Miss de Grande."

Lavinia rose to her feet and took the proffered hand.

"Ah, Henry! There you are!" Johnny Meredith appeared, his boyish face glowing with vitality. "What say you we take a turn about the dancefloor together?" He eyed Viscount Marlow. "Perhaps we could make a four with Miss de Grande and this fellow."

"I'm afraid I cannot," Henrietta replied. "My leg's not fully recovered."

"Then why come to a ball?"

"To see my friends. In fact, I have a friend who's not dancing, and I'm sure she'd be pleased to stand up with you."

"If you mean Lady Beatrice, I promised Phillip I wouldn't ask her. I believe he's half in love with her already."

"No, I meant Miss Howard."

"Heavens no!" He shook his head. "Miss Juliette's dance card's already full. And no wonder. She's such a beautiful creature—far too beautiful to accept an offer from someone like me."

"You do yourself a disservice, Johnny," Henrietta said. "You're worthy of any woman in the room. But I didn't mean Juliette. I meant her sister, Eleanor."

He wrinkled his nose and let out a laugh. "The *oddity*? Heavens no, I'm not so much at a loss."

"In which case, I withdraw my last comment," Henrietta said. "With that attitude, you're worthy of no one, though perhaps you and Miss Juliette have more in common than you think."

Henrietta rose to her feet, fighting the urge to plant a shiner on Johnny's face, which was already flushed with an over-indulgence of liquor.

Refusing his offer of help, she limped around the edge of the room in search of her friend, but Eleanor was nowhere to be seen.

The music started, and she slipped through the doors and out onto the terrace.

With summer at its height, the evening was still light. Pale orange streaks stretched across the sky, and the horizon glowed a soft pink color. She crossed the terrace, leaned on the balustrade at the end, and called out.

"Eleanor!"

No reply. Perhaps she'd slipped back inside. Eleanor had the habit of bolting for the door when an occasion overwhelmed her. And well she might, given how she was perceived by the others, including her own family. If the usually affable Johnny ridiculed her, what hope did she have among the more vitriolic members of Society?

She ought to return inside and seek Eleanor out, but the view across the garden held more appeal than a room full of strutting peacocks determined to outshine each other with their gaudy silks and inane chatter.

The doors opened, and laughter and music filtered through the air. Henrietta retreated into the darkness at the far end of the terrace as footsteps approached. Then she heard a laugh, its tone overly animated to affect interest.

"Oh, Your Grace! You're so amusing. How is it that you can be so charming?"

"I'm nothing of the sort."

Henrietta would recognize Juliette Howard's voice any-where, but she couldn't place the man's voice. Deep and rich, it held a tone of cold dislike and razor-sharp intelligence, as opposed to the inebriated slurring of the Duke of Dunton. Surely Juliette wasn't trying to maximize her chances of securing a match by following *two* dukes about with her tongue hanging out?"

Juliette's laugh echoed round the terrace again, and Henrietta shivered as the sound set her teeth on edge.

"Oh, Your Grace! If you believe yourself devoid of charm, why did you accept Lady Olyphant's invitation tonight?"

"I didn't."

The man, whoever he was, crossed the terrace toward the steps leading to the garden, Juliette trotting after him.

"But you came anyway," Juliette's voice continued. "To dance perhaps?"

Henrietta suppressed a snort at the desperation in Juliette's voice. The man turned, and Henrietta shivered as she caught a flash of cold blue eyes glinting in the fading light. Their sinister expression reminded her of a predator who showed no mercy when destroying his victims. Then he turned his back, strode down the steps, and disappeared into the gardens. Juliette stood still for a moment, then Henrietta heard a sharp huff as the woman turned and strode back inside.

The light had faded by now. Henrietta waited by the balustrade, watching the last streaks of orange fade, then disappear altogether. The strains of music continued inside, but she had no wish to return. The sight of Lady Elizabeth with Lord Thorpe had affected her more than she cared to admit.

Perhaps that was why he'd asked her if she was attending the ball, so she would see him dancing with his paramour.

Her cheeks burned with indignation—and shame, at how her heart had been so easily conquered—and she turned her head toward the breeze coursing through the terrace, to cool her face.

She heard the doors open once more, then footsteps approached. A heavy, irregular tread, most likely some drunken lout having slipped outside to relieve himself on the terrace.

"Ah, there you are!"

It was the Duke of Dunton. Even slurred with liquor, his voice was unmistakable.

Which unfortunate woman had secured his attention?

He moved toward Henrietta, and she caught a whiff of sour

wine.

"Miss Redford, what a pleasure."

She took a step back. "Your Grace, perhaps you should return inside."

"I've heard much about you," he said. "I hear you're something of a wild creature."

"That I am," she replied, "and I'm not above punching a lecher in the face."

He lumbered closer. "Oh, it's *so* much better when they struggle."

"You forget yourself, Your Grace," she said. "I believe Miss Howard is inside."

"Miss Howard!" He let out a snort. "She wants only one thing, and she seeks to arouse my ardor by trotting after Whitcombe."

He reached for her hand, and she pushed him back. "It appears that you only want one thing, Your Grace," she said. "And you certainly won't be getting that from me."

"Don't be so missish!" he laughed. "Women are too apt to tease without delivering the goods they promise."

"Then take the goods, as you put it, from Miss Howard, if she's willing to offer herself to secure your hand."

"Why would I take it from Miss Howard when there's easier prey to be had?"

"I'm no easy prey, Your Grace," she hissed, but he merely laughed.

"My dear Miss Redford, you have a reputation for lacking respect for social convention. I wouldn't be surprised if you slipped out tonight for a tryst. It's a shame your suitor has decided not to join you, but I can take his place. You'll find me an experienced lover."

He grasped her sleeve, and she tried to pull free.

"Get off me!"

"That's it, my little filly," he said, grasping her other sleeve. "Show me some of that spirit."

She struggled, and he released his grip, but she lost her balance and fell against the balustrade. Her foot twisted sideways, and she let out a yelp as a spike of pain shot through her leg.

Two thick, fleshy hands grasped her shoulders, and she wrinkled her nose at the stench of sour wine as he thrust his face closer.

"That's it," he said, his voice thick with lust. "If you stay quiet and give me a little kiss, then you'll not be discovered. You wouldn't want to be ruined, would you?"

"Leave me alone, you disgusting pig!"

He let out a laugh, his chins wobbling, and his big, heavy body pushed against her.

"Take your hands off her!" a voice roared.

Henrietta froze as she recognized Giles Thorpe's voice.

Dunton tightened his grip and glanced over his shoulder.

"I'm busy, Thorpe," he said. "Go back to your harlot. I've got one of my own here."

Henrietta caught a blur of movement, then her assailant was pulled off her.

"I *said*, take your hands off her." The cold, quiet calm of Giles's voice did more to strike fear in Henrietta's heart than when he had shouted in anger, for it spoke of a clear-sighted determination to vanquish a foe.

"Good God, Thorpe, must you be such a bore?" Dunton slurred. "A woman who ventures outside during a ball and sniffs around a dark corner is asking to be rutted—*you* know that."

"And I suppose you waited at the threshold for an opportunity to pounce on a member of the weaker sex," Giles said with a sneer.

"That's it," Dunton said, puffing out his chest. "Like a lion."

Giles let out a snort. "Lion, indeed! You're more of a hyena— or a vulture—scavenging for pickings, preying on the weak." He gestured toward Henrietta. "Can't you see she's injured? I suppose you thought you'd be in with a chance of besting her if she was incapable of freeing herself from your clutches." He shook his head. "You disgust me. A real man does not assert himself on a helpless female unless she's consenting."

"What's to say she wasn't consenting?" Dunton asked.

"Don't be a fool!" Giles scoffed. "She was crying for help."

Henrietta curled her hands into fists, her body shaking with indignation.

Helpless female?

Weaker sex?

How many more insults could he toss in her direction?

"I was *not* crying for help!" she said.

"As you see, Thorpe," Dunton said. "A willing partner."

"Don't be a fool!" Giles cried. "Of course, she's not willing. Go back inside, or I'll kick you inside myself!"

"I hardly think…" Dunton began, but Giles interrupted, squaring up to him in the manner of a stag facing his challenger.

"I didn't ask you to think," he said, coldly, "just leave the lady alone." He turned his gaze on Henrietta. "I take it you *want* him to leave you alone?

She nodded.

"As you see, Dunton, my rescue is welcome. If I see you attempting to compromise any other young ladies, I'll shoot you like a dog."

Grumbling, Dunton stumbled back inside. Giles waited for the doors to close before he spoke.

"Are you all right?"

Henrietta shook her head. "Arrogant boor!"

"He has a reputation."

He reached for her hand, and she snatched it free. "I meant *you!*" she cried. "I was perfectly capable of defending myself. I did *not* need rescuing!"

"It didn't look like it."

"I don't care what it looked like! Must you treat me like a child?"

"I don't understand."

"No, I suppose you don't. Your idea of the perfect woman is a delicate little lady with a tinkling laugh who needs a man to make all her decisions for her."

"That's not my idea of perfection at all."

"Or, perhaps, a widow who's overly free with her favors." She flinched at the petulance in her tone. "Forgive me," she said. "I didn't mean to impugn Lady Elizabeth's honor."

"Then what *did* you mean?" He sounded amused, which only served to anger her further.

"I meant that I can take care of myself. I don't need a man to rescue me at the slightest inconvenience."

"I'd consider the unwelcome advances of a drunken lecher to be more than a slight inconvenience."

"Nevertheless, I'm not weak," she said. "I could have easily fought him off. A knee to the groin would have rendered him incapable of forcing his unwelcome advances on anyone."

He threw back his head and let out a laugh.

How dare he make sport of her!

"Am I nothing but a joke to you?" she cried.

He shook his head. "On the contrary, Miss Redford— Henrietta."

Her body gave an involuntary shiver at his use of her name— the way his tongue curled around the syllables. Then, he moved closer, and she caught the aroma of raw, woody spices.

"I laugh because perhaps Dunton was the one in need of rescuing."

"You think it amusing?"

The moonlight cast sharp shadows across the angular planes of his face, giving him the air of a Grecian statue, as if a marble god stood before her, and his eyes glowed with a cold blue fire.

"Am I laughing now?"

He pulled her to him, chest to chest.

"Is it such a crime to want to protect you from danger?"

Though he spoke in a soft whisper, his voice seemed to penetrate her mind. The expression in his eyes deepened, revealing a deep chasm into which she felt herself being drawn—an ocean she would willingly drown herself in—filled with raw, primal desire.

He lifted his hand to her face and placed it against her cheek. Then he caressed her skin with his thumb before tracing a line around her face as if he wanted to memorize every contour, every feature.

"Your strength and courage are what I love most about you…" He placed his hand on the back of her head and buried his fingers in her hair. Then, he drew her close, dipping his head until their mouths almost met.

"Am I never to be given the pleasure of taking care of you?"

The raw, honest plea in his voice cut through her heart.

"Lady Betty is a friend, nothing more," he whispered, "and she understands my heart better than I. She knows that there's only one woman for me, and it's not the woman I've been dancing with tonight. It's the woman standing before me now."

"Giles, I…"

"Hush," he said, "let me take care of you."

She tilted her head upward, offering her lips, and he claimed her mouth swiftly and greedily. She parted her lips in invitation, giving a little mewl of desire as he thrust his tongue inside, moving it slickly against the roof of her mouth. He tasted of spices—pure, exotic spices—and she yielded to his strength, relishing the surrender.

A low growl of need vibrated through his body, and he pulled her close, his body hard and ready. Raw heat pooled in her center, where she was beset by an unfathomable need—a thick, pulsating ache that begged to be eased.

She shivered as her nipples hardened to painful little points. Relishing the abrasion of his jacket against the thin fabric of her gown, she parted her thighs, and arched her back—an instinctive motion, urged by the primal voice deep inside her mind.

"Oh, Henrietta," he rasped. "Sweet Lord, I want you—so badly. I want nothing more than to bury myself inside you. Here. *Now*."

She drew in a shuddering breath to ease the fog of need, but it only intensified, and she shifted position, rubbing her body against his, relishing the delicious friction.

Sweet heaven! Was this what drove women to ruination—the beautiful madness, lingering out of reach which promised untold, pleasure at the point of surrender?

"Giles!"

His body shuddered as she cried out his name, and with a strangled moan, he broke the kiss.

"I-I must stop," he said, his voice filled with pain. "Dear God, much as I want to…I cannot continue."

The nugget of pleasure began to fade, and she grasped his collar.

"No, Giles, please!" she cried. "Don't stop."

He shook his head. "You'll be ruined."

"You think I care?" she asked. "Why may I not be permitted a moment of pleasure?"

He closed his eyes and dipped his head as if in prayer. Then, he nodded. "I can deny you nothing, my love. But I'll not ruin you."

Her stomach twisted with disappointment, then he kissed her forehead and smiled. "I will leave you intact," he said, "but I can still give you pleasure."

"I-I don't understand."

He smiled and placed his hand on her cheek, caressing her skin—the light, intimate touch sending shivers through her body.

"Do you trust me?" he whispered.

"Always."

A glimmer of pleasure shone in his eyes, and they glistened with moisture. "There is no more precious a gift that a lady can bestow than her trust."

"You always said I was no lady."

He took her hand and led her toward the end of the terrace, to an alcove hidden deep in the shadows. The loss of sight heightened her other senses, and his heavy, labored breathing whispered through the air. Combined with the heady scent of him—of spices, desire, and raw, primal masculinity—her defenses had crumbled. The world around her disappeared, leaving only him.

"I care not whether you're a lady," he said, his voice deep and hoarse, seeming to resonate through her bones. "To me, you're a woman—all woman…"

He dipped his head and placed a kiss on her collarbone. She arched her back, her body urging him on.

"Are you *my* woman?" His hot breath rippled across her skin, and he nuzzled the neckline of her gown, his tongue flicking out, teasing, probing at her skin. A delicious ache swelled in her breasts, and an instinctive need to offer them to him overwhelmed her senses. She grasped her neckline in her fist and pulled it down. The cool air rippled across the skin of her breasts.

He dipped his head and flicked a nipple with his tongue.

"Oh!" she let out a gasp as pleasure fizzed through her.

Then his mouth came down on her breast.

A hot, insistent tongue swirled around the tip, drawing her nipple deep into his mouth, then his teeth grazed against the exquisitely sensitized skin, and she cried out as pleasure engulfed her. Fisting her hands in his hair, she held him close, urging him on, wanting—needing—him to devour her.

The unfathomable ache began to build once more, and she parted her thighs, trusting the instincts of her body.

"Are you ready for me?" he whispered, his voice swirling in her mind with the fog of need. Unable to speak, she nodded, digging her fingers into his hair to hold him close.

Delicate fingertips traced the edge of her stocking, then, with a swift, deft movement, untied the ribbon that held it in place.

The hand moved upward, toward the center of her need. His light fingertips grew more insistent, declaring ownership over every inch of her skin until he reached the top of her thighs.

Was he going to touch her…*there?*

She closed her eyes and surrendered to the sensation of those, expert fingers moving ever closer, and her body tightened in anticipation.

Sweet Lord…

The craving which had lain dormant in the back of her mind came to the fore—the need for his touch…

Then he stopped.

"No…" She let out a whimper of unmet need.

"Tell me what you want, Henrietta."

"I-I don't know."

"Oh, I think you do," he teased.

How could she utter the wanton, wicked desires in her mind?

"Giles, I…" Her cheeks flamed with shame, her voice catching in her throat, and she shook her head.

His teeth grazed against her nipple, and a bolt of need shuddered through her. She caught her breath and let out a low moan, overcome with shame at her wantonness—to offer herself like a harlot…

"Oh, sweet one," he gave a low chuckle, his voice reverberating through her chest while he licked and nuzzled at her breasts, "you must ask for your reward."

"I-I can't…"

"Where's my warrior gone?" he whispered. "The Valkyrie who fears nothing? Are you afraid to admit your desire—to ask for that which you crave?" He caressed the top of her thigh in light, delicate circles with the pad of his thumb, moving closer to the source of her need. "All you need do is ask. I am the servant of your pleasure."

The ache inside her intensified at his words, spoken with an urgency she'd not heard in him before, as if a primal beast lurked within him, striving to be unleashed.

He lifted his head and placed a kiss on the corner of her mouth. "Tell me," he demanded. "Tell me what you want."

Need overcame shame. "I want you to touch me," she whispered.

"Where?"

Must she say it?

"B-between my legs."

He drew a light fingertip across her skin, then slipped it between her thighs, moving slickly across the flesh, until he reached the sensitive little bud at the center of her need.

He drew his fingertip back and forth, and her body shuddered as the sensation—the delicious, unfathomable madness swelled within her.

"Mmm…" he murmured, "Does my warrior like her reward?"

How could he know where she ached for him?

"Y-yes…"

"Good," he said. "Shall I stop?"

He began to withdraw his hand.

"No!" Parting her legs wider, she thrust toward his hand, chasing the pleasure, ignoring the shame—ignoring everything but the desperate need to relieve the madness.

"Giles—please!"

He plunged his finger inside her, and her body exploded. Wave after wave of pure sensation rippled through her body, and she rode the tide, rocking back and forth.

His mouth claimed hers, swallowing her cries, and he thrust his tongue inside, mirroring the exquisite attention between her thighs.

Never could she have imagined the pure ecstasy to be had from yielding to another.

He deepened the kiss, savoring her as much as she savored the pleasure from his touch. At length, his caresses grew gentler.

A delicious languor settled over her, and when he pulled her close, she nestled her head on his chest, and let him take her in his arms as if she belonged there. Then, her heart beating to a deep, steady rhythm, she drifted into a dream-like state, relishing the moment of being safe in the arms of the only man she had ever loved.

GILES CLOSED HIS eyes, relishing the moment, the delicious serenity of a woman well pleasured. It was the difference between lovemaking and mere rutting—when they shared pleasures, not merely for the physical gratification, but for the deeper connection—a meeting of souls.

The woman in his arms let out a deep sigh, her chest rising and falling, as he gently lowered her skirts, then held her in his arms. He dipped his head and buried his nose in her hair, breathing in the soft aroma of rose mingled with the sweet, sharp scent of female satisfaction.

What bliss it had been to see her come undone at his hands, to see the joyous dissolution into pleasure. What might it be like to claim her fully?

His manhood surged with the need to be buried inside her, to claim that sweet body.

But he'd promised not to ruin her. He would leave her intact—at least, for tonight.

No other man shall have her. She belongs to me.

He stiffened at the voice whispering in his mind, as if by unleashing her passion he'd also freed his desires until they stood before him, and he could no longer deny them.

She belonged to him—and he belonged to her.

But, rather than honor her, he'd pleasured her in the garden, like a common harlot.

She stirred and looked up, her eyes glistening in the moonlight.

"What's the matter?" she asked.

"N-nothing," he said. "Forgive me, I shouldn't have done that. It was wrong. You deserve better."

"Better than this?" She shook her head. "It was wonderful. I-I can't describe it…" Then she narrowed her eyes, uncertainty in their expression. "Did you not…" she hesitated, "…enjoy it?"

"I…" He hesitated. "I took much enjoyment from witnessing your pleasure."

"Oh." The disappointment in her voice tore at his heart, and he captured her mouth in a swift kiss of reassurance. "A man cannot take his full pleasure without ruining a woman, and I value you too greatly to do that tonight. I have no wish to destroy your reputation."

"You've always said I have no reputation to speak of."

He took her hand and lifted it to his lips. "Every young woman has a reputation, which is ruined if she's caught alone with a man."

"What of the man's reputation?"

"That's different."

"Of course it is," she said, bitterness in her tone. "Men can behave as they like, with no fear of reprisal."

"Which is why we must tidy your appearance," he said, smoothing her hair. "I suggest you return inside now, discreetly, as if nothing happened. I'll follow a minute or so later so that nobody will draw any conclusions."

She withdrew her hand, hostility in her eyes.

"I see," she said. "You're ashamed of what we've done—ashamed of me."

He caught her hand and held it against his heart. "Dear Lord, no!" he cried. "I could never be ashamed of my feelings for you, but we must not be seen to have acted contrary to propriety."

"Why not?"

"Because reputation is everything," he said. "Yours, mine… And Beatrice's. She will be tainted by association." She tried to pull free, but he tightened his grip. "Believe me, I like it no more than you do, Henrietta. But it's the way of the world, and we must survive in the world as best we can."

"Then you wish me to go?"

The despair in her voice ripped through his soul. Did she think he cared nothing for her?

Tell her…

The voice whispered in his mind again—the voice of his soul.

Could he tell her? Could he swallow his pride and summon the courage to tell her, as she had summoned the courage to ask him to pleasure her?

"Let me go," she said, her voice cold.

"No," he replied. "Not until you permit me to tell you that I love you."

Hope flared in her eyes, then she looked away. "Please, don't make fun of me."

Did she, even now, think he cared nothing for her?

"I could never make fun of you, Henrietta," he said. "I value you too much." He shook his head. "I'm making a mess of this, aren't I? But for the first time, I find I'm unable to articulate what I mean. You do that to me, Henrietta. You've bewitched me— made me want to break the chains of convention and indulge in the pleasures of life. But, in turn, I wish to honor you as you deserve to be honored—to place you on a pedestal and let the world know how much you mean to me."

"Giles..." She shook her head. "Forgive me, I don't understand..."

"Hush, my love," he whispered, placing a finger on her lips. "I wish to court you."

She drew in a sharp breath, and her eyes widened. "You...*what?*"

"I wish to court you, as a respectable gentleman would court a young lady. I have no wish to claim you in a hasty union. I wish to do this properly and let the whole world see how I revere and worship you."

Her lips curled in a smile, then she let out a soft laugh.

"Do I amuse you?"

"I relish the irony," she said. "You have always berated me for being a tomboy, yet you seek to woo me by parading me about as if I were a fine lady."

"Do you object to the notion of being paraded about London and courted as if you were the premier debutante of the season?"

"No," she said, her eyes sparkling with joy. "I shall suffer the comforts that the premier debutantes indulge in if it makes you happy. I will take my own pleasure from witnessing yours."

"Then may I call on you tomorrow, good lady?"

"Why yes, good sir, I believe you can."

She straightened her neckline, then smoothed her hair until, with the exception of her flushed face, she looked like any respectable young lady who'd gone for a stroll to take in the air. Then, she blew him a kiss and slipped back inside.

He remained outside, drawing in a lungful of cool air, until his ardor—and the cockstand in his breeches—had abated. When he returned to the ballroom, the guests would be none the wiser to the fact that he'd awoken Henrietta to the joys of pleasure, or that he'd found his perfect companion.

And, after a period of courtship long enough to deem it respectable, he would ask Henrietta Redford to be his wife.

CHAPTER TWENTY-FIVE

"And *that*, my dear Beatrice, is how you parry a lunge."

Henrietta swept her foil through the air with a flourish, then bowed and set it aside.

"I think we're done for the day," she said. "Time for tea. Your aunt will be wondering what's happened to us."

Beatrice handed over her foil. Henrietta wrapped both swords in a cloth, then carried them inside from the sheltered spot in the garden where Papa permitted her to practice sword fighting unobserved.

Giles had been true to his word and had encouraged a friendship between her and Beatrice. Yesterday he'd arrived in his barouche, brandishing a posy of wildflowers to take her for a ride around the park. Though she'd felt ridiculous at first, like a specimen on display, she had basked in his attentive adoration and succumbed to the guilty pleasure of being wooed by a gentleman. Then he'd brought her home, indulged in tea with Papa and Aunt Agnes, then taken his leave, bowing over her hand and kissing it as if she were royalty, with a promise to call again.

Though she sought an independent life where she could control her own destiny, she couldn't fail to appreciate the pleasure of being tended to by a man in love.

In love…

He'd as good as said it, and she'd seen it in his eyes the night he'd taken her to the pinnacle of pleasure. And, in his active encouragement of her friendship with his young cousin—a marked contrast to his demands that she stay away from Beatrice.

Was he acclimatizing himself to the prospect of her becoming something more than a mere friend to Beatrice.

Such as a relation by marriage?

Beatrice was like the sister Henrietta never had—a loving friend with a lust for life, eager to experience new things and take joy in them—and she had blossomed during their friendship. Giles, also, had changed. The stern gentleman shouldering the responsibilities of his title still existed, but he revealed a different side of himself—a passionate man who admired her spirit. She smiled to herself at the notion of Beatrice sword fighting. The Lord Thorpe she'd first known would have had a fit of apoplexy had he known that she was encouraging his cousin in such an unladylike pursuit. But Giles—the man she'd fallen in love with— was happy to indulge her.

As for Beatrice, she was a willing pupil, and far more capable than the Meredith twins had ever been. Which just went on to prove that women should be permitted to enjoy the same pursuits as men for they were just as capable, if not more so.

But Beatrice still had much to learn. Her youthful enthusiasm needed to be tempered by restraint.

They reached the orangery and stepped inside, where Henrietta placed the swords in a trunk, together with the protective gauntlets. Then, arm in arm, they headed toward the parlor where Aunt Agnes and Lady Thorpe were taking tea.

"Can we practice again later today?" Beatrice asked.

"Perhaps another day," Henrietta said.

"But I'm determined to best you." Beatrice shook her head. "I know I've just begun, but how do you manage to block all my maneuvers? Can you read my mind?"

Henrietta smiled. "After a fashion."

"Is it because I lack the talent for it?"

"No," Henrietta replied, "you have a natural ability. But you have one fatal flaw."

"Which is?"

"Your artlessness."

Beatrice pouted, a sulky expression in her eyes.

"I meant no offense," Henrietta said, laughing. "It's an admirable quality, to be so open and honest. But it means that your intentions are there for all to see."

"Am I so easily read?"

"Only by those who know and love you."

Henrietta slipped her arm through Beatrice's. "I take it as a compliment, my dear friend, that you're comfortable enough in my presence to reveal your feelings. But you must remember only to have faith in those who have earned your trust."

"Such as Giles?"

Beatrice took her hand and interlinked their fingers.

"Is there anything in particular you wish to tell me, Henrietta?"

"Such as?"

A delicate bloom spread across Beatrice's cheeks, and she gave a shy smile.

"Giles is my cousin," she said. "I wondered if I might be in a position, in the future, to also call *you* my cousin."

Henrietta drew in a sharp breath.

"Oh, forgive me!" Beatrice cried. "I didn't mean to distress you, it's just that Giles has been so happy of late." She lowered her voice to a whisper. "I shan't mind if you don't wish to say, but, has he made you an offer? I know he took you out in his barouche-landau yesterday, and he hardly ever uses it."

Henrietta glanced at her friend, her heart melting at the love and hope in Beatrice's eyes.

"I knew it!" Beatrice cried. "He's asked you to marry him, hasn't he? Oh, I'm so happy! I always thought he liked you."

Henrietta placed a calming hand on Beatrice's arm. "He's not asked me," she said, "but, I believe he might. He said he wanted to court me properly."

"Oh, how romantic!" Beatrice cried. "Did you know that he

pretended to be out when Lady Fairchild called on us yesterday? I'm so glad! I was worried he'd ask *her* to marry him. He kept going on about how perfect a lady she was, and how beautiful. Personally, I think she has a face like a duck's rear end."

Henrietta suppressed the urge to laugh.

"It's true," Beatrice continued. "Aunt's been reading Bewick's *History of British Birds* and there's a picture of a mallard's…"

"Beatrice!" Henrietta cried, unable to contain her mirth. But, she could afford to be generous toward Lady Irma, given that she was on the brink of attaining her heart's desire.

"Beatrice, I'm sure Lady Irma is charming."

Beatrice snorted. "Well, *she's* not someone I want in the family. That's why I admire you so much, Henrietta. You're not afraid to defy convention, to be adventurous, and daring…so reckless!"

"Perhaps not reckless, Beatrice," Henrietta said, "but I firmly believe that a young woman should strive for what she wants, rather than what she believes others expect of her. Otherwise, she'll become a characterless, obedient mannequin, of whom there are far too many in the world already."

"I quite agree with you," Beatrice said. "Oh, I can't wait to wish you joy!"

"Hush!" Henrietta hissed as they neared the parlor. "Your cousin has not made me an offer, so it would be improper to speak of it. Sometimes, even *I* must restrain myself."

"But you'd counsel against restraint if it were in the pursuit of love?"

Henrietta looked into Beatrice's eyes, their expression full of hope and happiness.

"Yes, Beatrice," she said. "I would—every time."

CHAPTER TWENTY-SIX

G ILES PULLED OUT his pocket watch, then tutted in irritation. Beatrice was late for breakfast. Again.

"She'll not be long," Mother said from across the table. "I've told you before, this isn't the militia."

"Perhaps not," he replied, "but she's been preoccupied of late."

Mother sipped her tea and smiled. "Perhaps she has something particular on her mind," she said. "Something we *all* have on our minds?

"Such as?"

She set her cup down with a clatter. "Oh, Giles!" she cried in exasperation. "Surely you know what I'm speaking of?"

"Enlighten me."

"You've always delighted in vexing me," she said. "Even as a small boy, you were so…" she hesitated, "so…"

"Vexing?" he teased with a smile.

"Yes," she said, leaning back in her chair. "And I know the reason why."

He raised his eyebrows. "You do?"

"Stop it!" she cried, laughing.

He'd not heard such mirth in her voice for a long time.

Except once, when he'd come across her on the grounds of Thorpe Hall, indulging in a picnic, with…

With *her*.

Henrietta.

"She's perfect for you, Giles."

"Who?"

"You know perfectly well who," she said. "I can't guarantee Miss Redford will always make you happy. After all, a strong-minded young woman determined to get her own way will be a considerable challenge for a man such as yourself who wants everything to be just so. But, only through challenge can we grow and develop, and realize our full potential. She taught me that, from the day she climbed through my window."

She leaned forward. "And, my boy—she'll be the making of you."

He smiled. "I'm glad you approve."

"I couldn't imagine a better helpmate to restore Thorpe Hall to its former glory," she continued. "Granted, her fortune is not as large as some, but that's all for the good, for it will free you from the temptation to which your dear papa succumbed. And, though she appears something of a hellion, she has the decency to know when to temper her behavior. You will steady her with your good sense, and she will bring light and joy into your life."

"Mother, I've not asked her to marry me yet. She might say no."

"Pshah! She'd be a fool to refuse you. Who else would she choose? Those rambunctious young pups who live near Thorpe Hall—what are their names? The elder one keeps asking Beatrice to dance. I think he's a little taken with her. A pleasant enough fellow, but..."

"Phillip and Jonathan Meredith?" he interrupted. The elder twin had asked Beatrice to dance once or twice and, to be honest, he'd taken little notice, having merely been grateful that the young man hadn't danced with Henrietta.

"Ah yes, that's it!" she cried. "Viscount Meredith's boys. They could never handle a passionate woman such as her. Whereas *you...*"

"Mother, please!" he cried as memories of the night on the

terrace, and Henrietta's cries of passion sent a flush of heat to his groin.

She raised her hand in appeasement. "Very well, Giles," she said. "I'll leave you to ask her in your own time. But don't tarry too long, for she's a woman intent on seeking her own destiny rather than waiting for destiny to fall into her lap."

After making her little speech, she nodded to the waiting footman and asked for a little scrambled eggs. When he placed her plate in front of her, she picked up her knife and fork and ate in silence, a smile on her lips.

He listened to her chatter with loving indulgence. Mother had been transformed. The sorry creature who hid in seclusion at Thorpe Hall had gone, and the vivacious woman had returned. In fact, he barely noticed her frailty. Though her eyesight would never be fully restored, she managed to maneuver herself about the house without assistance, having memorized the layout, with Beatrice's help.

The Thorpe family was finally on an upward trajectory—able to put past tragedies behind them and look forward to a prosperous future.

Hurried footsteps approached, and Beatrice's maid burst through the door. Body shaking, she held up an envelope.

"Master Giles!" she cried. "It's too terrible!"

"Kitty, what the devil's happened?" Mother cried.

"It's Miss Beatrice. She's…" The maid burst into sobs.

A cold hand of fear clutched at his insides. "What's happened? Has she been taken ill?"

Kitty shook her head. "N-no, your lordship. She's…" Her voice caught, and she shook her head. "I'm so sorry. She's gone!"

"Gone?" Mother asked. "You mean for a walk?"

"N-no," Kitty sobbed. "She's run away. Her valise and several of her gowns are missing!"

"You must be mistaken, Kitty dear," Mother said.

"She's written a note." The maid held out the envelope on which was written a single word.

Giles.

Giles leaped to his feet, snatched the envelope, and tore it open, his heart almost stopping as he read the first line.

"Giles!" Mother cried, her face ashen. "What does she say?" He unfolded the note, and read the words.

Dear Giles,

I ask forgiveness for what I have done, but I trust you'll understand. I have learned that in order to find true happiness, I must go out into the world and seek it. You may be surprised that I have acted on impulse, but is that not how we find true happiness? I think it is. It's become increasingly clear over the past few days that convention and propriety are the chains that bind a woman to a life of servitude and submission.

In order to find fulfillment, a woman must break convention so that she can fly and be free. I have, therefore, listened to the impulse of my heart and sought adventure. I have broken free and sallied forth into the world.

Please do not worry for me. I am in love, and so is he. I shall return a married woman and trust that you will understand my desire for adventure. You yourself have discovered the joy to be had from defying convention and following your heart.

Sometimes reason must be abandoned in order to find happiness. You have done this yourself, and I am so happy for you! I pray that you will also be joyous for me and will welcome us back into your home.

Your ever-loving cousin,
Beatrice.

The initial shock on reading the first paragraph gave way to fear, then anger. How could Beatrice be so foolish? Was she under the influence of a cad or some sort of adolescent madness? But as he continued to read, it became clear what—or rather, *who*—had persuaded her to undertake such a ruinous act with no thought for propriety, or her family.

"Sweet heaven, she's eloped!" Mother cried. "The family

name will be in tatters…oh, Beatrice, what have you done!"

The maid burst into tears, loud wails which grated on his senses.

"For heaven's sake, girl, must you torture us with your caterwauling?" he roared. "As if we've not got enough to deal with!"

Kitty let out another wail.

He strode across the breakfast room and grasped her by the shoulders.

"Do you know where she's gone? Or who with?" Kitty stared at him, terror in her wide-eyed expression. He shook her roughly. "Did you hear me, girl? I demand to know!"

Tears streamed down the maid's face, and she shook her head. "I'm sorry, sir, I-I don't know. She said nothing to me."

"If I find you're lying, I'll have you thrashed so hard, that you'll…"

"Giles!" Mother screamed. "Leave poor Kitty alone!"

He released the terrified maid, and she stumbled backward, trembling.

Mother held out her arms. "Kitty dear, come here." The maid ran toward her, sobbing. "I know nothing, ma'am, honest, I don't!"

"I know," Mother soothed, caressed the crying girl. "It's not your fault."

In that, at least, Mother was right.

It wasn't the maid's fault. Nor was it Beatrice's.

It was clear who the instigator of this particular disaster was.

Henrietta Redford.

CHAPTER TWENTY-SEVEN

HENRIETTA PLUCKED A rose and placed it in her basket. A week before, she'd have laughed at the notion of a pastime so ladylike. She'd even, to Aunt Agnes's surprise, made a passable attempt at embroidery last night.

And it was all down to one man.

Giles.

A secret thrill coursed through her. He accepted her—loved her, even—for what she was. A tomboy adventuress. And, in turn, she'd decided to at least attempt a handful of ladylike pursuits. She found that the notion of pleasing *him* was not as unpalatable as she had at first thought.

And, perhaps, there might be other ways of pleasing him. Such as that night on the terrace, when he'd held back while she cried out his name in unashamed passion. How might *he* sound, his voice filled with passion, crying her name?

Henrietta…

A voice floated through the air.

Yes, just like that.

"Henrietta!"

The voice called again—an angry voice—and she looked up. The door to the garden flew open to reveal Giles Thorpe. He strode toward her, a footman in his wake.

"Sir! I beg of you…" the footman pleaded.

Giles glanced over his shoulder and held up his hand.

"Do *not* try to stop me," he snarled. "Go back inside. This is between me and Miss Redford."

Henrietta flinched at the anger in his voice and the manner by which he almost spat out her name.

He stopped a few feet away, and she shivered at the fury in his eyes.

"Giles, is there something wrong?"

"Send your man back inside."

The footman stood beside him, fear in his eyes. Was he afraid for himself or for her? He glanced nervously at Giles, then returned his attention to Henrietta.

"Shall I fetch the master?"

"No, Charles," she replied. "I'll be fine. Tell Papa we have a guest, in case he'd like to take tea?"

"I don't want tea," Giles growled.

"In which case, Charles, you may go," Henrietta said.

"Are you quite sure, Miss?"

"She told you to go!" Giles snapped. The footman bowed and scuttled back to the house.

"What's happened?" she asked.

He let out a snort. "As if you didn't know!"

"I don't, as it happens."

He shook his head. "What a fool I've been. Are you proud of what you've done?"

"Done what?"

"Don't treat me like a simpleton!" he snarled. "You know damn well what you've done. Beatrice has eloped."

She drew in a sharp breath.

"She's *eloped*? Who with?"

"I'd hoped *you* could tell me."

"Dear God!" she cried. "Not Philip Meredith?"

"So, you *have* known," he said. "Did you plan it with him?"

"Of course not!" she cried. "I've never really trusted Philip."

"What nonsense! You've been horsing around with him and his brother from the moment you were out of leading strings.

You're quite capable of using him in your quest for revenge."

"Revenge? Against who?"

"Against *me*, of course!" he cried. "All your ridiculous little tricks and japes, all designed to irk me. How long had you been planning *this* one?"

"Why on earth would I want to harm you?" she demanded. "Are you so arrogant to believe that you occupy my every waking moment?" She shook her head. "What's worse is that you'd think I'd place Beatrice in danger."

He drew a sheaf of paper from his pocket and thrust it at her.

"Read it," he said. "Read what your handiwork has achieved."

She took the note, and her cheeks burned as her gaze moved across the page and fell on the familiar words.

A woman must break convention so that she can fly and be free…

"Oh, no, Beatrice, what have you done?" she murmured.

"You know damn well what she's done!" he cried. "A woman must break convention. Are those not your words? Have you not uttered them yourself to justify your outrageous behavior?"

"Yes, but, I never meant Beatrice to…"

"Don't be so naïve!" he cried. "Beatrice looks up to you, she has from the moment she set eyes on you. And you took advantage of that, encouraging her into all sorts of wild behavior." He shook his head. "I should have known it when I saw her halfway up that bloody tree, that you had an unhealthy influence over her."

"What will you do?" she asked.

"Do? I ought to have you thrashed! It should have been done years ago, but your father's too soft on you. The poor fool thought you could be controlled by packing you off to your aunt, but a bloody good hiding might have beaten the willfulness out of you. I'm minded to do it myself."

"I'd like to see you try!" she cried. "But rather than taking your revenge on me, you should be concentrating your efforts on finding Beatrice. Her welfare should take precedence over your thirst for revenge!"

"How dare you speak to me as if I'm the one at fault!" he roared. "I'm the one in the right, here!"

"We should make inquiries," she said.

"There's no 'we,' Miss Redford," he said. "*I'll* inquire, discreetly. As soon as they're found, I'll make them marry, to preserve her reputation."

"Shouldn't her safety and her happiness, come first?" she asked.

"My objective is to preserve the Thorpe family name," he said, "to see her discreetly married before she sets foot in my house again."

"Finding them quickly, rather than discreetly, should be your objective. And I'd advise against Philip as a husband. He'll not make her happy."

"And there lies the problem," he said. "You've never understood the need for discretion or propriety." He shook his head in disgust. "How in heaven's name could I ever have thought you'd make a suitable wife? You're nothing more than a willful child. I thank the Almighty I didn't make the mistake of offering you my hand!"

"How dare you?" she cried. "As if *you'd* make a suitable husband! I couldn't think of anything worse! I pity the woman who does accept you, for she'll be subject to a life of misery and incarceration, just like that which you subjected your poor mother to! No wonder Beatrice ran away. Any woman in her right mind would want to escape from you!"

"Why, you little…" He stepped closer, his expression darkening, but a voice interrupted him.

"I say, Thorpe! What the devil are you doing?"

Papa stood by the doorway, the red-faced footman beside him.

"I'm doing what should have been done years ago," Giles said. "Teaching your brat of a daughter a lesson."

"You'll do no such thing," Papa said. "She's not your responsibility."

"Perhaps you should take more responsibility, given her behavior," Giles said. "I always said you should have had her thrashed when she started to display her wild tendencies, and now she's placed my ward in danger."

"I've done nothing!" Henrietta cried. "I've even cautioned Beatrice against recklessness."

"Save your falsehoods," Giles said. "But I'll tell you this. Spread one word of what you've done and, so help me God, I will seek retribution. I knew you were badly behaved—I just didn't realize the extent of your evil."

She shrank back at the raw fury in his voice, his words cutting through her heart.

"That's enough!" Papa roared. "Charles, please escort Lord Thorpe off the premises, and make sure he never returns."

"Have you no interest in hearing about your daughter's crimes?" Giles asked.

"I shall hear it from her own lips," Papa said. "Henrietta may be a little spirited, but despite what you think—and, frankly, I don't give a damn what you think—she's not a liar, and she's not evil."

"Then curse the both of you!" Giles cried. "I'll see myself out." He turned on his heels and strode across the garden and back into the house, pushing the footman aside. Moments later, a door slammed in the distance.

Papa drew Henrietta into his arms, and she took comfort from his familiar aroma of brandy and cigar smoke.

"Oh Beatrice, what have you done!" she cried.

"Hush, daughter," Papa said. "It needn't concern you."

But it did. Not only had Beatrice most likely thrown herself into ruination, she had also destroyed Henrietta's one chance of happiness. For despite his obvious hatred of her, Giles Thorpe was, and would always be, the only man she could ever have been happy with.

CHAPTER TWENTY-EIGHT

Papa MADE NO demands on Henrietta. He merely led her inside, asked Charles to arrange some tea and to fetch a vase for the roses. Then he escorted her into the morning room.

When Charles reappeared, complete with tea tray and vase, Papa poured the tea in silence, while Henrietta arranged the roses and set the vase on a table by the window.

When she'd finished, he gestured to a chair and handed her a cup. He sat and sipped his tea, his gaze fixed on her.

He raised his eyebrows. "Well?"

"I've not done anything if that's what you're asking."

"I'm not asking anything in particular," he said, "though I would like to know why Lord Thorpe was so angry. Only yesterday you seemed so close…" He hesitated. "I'd almost go so far as to say that you looked as if you were falling in love."

The tears she'd kept at bay threatened to escape, and she turned her head aside.

"I'm sure whatever has angered him is down to a misunderstanding," he continued. "The two of you have always argued. People in love often do."

She bit her lip to stop it from trembling, then a warm hand covered hers.

"Hen, my dear, what's the matter?"

"It's Beatrice," she said. "She…she's eloped with Philip Meredith."

"That coxcomb!" Papa scoffed. "I'd have credited the girl with more sense. I suppose Lord Thorpe thinks it's your doing." He let out a snort. "As if you'd be so reckless. How dare he!"

"You don't blame me?"

"Of course not!" Papa said. "You've always been a little wild, but you have a sensible head on your shoulders. I suppose Thorpe objects to the Meredith lad being a suitor for his cousin. But if they're in love, I see no harm in it. Philip will inherit a title, and he's a respectable young man."

"What if they're not in love?" Henrietta asked. "Phillip's never struck me as the kind of young man to marry for love. What if he only wants Beatrice for her fortune?"

"That is the way of the world," Papa said. "Most marriages are based on far more practical concepts than love."

"You loved Mama, didn't you?"

"Of course," he replied, patting her hand. "Your dear mother and I were in love before we married, but I have no title. I'm of a very different class to the Thorpes and, for that matter, the Merediths. Men with titles expect to marry for reasons other than love."

"But I know Beatrice wants to marry for love."

"Perhaps she loves Phillip Meredith."

Henrietta shook her head. "Papa, it just doesn't *feel* right."

"I'm sure Lord Thorpe will put all to rights when he finds them."

She shook her head, "He said he doesn't care whether they love each other, he's going to make sure they marry regardless."

Papa sighed. "There's nothing you can do to stop it."

"What if I find her before Giles does?" Henrietta rose to her feet. "I might be able to prevent her from making a mistake she'll regret for the rest of her life. Or, at least, I can find out if it's what she really wants."

He shook his head. "How would you even know where to start looking?"

"I know exactly where."

PELISSE IN HAND, Henrietta stood on the doorstep of the Meredith townhouse. As she lifted her hand to knock on the door, she caught sight of a curtain twitching in a second-floor window.

Oh, Johnny, you always were a coward.

An image crossed her mind—Johnny crouching and shivering like a frightened rabbit, clutching the curtain for comfort while Lord Thorpe hammered at the door demanding entrance.

After a minute, the door opened, and a footman appeared.

"Lord and Lady Meredith are not at home," he said. "They're in Bath, on account of his lordship's health."

"I'm come to pay a call on Master Jonathan."

The footman hesitated, then glanced over his shoulder.

"Master Jonathan, and..." he hesitated, "Master Phillip, are not at home."

She leaned forward and lowered her voice. "I know what's happened," she said, "and I think I can help."

"I don't know..."

"Well, I *do*," she said crisply. "Be reasonable, Harry, how many times have I been here before, sparring with Johnny and Phillip? They're my friends, and I'd never betray a friend."

"It's all right," a voice called out. "Let her in—quickly!"

The footman ushered her inside.

Johnny stood at the foot of the stairs. "That'll be all, Harry," he said. He waited for the footman to disappear before speaking.

"What are you doing here, Henrietta?"

"I'm here to help."

"What with?"

Henrietta curled her hands into fists to control her anger. Johnny had always been a poor liar. Guilt was written all over him, and doubtless, he'd been party to Phillip's scheme. She needed a confession and an admission of their whereabouts. And, in order to do that, she'd have to deceive him by convincing him that she'd come with friendly intent, even if all she wanted to do was knock him senseless.

"I've just had Lord Thorpe bursting into my home," she said. "I've never seen him so angry."

That, at least, was true.

"Oh."

"Oh, indeed," she said. "I take it you know about your brother and Beatrice?"

He shifted from one foot to the other—his usual sign of guilt.

"Shall we go into the morning room at the back of the house?" she suggested. "If you're not at home to visitors, it would be a shame to be seen from the road. I'm already risking my reputation by coming here unchaperoned."

He glanced at the window and shrank back, then led the way to the back parlor, waiting until she took a chair before he sat on the edge of a chair, back straight, body tensed.

She needed him to relax. She placed her pelisse on her lap, feeling it to check the contents, then relaxed into her chair, waiting for the right moment. With luck, she wouldn't need it, but Johnny was a faithful younger brother—faithful to a fault—which was why he'd always taken the blame for Phillip's schemes.

But this time, Phillip had undertaken one scheme too far.

"I take it you're hiding from Lord Thorpe," she said. "Has he called?"

He flinched at the name and glanced at the door. "Well, not exactly *hiding*..."

"Cowering behind the curtain, then."

His mouth set in a stubborn line. "I wasn't..."

"I don't blame you," she said. "Lord Thorpe has a vile temper. I lost count of the number of times he threatened to thrash us when we were younger. Did you know he came round threatening *me* this morning?"

"Ah, so *that's* how you knew," he said. "I thought Phil might have told you, seeing as you're so friendly with Lady Beatrice."

"If he'd told me, I would have stopped them from eloping," she said. "Do you know where they've gone?"

He hesitated, shifted his gaze to the left, then shook his head.

"To Scotland, perhaps?" she suggested. "It's a long way from London, so they can't have reached there by now."

"They're not in Scotland. I'm sure of it."

That question, he'd answered a little too quickly.

Whatever he might say, he knew where they were.

She waved a dismissive hand in the air. "It matters not if they're to marry," she said. "They'll return home eventually. I take it he intends to marry her?"

He nodded. "Of course."

"Does he love her?"

His gaze shifted again, and he nodded. "Of-of course. And she loves him."

"Did he tell you that?"

Another glance to the left.

"H-he told me she's the prettiest girl in London, that she's a beautiful rose and he wants to worship her forever."

Hardly the sort of words Phillip would use. But Henrietta played along, nodded, and forced a smile.

"It'll soon blow over," she said. "Lord Thorpe told me he expected them to marry, so as long as they do, he'll come round."

"Did he send you?" Johnny asked.

"Of course not!" She forced a laugh. "That arrogant fool! I'm not here for him."

He smiled and relaxed back in his chair. Her time had come.

In favoring discretion, Giles had it all wrong. Henrietta had always preferred the direct approach.

She reached in her pelisse and drew out the knife she'd procured from Papa's kitchen. Then she sprang forward. Before Johnny had time to move, she was upon him, one hand on his throat, the other brandishing the knife which she pressed into his groin.

"Hen…"

"Hush," she hissed. "I'll cut them off if you say another word. Nod if you understand."

Eyes widening, he nodded.

"Good. Now, first, tell me where they are."

He shook his head. "Phillip will be angry if I tell."

She twisted the knife, and he let out a whimper. "What would you prefer? Your brother's anger…or castration?"

"You wouldn't—ouch!" He squeaked as she pushed the knife against him.

"Where are they?" she demanded. "Has he taken her to Bath with your parents?"

He shook his head.

"Where? I take it they're not in Scotland."

"W-Wilton-on-Sea," he stammered. "Near Southend."

Of course! Lord and Lady Meredith owned a small property there, which she had visited once with Papa when they'd taken a vacation in Southend.

"That's barely a day's ride away," she said. "Why there?"

"The Aberdeen coach is due to pass through there next week."

"Next week?" she cried. "Dear God, Beatrice will be ruined."

"It doesn't matter if they're going to marry."

"Do they love each other? Really?"

He hesitated and lowered his gaze to the knife in her hand.

"I've always been able to discern whether you're telling the truth, Johnny," she said. "It's a simple question."

"I-I can't speak for the lady," he said, "b-but Phil…well, you know what Phil's like."

"Oh, hell and damnation!" she cried, and he flinched at her profanity. "He doesn't love her at all, does he? What is it he wants. Her fortune? Vengeance on Lord Thorpe?"

When he didn't respond, she pressed the knife harder.

"All right!" he cried. "He wants both! He's never liked Thorpe, none of us have. I thought you'd find it funny."

"Am I laughing?"

He shook his head.

"Whatever your brother's feelings toward Lord Thorpe, he has no right to drag Beatrice into it. There's plenty of soulless debutantes with fortunes who'd be happy to marry him for his title. But Beatrice is not one of them. She's my friend."

"What are you going to do?" he asked.

"I'm going to bring her home."

"You'll have a challenge on your hands," Johnny said. "Phil won't give her up without a fight."

"Oh," she said, giving him a cold smile, "that's exactly what I'm counting on."

HENRIETTA CHECKED THE saddle of Papa's horse for the fifth time, then took the reins and led the animal out into the livery yard.

Oh, Papa, please forgive me for what I'm about to do.

The stable master seemed unconcerned by her attire—riding jacket, shirt, and breeches—and he tipped his hat as she strode past.

With her confident stride and hair tucked into her hat, Henrietta looked every inch the young man indulging in a dawn ride. Doubtless, she'd be ruined if anyone recognized her. But it was a sacrifice worth making if it prevented Beatrice from ruination, or worse—making a mistake she'd regret for the rest of her life. All that mattered was she reach Beatrice before the girl was lost forever. For, despite what she'd asserted to Giles, and what Papa had said, it was *her* fault that Beatrice had run off. She alone had encouraged Beatrice to seek out adventure and independence and, though she'd tempered her encouragement with caution, poor Beatrice had succumbed to the one fatal enemy of every innocent heart.

Infatuation.

And poor Beatrice had fallen victim.

Grasping the pommel of the saddle, Henrietta placed her foot in the stirrup, then swung herself up into position. She steered her mount out of the yard.

Dawn had not long broken, and the sun had yet to boil away the shroud of morning mist. But, nevertheless, she prayed that she wouldn't encounter too many folks on the streets.

Though she cared little for her own reputation—which would, in all likelihood, be ruined by her escapade—Henrietta had no wish to disappoint Papa. Guilt gnawed at her at the thought of the note she'd left for him, and what he'd think of her when he read it, and when he discovered that she'd taken her sword. She only hoped he'd forgive her and understand that she was making amends for what she'd done, albeit unintentionally, to Beatrice.

And what she'd done to *him*. To Giles.

Like it or not, Giles valued propriety and appearance, and though Henrietta couldn't understand his priorities, she recognized them and could acknowledge the pain that Beatrice's elopement had caused him—even if that pain had manifested itself in the fury which he'd directed at her.

She spurred her mount into a trot, the hooves echoing on the street. Once out in the country, she could increase the pace and she'd reach Wilton-on-Sea well before nightfall.

In all likelihood, Beatrice would greet her with hostility, if she was still under the spell of her infatuation. As for Phillip—Henrietta smiled to herself at the prospect of finally having their long-anticipated confrontation. He'd always shied away from sparring with her when they'd played at sword fighting. But this time, she would fight him for real.

CHAPTER TWENTY-NINE

HENRIETTA RECOGNIZED THE landscape before she saw the sign.

Wilton-on-Sea was a small resort, situated north of Southend, and surrounded by lush, green countryside.

The landscape stretched in front of her, beyond which the sea glistened in the sunlight, a deep blue that met the lighter blue of the sky. The tall, square tower of a church rose up among a copse of trees to dominate the skyline, and she smiled at the memory of the Sunday service that she'd attended during a vacation as a child when Papa had admonished her for giggling. The parson had delivered his sermon with all the pompous monotony of the morally superior while the sunlight had streamed through the medieval window, illuminating his bald head, and giving it the appearance of a boiled egg.

As she neared the village, the sounds of activity filtered through the summer air—excited chatter as a gaggle of school-children skipped across the road, running toward a small, squat cottage, the hammering of metal against an anvil from the blacksmith, and cows lowing in a distant field.

From memory, the Merediths' cottage was near the coast, but it had been several years since Henrietta had visited it with Papa. She recalled the view of the sea from the front parlor window, and that the church tower had been visible from the gardens. With luck, it wouldn't take long to locate it.

Entering the village, she spied a couple, arm in arm, dressed in the easy, comfortable clothes of farm laborers, most likely returning home from a day's work in the fields. She reined her horse to a halt. The man tipped his hat as they approached her, and the woman bobbed a curtsey.

"Good afternoon, young sir," the man said. "Are ye wanting assistance?"

She removed her hat, and her hair cascaded about her face.

"Heavens above!" the woman cried.

"Forgive me, Miss," the man said, his eyes widening in alarm. "I had no idea…"

"No matter," Henrietta said. "I was hoping you'd be able to help me. I'm looking for some friends of mine. They've invited me to a house party, but I mislaid the directions."

"Ah, that'd be Highleigh Manor—the big house yonder." He pointed back along the road in the direction she'd come.

She shook her head. "My friend said it was at a smaller dwelling, overlooking the sea. But I can't recall the name. You don't happen to know of such a property where a party of young people has recently arrived?"

He shook his head. "I know of no such property, Miss."

Henrietta's heart sank, but the man's wife gave him a nudge. "Oh, ye do, Frank," she said in a thick country accent. "That'll be Eastview cottage on the road leading south."

"That's been empty for years."

The woman rolled her eyes. "Bless me, Frank! Why do ye never listen to a word I say? Don't ye remember what I told ye last night, about Anna's ma having seen a young couple in a hired coach?" She let out a sharp breath in the huff of a long-suffering wife and glanced at Henrietta, as if looking for female solidarity, before resuming her attention on her husband.

"I *knew* ye were asleep when I told ye about it last night."

"I wasn't."

"Yes ye were," she said. "Yer snoring was enough to wake the dead."

"Why ask me if I could remember yer gossiping if I were asleep?" the man asked. "Lord, woman, 'tis a wonder I've not been rendered deaf, the battering my ears have had."

"Perhaps you could tell *me*?" Henrietta suggested in her sweetest voice. She reached into her pocket and fished out a coin. "There's a shilling for your trouble."

She tossed it at the woman, then winked at the man. "I daresay a shilling would help cure your deafness if your good lady wife were to suggest you spend it on a good supper at the inn—the Crown, isn't it, if I recall correctly?"

"Aye, the Crown, that's right," he said. "Have ye visited here before?"

"When I was a child. The landlord's wife served an excellent mutton stew."

"That'll be Mrs. Prosser," the woman said. "She has a rare talent for making the tastiest, tenderest dishes out of the scrawniest animals. Why, only last week, she…"

"Nellie, my love, the young lady has no wish to listen to your prattling," her husband interrupted. "Tell her what ye know, and she can be on her way."

Henrietta suppressed a laugh. Perhaps she should have given the husband the shilling after all, given that his wife clearly loved to talk—both to and at—everyone within earshot.

The couple exchanged a glance, and Henrietta's heart twitched to see their mutual affection, even after they'd been bickering. That's what she'd wanted—a partnership with a man who loved her, where they enjoyed each other's company, walked arm in arm everywhere, and engaged in a little banter to maintain a little spirit, rather than always being in agreement.

The woman pointed along the road. "Keep going until you pass the church, Miss, then take the first road on the right and follow it past the Crown Inn, and the row of houses, until you leave the village. Eastview cottage is in a dip to the left of the road, sheltered by trees, with a red roof and a climbing rose surrounding the front door—in need of a trim, it is. Ye can't miss it."

"Thank you." Henrietta replaced her hat, gave them a nod, then spurred her mount toward the church. The woman's voice echoed through the air as she chattered away to her husband, fading as Henrietta entered the village.

The woman was right. Eastview cottage was unmistakable and stood out against the landscape, overlooking the sea. It seemed smaller than Henrietta had remembered and more forlorn. The rambling rose bush was overgrown, the windows dark, and the roof was missing several tiles. It looked as if it had been abandoned for years, which it had been since Lord Meredith's health had begun to fail and the family had preferred to split their time between Bath and London. But, as she approached the building, she noticed a wisp of smoke spiraling into the air from the chimney.

She dismounted, led her horse toward the building, and tethered the animal against the gate. Then she reached into the panniers for her sword belt and strapped it round her waist. She was unlikely to be greeted with a warm welcome, or any degree of civility. And, as her victory against Johnny had confirmed, surprise was the best form of attack.

She approached the front door, hand on the hilt of her sword, and listened.

Voices came from within—a man's voice, and another voice, a female voice, high-pitched, filled with distress.

"I want to go home!"

"It's a bit late for that," the man's voice said.

"I've changed my mind."

"Don't you love me?"

"I-I do, but my cousin will be so angry!"

"That didn't bother you yesterday. Why should it bother you now? There's nothing for it, we must stay here and wait for the coach."

"Can't I go out, at least? I need some air."

"I already told you!" the man cried, anger creeping into his tone. "Do you want to risk discovery? We stick to the plan." He paused and let out a snort. "Dear God, not the tears again!"

Muffled sobbing came from within. Unable to bear it any longer, Henrietta knocked on the door.

The sobbing stopped, replaced by urgent whispers. She waited a few heartbeats, then knocked again.

Footsteps approached.

"Who's there?" a voice asked.

"I be Mrs. Prosser from the Crown," Henrietta said, lowering the tone of her voice and affecting her best attempt at country dialect.

"Wh-what do you want?"

"I'm come to check over the house for Lord Meredith's steward, to keep it tidy, like. I can bring some logs if you're needing any." Henrietta winced at her accent.

Eventually, she heard a sigh. "Oh, very well."

The door opened a fraction, and Phillip's face appeared.

His eyes widened. "You!"

Before he could slam the door in her face, Henrietta wedged her foot in the door and rammed it open with her shoulder.

He jumped back, and she followed, entering a narrow corridor, with a flight of steps in the background.

"What the devil are you doing?" he asked. "How dare you!"

"Oh, be quiet!" she snapped. "You've no right to question what I'm doing. What the devil have *you* been up to, Phillip? Did you think you'd get away with it?"

"Get away with what?"

"Oh, for heaven's sake!" she cried. "Beatrice—Beatrice!"

"She's not here," Phillip said.

"Come out!" she cried. "You're not in any trouble. I've come to see if you're all right."

A face appeared at the top of the steps.

"Henrietta? Oh, thank goodness!"

"Stay where you are!" Phillip roared.

"How *dare* you speak to her like that!" Henrietta cried.

"I'll speak to her how I like. She's my fiancée."

"Is that so?" Henrietta asked. "She doesn't seem all that willing to me. Abduction is frowned upon in polite society."

"You came willingly, didn't you, Beatrice?"

"Oh, Henrietta, forgive me!" Beatrice cried. "I've made a terrible mistake! Is Giles with you?"

"No, but he's very worried."

"Is he angry?"

"Not with *you*," Henrietta replied. "If you come with me now, there's no harm done."

"I think you've forgotten one thing," Phillip said. "Beatrice is ruined. She has no choice but to marry me."

Beatrice burst into tears. "I don't want to!" she cried. "I want to go home!"

Henrietta turned to Phillip. "Have you ruined her?"

He let out a laugh.

"Beatrice, has he touched you?"

"I-I don't understand," Beatrice said, sniffing. "What do you mean *touched* me?"

"What's happened since you left London?" Henrietta asked. "Has he kissed you…" she hesitated, then forged ahead—this was not the time for delicacy, "…have you shared a bed?"

Beatrice shook her head. "H-he said he loved me and asked me to elope. He hired a coach at midnight, said it would be terribly romantic, and everyone would think me brave and adventurous like I want to be—like *you* are."

Henrietta glared at Phillip, who shrugged. "What can I say?" he said. "She admires you."

"Oh, be quiet!" Henrietta snapped. "Go on, Beatrice."

"Even before we left London, I changed my mind. But when I asked him to turn back, he said there was no going back—that I had to marry him, because Giles would throw me out on the street if I didn't."

Henrietta curled her lip in disgust. "So, you abducted her, Phillip."

"I told you, she came willingly."

"Under coercion," she replied. "Under false declarations of love. Or, am I wrong? Do you love her?"

He opened his mouth to reply, and his gaze flicked down to the sword in her hand.

"Think very carefully before you speak, Phillip."

He glanced at Beatrice. "Oh, very well," he said. "Of course, I don't love her."

"Why whisk her away in the middle of the night to marry her?"

"Are you a complete simpleton? For her fortune, of course! A man will put up with a lot for thirty thousand."

Beatrice let out a wail.

"You unimaginable bastard!" Henrietta cried. "Well, you've failed, Phillip. You'll not get your filthy hands on Beatrice, or her fortune."

A slow smile curled on his lips. "Oh, won't I? I suppose I might be persuaded to leave the lady with her reputation intact, but you—and the highly respectable Lord Thorpe—will have to make it worth my while."

"What do you mean?"

"Oh, please!" He let out a mocking laugh. "In all likelihood, Lady Beatrice is, by now, the talk of the town. But I'm not a greedy man. I'll release her for twenty thousand. The remaining ten should be enough to purchase a husband if you can find one who doesn't mind soiled goods."

"Why you..." Henrietta drew her sword. "I should cut you down, here and now, for dishonoring her. In fact, why don't we settle the matter outside?"

He let out a laugh. "You don't mean a duel? In a cottage garden?"

She set her mouth into a grim smile. "A cottage garden is as good as anywhere. I'd suggest dawn tomorrow, but I couldn't rely on a dishonorable man such as yourself not to bolt in the night. I take it you have your sword?"

"I'm sorry to disappoint you, but no."

"He does!" Beatrice cried. "I asked him about it, and he said he needed it to protect me."

"To threaten you, more like," Henrietta said.

"You little blabbermouth!" Phillip cried. "How dare you!"

"How dare *you*!" Beatrice yelled, having clearly regained some of her courage. "Hen's right. You took advantage of me. I only regret being foolish enough to believe your lie. What must my cousin think of me? He'll be heartbroken."

"Let's hope so," Phillip said.

"That settles it," Henrietta said. "Outside, now!"

"What are we fighting for?" he asked.

"Honor," she said, "if you understand the concept. But let's make it worth your while. Either way, you return to London without Beatrice and say that you visited the country on your own and have no idea where Beatrice is. If you win, you can have your twenty thousand. But, if you lose, you return with nothing."

She held out her hand.

He stared at it with narrowed eyes, as if in thought. "Nothing?" he asked. "It sounds like a poor deal."

"Only if you lose," she replied. "It's a better deal than having me cut your balls off."

A flare of fear ignited in his eyes, then he let out a sigh and took her hand.

She curled her fingers round his wrist and squeezed it firmly. "No reneging."

"No reneging," he repeated, tightening his own grip until she could feel the bones in her hand scraping against each other. Most likely she'd be left with a bruise. "It'll be the easiest twenty thousand I've ever earned."

"Henrietta, no!" Beatrice cried. "You can't do this on my account."

"Yes I can," Henrietta said. She turned to Phillip. "What do you suggest? First to disarm, first hit to the torso, or first blood?"

His eyes glowed with relish. "First blood."

He disappeared into a side room, then emerged moments later, holding a foil. He gestured toward the open door.

"Ladies first."

As Henrietta turned toward the door, Beatrice ran down the stairs, almost tripping, and tugged at her sleeve.

"Please Henrietta, don't endanger yourself on my account. This isn't your fault."

"Your cousin thinks otherwise," Henrietta replied. "I must take my share of the responsibility and do what I can to make amends. Make sure you stay at a safe distance. May I borrow a ribbon as a token of luck?"

Beatrice nodded and plucked a ribbon from her hair and handed it to her. "Like a favor for a champion in a tournament," she said, giving Henrietta a watery smile through her tears.

Henrietta returned the smile in an attempt to reassure Beatrice. "If you like."

Phillip strode past them, pushing Henrietta aside, and he led the way to the garden at the back of the cottage, which overlooked the sea. The wind from the sea cooled Henrietta's burning cheeks, and with trembling hands, she tied her hair back, securing it with Beatrice's ribbon.

What the devil had she got herself into? But there was no time for a loss of courage. Beatrice relied on her, and it was always easier to remain strong for others than for oneself.

She entered the garden where her opponent waited, standing to attention, sword in hand. As she had done many times before with his brother, she moved to stand opposite him, saluted him with a flourish of her own sword and bowed. He mirrored the gesture, and they stood, staring at each other.

His expression was filled with the self-assurance he'd always possessed, bordering on arrogance. Being several inches taller and of heavier build, he was undoubtedly stronger than her. But he knew it, and complacency was the failing of the strong.

For a moment, he stood still, then he lunged toward her.

The fool! She'd seen it in his eyes, which had narrowed and

glanced to her left just before he moved. She dodged to the right, lifting her weapon to deflect the blow, as Beatrice let out a cry. He tried again, this time aiming for the right, and she parried the blow again. They circled each other for a few steps.

He had the disadvantage. While growing up, he'd take little interest in her abilities, refusing to fight her because she was "only a stupid girl." That arrogance had never left him, and while she'd observed him time after time sparring with Johnny, he'd paid little attention to her, thinking her beneath his notice, and only showing any interest when he'd wanted her to carry out his schemes, such as dropping water-bombs on Giles Thorpe.

She leaped toward him, aiming her weapon to one side and, with a shriek, he jumped backward. She repeated the gesture, aiming wide on the other side. Again, he leaped back, letting out a sneering laugh.

"Is that all you can do, little urchin? Hardly proficient."

"Henrietta, please!" Beatrice cried. "I beg you not to get hurt. Can't you surrender?"

"Oh, be quiet, and let me win my twenty thousand!" Phillip cried.

"Giles will never hand over the money," Beatrice said.

"Oh, he will," came the reply. "He's a man of honor, and he'll do everything he can to protect yours. Either that, or he'll force you to marry me, and I shall have thirty thousand. An extra ten is ample compensation for being saddled with you."

The simpleton! Didn't he realize she'd deliberately aimed wide?

He lunged forward again, this time, aiming for her torso. Had his aim hit true, he would have sliced her across the chest. But she dodged the blow and, with a flick of the wrist, knocked his sword out of his grip. The weapon flew through the air and fell onto the nearby path with a clatter. Caught off guard, Phillip lost his balance and toppled backward, landing in the grass.

Henrietta darted forward and placed her sword at the tip of his throat.

"Damn you!" he cried.

"Do you yield?"

He shook his head.

"You gave me your word," she said. "We shook hands. You're supposed to adhere to the ridiculous codes of honor that gentlemen indulge in."

"You've merely disarmed me," he said, panting. "First blood, remember?"

With a flick of her wrist, she executed a maneuver with her weapon, the tip moving in a blur, before settling once more on his throat.

"I don't think you're in a position to object," she said.

"Are you so dishonorable that you'll renege on our agreement?" he asked. "First blood."

She gave him a cold smile. "Take a closer look."

His gaze flicked down, and his eyes widened. The letter 'X' was carved into his flesh, just below the throat, where thick red droplets were already swelling.

"I don't think…" he began, then stopped, as she pressed the tip of her sword against his neck, causing an indent in the skin.

"Did I not draw enough blood?" she asked. "Should I perhaps add a sliced throat to the mix as well as taking your balls? I'm happy to oblige if you need further proof of my victory. What would Lord Meredith say if I presented your balls to him on a silken cushion?"

He sank back to the ground, defeat in his expression.

"Have it your way," he said.

"You yield?"

"I do."

"And you accept my terms?" she asked. "You must take the first coach to London and tell everyone that you were visiting your parents in Bath, but you went alone and you haven't seen Lady Beatrice."

He glanced at Beatrice, a plea in his eyes, but Beatrice had been cured of her infatuation, and she merely stared back, dislike in her expression. He nodded. "Very well," he said. "What will you do?"

"That's none of your business," she said. "But, for my part, I promise I'll say nothing about your having abducted Lady Beatrice against her will…" He opened his mouth to protest, but she ignored him and continued, "…or," she added, "that you were beaten in a fair fight, by a *girl*."

Beatrice let out a giggle.

"I wouldn't laugh if I were you," Phillip said. "I could still ruin you."

"Go ahead," Beatrice said. "I care not. I'd rather be ruined than married to *you*."

"Don't worry," Henrietta said. "He'll not tell. He values his hide too much. Your cousin would rip him apart if he realized what he'd done. And, he knows that he's at risk of waking up in the middle of the night with a knife at his groin if he doesn't honor his promise."

Phillip drew in a sharp breath, and Henrietta glanced at Beatrice. "Do you need long to pack your valise?"

Beatrice shook her head.

"Good. Meet me by the gate as quick as you can. I'll secure us rooms at the Crown Inn. Phillip can meet us there tomorrow morning."

"What for?" Phillip asked.

"So we can make sure you're on the London coach," Henrietta replied. "You may be surprised at the notion, Phillip, but I don't trust you. I'll not be satisfied until I see you climb aboard the coach with my own eyes."

"And you're not returning to London?"

"Not right away," she replied. "If we returned to London with you, it would only fuel the rumors that Beatrice left with you. I must do everything I can to preserve her reputation."

"Why?" he asked.

"Because you've ruined it!"

"No, I mean why *her*? I thought you hated her. What's she to you?"

"She's my friend."

"Or, is it because of who her cousin is?" he asked. "I always wondered if you'd set your cap at Giles Thorpe." A sneer crept across his face. "Aha, that's it! Are you trying to ingratiate yourself with him? You've *no* chance. He'll end up marrying someone like Lady Irma Fairchild."

Henrietta chose not to dignify his taunts with a response, but a voice whispered in her mind that, given what Giles had said during their last encounter, Phillip was right.

And, with what she had planned for the restoration of Beatrice's reputation, she'd sacrifice any chance of Giles viewing her with anything other than loathing.

Moments later, Beatrice appeared, complete with valise. Without a backward glance at her defeated adversary, Henrietta led her friend toward the gate where the horse stood patiently waiting, then they set off toward the inn.

Once there, she could set her plan in motion. It was a plan that had a small chance of restoring Beatrice's honor, but would, almost certainly, destroy Henrietta's reputation, and with it, her only chance at love.

CHAPTER THIRTY

"WILL YOU BE wanting some more toast, Miss?"

Henrietta leaned back in her chair and pushed her plate aside. "I don't think I could eat another morsel, Mrs. Prosser. I've already had two slices too many. How do you get your elderberry jam to taste so good?"

"A pinch of cinnamon," the landlady said. "A recipe from my grandmother, who lived in Burma before she married."

"May I have another slice, please?" Beatrice asked.

"Very good, Miss," the landlady said. "I must say you look much better than you did last night."

Beatrice blushed and sipped her tea. When they'd arrived at the Crown last night, inquiring about a room, the poor girl was shaking with distress, having finally realized the enormity of what she'd done. A good dose of Mrs. Prosser's venison stew washed down with a glass of wine, had settled her nerves a little, but it had taken Henrietta most of the night to convince Beatrice that her plan would work. Beatrice had been all for returning to London with Phillip and throwing herself at her cousin's mercy, but the risk that she'd end up being forced into a marriage with Phillip was too great.

Beatrice had woken that morning in the low-ceilinged bed-chamber they shared, with the sun on her face, and a determination to do better. There just remained one obstacle to overcome.

"When does the mail coach leave for London?" Henrietta asked. Beatrice dropped her teacup with a clatter, and the landlady gave her a sharp glance.

"Have you changed your mind about your stay, Miss?"

"Not at all," Henrietta said, "but I have a number of letters to post, and I'm anxious that they go today. You see, my friend and I came here on something of a whim, and I wish to reassure my family of our whereabouts, and that we'll be home at the end of the week."

In that, at least, Henrietta spoke the truth. Last night, Beatrice had written a letter to Giles under her direction, and Henrietta had written another letter to Papa.

The landlady gave a smile of good-natured indulgence. "The coach leaves on the hour," she said, "so you've not got long. If you'd like to give me your letters, I can pass them to the driver and add the postage to your account."

"Please don't trouble yourself," Henrietta said. "I can do that myself." She glanced at her friend, who had turned pale and was staring at the window as if she expected Phillip to appear at any moment to abduct her.

"Shall I come?" Beatrice asked.

"No, finish your breakfast," Henrietta said. "We've a long excursion planned for today. I thought we might visit Southend. What do you say, Mrs. Prosser?"

"Oh yes, a fine idea," the landlady said, "but mind you wrap up warm—the wind from the sea has a distinct chill to it which can catch a lady unawares. And, if I may be so bold, I'd highly recommend the tearoom at the end of the Royal Terrace. Ask for Mrs. Booth. Tell her I sent you, and she'll see you're looked after." She bobbed a curtsey. "I'll go and see about your toast now."

After the landlady exited the room, Henrietta placed a hand on Beatrice's arm.

"Stay here while I make sure he's on the coach," she said. "We can forget about him and enjoy a little vacation away from

London, society, and propriety."

Beatrice gave her a small smile and nodded. Then Henrietta rose to her feet, exited the breakfast room, and stepped out into the morning sunshine. In the distance, she spied the silhouette of the mail coach approaching from the road.

Standing in the courtyard, waiting for the coach, next to an elderly gentleman, was Phillip Meredith. The elderly gentleman tipped his hat on seeing Henrietta, then resumed his attention on his newspaper as Phillip watched her approach.

"So, you're here," Henrietta said.

"Did you think I wouldn't be?"

"Given what you've done, can you expect me to trust you?"

He colored and looked away.

"What's wrong with you, Phillip?" she asked. "There's dozens of young women who'd marry you for your title alone. You had no need to persuade one into an elopement."

"She might have changed her mind after we left," he said, "but she took little persuading at first. The fault is not all mine."

"She's young and impressionable, Phillip," Henrietta said. "You had no right to take advantage. You could have petitioned Lord Thorpe for her hand."

"He'd have refused, and then I'd have been the laughingstock of London. I thought it would be fun to snatch his cousin from under his nose. She was willing."

"She was infatuated," Henrietta said. "Her only crime is naïveté, nothing more. In time, she'll get over it."

"And you'll be the one to pay for her transgression."

"So, what's new?" she replied. "I paid for your crimes when we were children, if I recall. You always slipped your way out of trouble, leaving Johnny and me to take the blame. But you're going to have to take responsibility for your actions at some point, Phillip."

"Because I'm the eldest?" He let out a sigh. "Johnny can do what he damn well likes with no retribution. Whereas I…"

"That's your burden to bear as the heir," she said. "Is that why you've always shirked responsibility? Because you know that the ultimate responsibility awaits you?"

"Papa's not getting any younger," he said. "I overheard Dr. McIver telling Mother to prepare herself. I don't know if he'll return from Bath this year—alive, at least."

She placed a hand on his arm. "Oh, Phillip, I'm sorry," she said. "Does Johnny know?"

He shook his head.

"Go back to London and tell him. He deserves to know. The title cannot be shared, but the responsibility can. It's time to grow up." She gave him a grin of mischief. "Little did I think I'd be telling anyone to grow up and take responsibility. It seems as if we've both changed."

She hesitated, then drew the letters out of her pelisse.

"Can I trust you to post these for me when you arrive in London?"

"What are they?"

"They're letters, explaining that I arranged to take Beatrice away on a whim, and persuaded her to concoct a tale of elopement for a jape."

His eyes widened. "Why the devil would you write that?"

"To clear Beatrice of any wrongdoing. She doesn't deserve to have her reputation or her family name ruined for a silly mistake."

"But you do?"

"I have less to lose than she does."

He stared at the letters and nodded.

"I'm sorry," he said. "I acted like a fool—have done for most of my life. If I could change what I did, I would. Beatrice deserves better, and I hope she finds it. Will you tell her that, from me?"

"Of course."

"And what about you?" he asked.

"I have a few days' respite by the seaside to look forward to," she said with a smile. "I shall take this opportunity to enjoy the sea air and to persuade Beatrice that she's not ruined her life."

He shook his head. "I meant you and Giles Thorpe."

Her stomach gave a little jolt at the mention of his name. How he'd hate her when he read the letter!

"*Bloody hell*, you love him," he said, "don't you?"

She gave a smile of resignation. "In time, I'll get over it," she said. "As you say, he'll most likely marry Lady Irma."

With a rattle of wheels and clatter of hoofbeats, the coach drew up alongside them, laden with trunks and packets, and a young traveler clinging to the outside. Henrietta pressed the letters into Phillip's hand while a footman loaded the elderly gentleman's trunk onto the already top-heavy coach, and ushered him inside. Phillip dropped a coin into the footman's hand, then followed suit.

The coach set off with a lurch, the traveler almost losing his balance. Phillip's face appeared at the window, and he raised his hand in salute.

Henrietta watched the coach disappear along the London road, then she turned and went back inside the inn to join her friend, praying that her last words to Phillip would prove to be true—that she would get over losing the man she loved.

But a voice inside her head whispered otherwise.

CHAPTER THIRTY-ONE

GILES CLIMBED THE steps leading to his townhouse and shouldered his way past the waiting footman, who nearly toppled over.

"Out of my way!"

"Sorry, your lordship."

He pulled off his jacket and threw it at the footman, then strode into the parlor where his mother sat, her nose in a book.

She looked up. "Have you found Beatrice?"

"No."

He crossed the floor to the bureau, picked up the brandy decanter, and poured some into a glass. He drained the glass in a single gulp before pouring another.

"Better?" she asked.

"Not really." He drained the glass again and refilled it.

"It's not like you to drink at all in the afternoon, let alone take two glasses at once," she said. "Whatever it is, it must be serious."

"Well, aren't you observant?" he quipped.

Immediately, he regretted the words.

"Forgive me, Mother. I'm not myself."

"Regarding the drinking, perhaps not, but the air of superiority is very much my boy."

He flinched at the sharp edge of her voice. Then he set the glass aside and flopped down in a chair beside her.

"Are you *reading*?" he asked.

"As you see." She held up a pair of lorgnettes. "These are a wonder. They've enabled me to read by myself, provided the light is good—which it is, in this parlor." She cast him a sharp glance. "Miss Redford gave them to me not long after we arrived in London."

"Why?"

"As a gift," she said. "Believe it or not, Giles, there are some people in this world who take pleasure out of giving and expect nothing in return. Where have you been?"

"The Meredith townhouse."

"Again? I thought they were not at home."

Lord and Lady Meredith are in Bath," he said. "It seems the rumors about his lordship's failing health are true."

"How do you know that?"

"Because their sons *were* at home."

"*Both* of them?" Abandoning her needlework, she sat up straight. "Was Beatrice with them?"

"No."

"Have they seen her? What did they say?"

He hesitated and moved his hand out of Mother's view to conceal the broken skin around his knuckles. While he didn't mind her knowing he'd confronted the Meredith twins again, or that the elder of the two had managed to convince him that he had no idea of Beatrice's whereabouts, he had no wish for Mother to know that he'd lost his temper and planted a shiner on Phillip Meredith's face.

Phillip's account of having spent a few days sparring with friends in Brighton seemed plausible, particularly given the recent wound running along his collarbone, which looked as if it had been sustained at the tip of a foil.

Which meant that Beatrice was still abroad somewhere.

Where the devil was she? Had she run off with someone else? But he couldn't recall her having shown a partiality for any young man save Phillip Meredith.

Foolish child! Not only was she endangering herself, she was making a mockery of the family name. The longer she was away, the greater the chance of the scandal getting out. And, if the rumors were true, Miss Redford had disappeared also.

There was some devilry afoot, if only he could piece together the puzzle.

But he had no wish to alarm Mother.

"Shall I ring the bell for tea?" he asked, forcing his voice to remain calm.

"Yes," Mother replied, "and I'd recommend a slice of fruit-cake to soak up that brandy."

Before he could ring the bell, the footman appeared, holding a silver salver containing a single envelope, written in Beatrice's handwriting.

"What the devil is this?" Giles demanded.

"It was delivered while you were out." The footman glanced at Mother and lowered his voice. "I thought it best to wait until you returned, on account of her ladyship's nerves."

So—even the servants knew of the impending scandal. With a sigh, he plucked the envelope off the tray, ripped it open, and read the first line.

"Dear God!" he cried. "Foolish brat—and that damned ur-chin! I might have known. She's gone too far this time."

"Sweet lord, what's happened?" Mother cried, her features twisted with distress. "Is it Beatrice?"

"Yes."

He read the letter again to be sure of its meaning.

"What does she say?" Mother asked. "Is she safe? Dear God, Giles, tell me, is she in danger?"

"She writes to say that she's been enjoying a vacation by the sea," he said.

"A vacation? With whom?"

"With Miss Redford." He spat out the name with gritted teeth.

Curse her!

"With Henrietta? Does Mr. Redford know?"

"It would seem not. Miss Redford apparently suggested they leave in secret because she feared her father and I would not allow it. What the devil has she been playing at?"

"I don't understand," she said. "You saw Henrietta after Beatrice had left. They can't have gone together."

"It seems as if Beatrice went ahead. Miss Redford followed," he replied. He shook his head. "I can't make sense of it—but then, I've never made sense of *her*."

"I thought you were fond of Miss Redford."

I loved her.

"Does she say when they're returning?" she asked.

"Saturday," he said. "After which I'll never let Beatrice out of my sight again until she's been safely married off."

"And Henrietta?"

"I'll make damned sure she understands the enormity of what she's done," he said. "I only thank the Almighty that I've been spared from making what would have been the biggest mistake of my life. To think that I once thought…"

No.

He stopped himself. There was no point in letting in the image he'd conjured up in his mind—of Henrietta, his Henrietta, naked and pliant beneath him, moaning as he buried himself between her thighs and brought her to pleasure…

Stop it!

He screwed the letter into a ball and rammed it in his pocket.

"What will you do?" Mother asked.

"First, I'll ring the bell for tea," he said. "Then, I'll do what I should have done the moment we came to London."

"Which is?"

"I'll ask Lord Fairchild for permission to court his daughter. Beatrice needs a steadying influence of a woman such as Lady Irma, and I need the right sort of wife."

Pleasure and passion came with too much risk. It was time to listen to his head and ignore the calling of his heart.

CHAPTER THIRTY-TWO

ARM IN ARM with Beatrice, Henrietta walked along the pavement of Sussex Gardens. The walk from the livery yard had done nothing to steady her nerves, and her heart rate increased further as the façade of the Thorpe townhouse came into view.

Beside her, Beatrice tripped against the pavement, and Henrietta squeezed her friend's hand.

"*Courage*, my friend."

The merry young woman who had blossomed during their brief vacation—and had even been adventurous enough to undertake sea bathing at Southend—was gone. She had been replaced by a trembling girl, terrified of the reception that awaited her.

With Henrietta's sword concealed beneath her redingote, and her riding clothes tucked into her valise, the two of them looked like any other pair of respectable young women taking a morning constitutional.

A handful of people milled about the street, a couple strolling, a butcher's boy scurrying along with a basket laden with goods. All going about their daily business, indulging in the simple pleasures of a walk or an errand.

How she envied them!

"I don't know if I can face him," Beatrice whispered.

"Remember what we agreed," Henrietta said. "I persuaded

you to come away with me for a vacation and play a trick on your cousin. Just tell him it was *my* fault, and you'll be unharmed."

"I-I can't tell a falsehood."

"You can, Beatrice," Henrietta replied. "You look your cousin in the eyes and think of your future. Your reputation depends on everyone believing what we say. If we succeed, you'll maintain your footing in Society."

"And what about you?"

"I have no problem telling a falsehood plausibly if it's in a good cause."

"No," Beatrice said, "I mean, what about you and Giles?"

"Anything we had is over," Henrietta said. "Truth be told, your cousin never liked me."

They continued in silence toward the house.

"You're wrong," Beatrice said.

"About what?"

Beatrice met her gaze. "You *can't* tell a falsehood plausibly. And, I know what I saw. Giles likes you."

Not anymore.

Beatrice tightened her grip on Henrietta's hand and whimpered. "Giles…oh *no…*"

Striding toward them along the pavement, was a familiar figure. Though silhouetted against the sunlight, there was no mistaking him—his body exuded power. He must have been out for a morning walk.

Henrietta's stomach twisted with apprehension.

He reached the bottom of the steps leading to the door, glanced in their direction, then froze.

"So, you've decided to grace us with your presence, at last."

Henrietta shivered at the ice-cold calm in his voice. It would have been better if he'd shouted. At least they'd have been on familiar turf, and she could have shouted back.

Henrietta drew to a halt, clutched Beatrice's hand, and glanced across the street where a couple was taking a stroll.

"Too much of a coward to look me in the eyes, I see," he

said.

"Not at all," she retorted.

He held out his hand.

"Come here, Beatrice."

"Cousin, I…"

"*Now.*" Though he'd lowered his voice, it exuded anger. His whole body shook with it—a suppressed fury that the casual observer might miss unless they looked into his eyes.

Henrietta shivered as she met his gaze. She had never seen such loathing. "Do as he asks, Beatrice," she whispered.

Beatrice hesitated, nodded, and approached her cousin. He grasped her hand and pulled her close, glaring at Henrietta as if she carried the plague.

The door opened, and a footman appeared. He let out a cry.

"Good grief, Miss Beatrice!" He glanced at Henrietta, opened his mouth as if to speak, then frowned, and shut it again.

"Beatrice, go inside," Giles said.

"But, Giles, I…"

"Don't argue!" he snapped. "Not after what you've done. Dear God, girl, have you taken leave of your senses?" He turned to Henrietta. "As for *you,* I want you out of my sight."

Henrietta glanced at the couple across the road. They'd stopped walking and were staring at her.

"Might we continue this conversation inside?" she asked. "I can explain…"

"No," he said. "We will *not* continue this conversation. I'll be damned if I'll admit you into my home again. What the devil were you thinking? Do you hate me so much as to want to destroy my family completely?"

"I fail to see how…"

"No!" he cried, holding up his hand. "Do not attempt to poison me with your words. Beatrice might be a naïve little fool, but you'll not find me so. I can't make out whether you're a complete simpleton, or if you're inherently evil and have resolved to ruin my family."

"I've not ruined…"

"Yes, you have," he hissed through gritted teeth. "Beatrice's reputation is at risk because of your recklessness. I thought she'd been abducted by a rake, but the reality is far worse. And to think I once considered you as…" he shook his head, "…that is my misfortune, but I thank the Almighty I didn't fall for it. Your father should never have brought you to London in the first place. You're rotten to the core—irredeemable."

"What about you?" she cried. "Your obsession with propriety resulted in your poor mother's incarceration and it's stifled your cousin. No wonder she sought freedom!"

"Better that than ruin the lives of those around me," he snarled. "You might think you're adventurous, breaking with tradition and rules, but you're not. Rules exist for a reason. They ensure that humanity remains civilized, and doesn't descend into savagery. You have no place here, for you're nothing more than a savage yourself. If your father has a shred of sense in him, he'll remove you from Society before you destroy even more lives. I pity the poor man for having you as a daughter. How he must have suffered from the day you were born!"

"Giles!" Beatrice cried. "How can you say such things? You're wrong about Henrietta. I left for Wilton-on-Sea with…"

"Beatrice!" Henrietta interrupted. "Remember your promise."

The couple across the road were no longer alone. A small crowd of onlookers had formed. At all costs, Beatrice mustn't admit her indiscretion in public, for she'd be irrevocably ruined.

Beatrice glanced across the road and paled. She met Henrietta's gaze and nodded, her eyes filling with tears.

"Beatrice, go inside. It's all right," Henrietta said.

"No, it bloody isn't," Giles said. He gave Beatrice a shove, and she stumbled up the steps, tripping at the top and dropping her valise. The footman grasped her arm before she fell.

"Get her inside—now!" he roared.

"Yes, your lordship." The footman picked up the valise.

"I hate you!" Beatrice cried.

"As if I care what a silly brat thinks!" he scoffed. "You'll hate me a good deal more by the time I've finished with you."

Beatrice burst into tears and ran inside.

Henrietta backed away, but a strong hand gripped her arm.

"You're not going anywhere until I've had my say."

"There's nothing more you *can* say," she replied. "You've made your hatred plain."

"Hatred?" He let out a cold laugh. "I don't hate you, Miss Redford. You don't matter enough to elicit such emotion. But rest assured, if you come near me or any of my family again, I swear you'll regret it."

"No need to swear," she retorted. "I already regret ever knowing you. But at least I'll not have to endure your company anymore. Please pass my deepest sympathies to your mother and to Beatrice."

Before he could respond, she walked away, aware of several pairs of eyes watching her.

By the afternoon, all of London would know the particulars of their argument, and the gossipmongers would be dining on it for weeks. She'd be known as a wild, untamed creature, unfit for Society.

Her reputation was ruined, and no respectable man would want anything to do with her.

As if she cared!

Yes, you do care.

As she rounded a corner, she succumbed to the emotions she'd fought to conceal, and by the time she approached Papa's house, her face was wet with tears.

THE RECEPTION SHE received at Papa's townhouse couldn't have been more different than that at the Thorpe residence.

As she climbed the steps, the door flung open and Papa stood on the threshold, arms outstretched, a footman at his side.

"Oh, Henrietta!" he cried. "I'd been so worried. Thank the Lord you're home safe. Charles, take her bag, then ask Mary to bring some tea to the morning room, and perhaps a little brandy?"

"Very good, sir."

The footman took her valise, and Papa led her inside.

"Was your mission successful?" he asked. "I understand the Meredith boy returned shortly after you left, or so Thorpe told me. I've never seen him so angry."

She nodded, fighting back tears.

"And you're unharmed?" He held her at arm's length and looked her up and down. "You *look* unharmed, but my girl has always been able to take care of herself. What about Beatrice? Is she safely home?"

"She is, and it seems that they believe my story. Nobody knows that she eloped."

Henrietta waited for the reprimand, but none came.

"It was well done," Papa said, "though, I'm sorry for it."

She stared at him, unable to voice a reply. She'd expected anger, threats—but not this. His voice was filled with regret, but also something else entirely unexpected.

Admiration.

He shook his head and sighed. "What the devil were you *thinking*, risking your reputation like that, riding halfway across the country, for the sake of a girl who's most likely already ruined?"

"Papa, we both know that I care little for my reputation. Beatrice, on the other hand, had much more to lose than me. It was a chance I had to take."

"Your Aunt Agnes took to her bed the day you left."

"Is she recovered?"

He nodded. "Sufficiently enough to return to Bath, where she intends to stay for the rest of the Season."

A ripple of fear threaded through her. "Am I to be sent there to learn the error of my ways?"

Papa let out a laugh. "No, my dear. Your aunt has given you up as a lost cause."

"I'm sorry, Papa," she said. "I had no choice."

"We all have choices, Hen," he replied, "and we must use them wisely. You're not unintelligent, and I suspect you made your choice understanding what it would do to your reputation. I should have realized that you could never be turned into a society lady, or make a society marriage. Perhaps I should have listened to my heart and not my head. Had you been a son, I would have taught you how to run my business. But, as the Almighty saw fit to furnish me with a daughter, I had assumed that I'd need a son-in-law to hand the business to."

He took her hand and patted it. "We both made mistakes. In trying to mold you into the ideal of a young woman, rather than give free rein to your tomboyish ways, I made a grave mistake, for which you have suffered."

"You've nothing to reproach yourself over, Papa."

"I beg to differ," he said. "But at least I can redeem myself a little with regard to *my* choice, by listening to you now. What is it that you want in life?"

For a moment, the image flashed across her mind—of *him*—then she shook her head to dispel it.

"I want to go home," she said. "To the country, free from the confines of London and Society. And I want to live an independent life."

"You have no wish to marry? Is there no one who you could imagine being happy with?"

Henrietta began to shake her head in denial, then she checked herself. Papa deserved to know the truth, however painful it might be. She squeezed his hand and let out a sigh. "The only man I could have ever considered spending the rest of my life with hates me. And he has good reason to."

Understanding gleamed in his eyes, and he drew her to him.

"My poor child," he said. "You must have known that he'd

not look upon your actions with any favor, particularly given that he thinks *you're* responsible for his cousin's disappearance. Could you not at least tell *him* the truth?"

"It makes no difference," she said. "Whether Beatrice ran off with Phillip Meredith or with me, Giles views me as a bad influence, who's planted unsavory ideas of freedom into his cousin's head. At least this way, Beatrice's reputation has a chance of survival."

"You sacrificed your happiness for her," he said, nodding in understanding, "and perhaps, also, for him?"

She looked away, tears stinging her eyes.

"I'm sorry, Papa," she said. "I never wanted to be a disappointment to you."

He held her face in his hands and kissed her forehead. "You could never disappoint me," he said. "In fact, I'm proud of you."

He drew her into his arms. "I am resolved to be a better father," he said. "And whatever anyone may think, always remember that *I* love you."

She nodded.

"And," he added, "you've lost nothing of note, my dear. Your quality lies in your courage and strength of character, and nobody can take that away from you. If anyone's lost, it's him—for he has let slip through his fingers the most remarkable young woman."

A maidservant entered carrying a tea tray and a bottle of brandy.

"Ah, excellent," Papa said. "Just set the tray down, Mary."

The maid bobbed a curtsey, placed the tray on the table, and scuttled out of the room, but not before she cast a glance at Henrietta.

"Am I the subject of the servants' gossip?" Henrietta asked.

"You can hardly expect them not to react," he replied. "Your Aunt Agnes had rather a lot to say about you. But it'll blow over. Mark my words, next week, some other poor soul will earn the disapproval of the world, and they'll turn their attention elsewhere."

"But before they do…"

"It won't concern us," he said. "Before the week is out, we'll have left London." He poured a cup of tea, shook a few drops of brandy into it, and handed it to her.

"If you wish it, you need never set foot in Society again," he said. "I'm taking you home, where we can work on building your future."

Henrietta sipped her tea, letting the brandy warm her throat. She should count her blessings. How many fathers would show the kind of indulgence toward her tomboyish tendencies as Papa did?

But a voice in her mind whispered that while her future and freedom looked brighter than it had ever before, her heart would have to survive in the darkness.

That was the burden of sacrifice.

CHAPTER THIRTY-THREE

"Would you care for a cup, Beatrice dear?"

Lady Irma glided across the parlor, resplendent in pale pink silk. She gestured toward the tea tray. "If you please, my man."

The waiting footman glanced at Giles, eyebrows raised in inquiry, and Giles nodded.

A true lady, Irma had declared on many an occasion, did *not* sully her own hands with serving the tea. She directed others to do so.

A sigh came from the corner where Beatrice sat, slouched in the chair beside the window, her attention focused on the view outside. But, other than that, she made no reply.

"Beatrice," Giles said. "Lady Irma asked you a question."

Beatrice continued to stare out of the window. "I can pour my own tea."

Lady Irma's smile slipped a little, but she maintained her poise.

"Beatrice, dear, do you remember what I told you the other day? If you are to run your own home, you must gain the respect of your subordinates, even the *lower* servants. You cannot be seen to undertake tasks that are so far beneath you."

Beatrice turned her attention to Lady Irma, her brown eyes pale in the afternoon sunlight.

"Can I not?"

Lady Irma gave the delicate laugh which Giles had grown accustomed to.

Too accustomed to, in fact. The affected tone might elicit gasps of admiration from other ladies who aspired to her particular style of elegance, but, to him, it had begun to grate on his nerves in the manner of a knife scraping across a plate.

How had Beatrice described it?

Oh yes, that was it—*like a herd of sheep emptying their bowels on a summer's eve.*

He glanced at Beatrice, and their eyes met. She let out a snort, her eyes sparkling. Then she resumed her attention on the view outside.

"There must be a flock of sheep in the park today, Lady Irma," she said. "I swear I heard one just now."

Giles drew in a sharp breath to suppress the bubble of mirth swelling inside him.

"Beatrice!" Lady Irma snapped. "Tea?"

"I'm not thirsty."

"Thirst has nothing to do with it. It's to do with what is expected of young ladies of our class." She gestured to the footman. "John—whatever your name is—pour Lady Beatrice a cup."

"Yes, Miss."

Beatrice huffed, and Lady Irma cast a sharp glance in her direction.

"Giles, darling," she said, "I see I'll have a challenge on my hands with the child. But, it's not insurmountable. The lapse in her education is understandable, of course, but it cannot be allowed to slip any further."

Lady Irma rattled on, and his mind drifted elsewhere. She had uttered those exact same words during their stroll in the park that morning while clinging possessively to his arm and shouting her greetings to every acquaintance they'd met as if she wanted the whole world to know to whom he belonged. Her little speech had seemed fatuous when he'd first heard it. But now, spoken in front of Beatrice, the words had taken on a note of cruelty.

In the three weeks since Beatrice had returned—and since…*she*…had disappeared to the country—Lady Irma had become a semi-permanent fixture in Giles's life. His decision to court her had been born of anger, as if he'd wanted to punish himself for having fallen for the wrong woman, by actively pursuing her antithesis.

But lately, Lady Irma's blandness had been replaced by cunning. At first, he'd considered her to be the sort of woman who mirrored the behavior of those she sought to ingratiate herself with. But, as their acquaintance progressed, a more calculating nature emerged. It was as if, now assured of his attention, she'd decided to assert her own opinions. What had, at first, seemed to be Lady Irma's genuine concern for Beatrice's welfare, he now saw as an obsession with social niceties, and a determination to have Beatrice married as well as possible.

And as *soon* as possible.

It was as if Irma wished to rid herself of Beatrice so she could have Giles all to herself.

An elbow dug into his ribs.

Oh Lord, what the devil had she been saying?

"Giles, do you not agree?"

"Of course," he replied.

Whatever Lady Irma had said, it was better to nod and agree in order to stop her prattling. Her voice often took on a sharp, shrewish tone, which intensified until she found the agreement she sought.

Or a herd of sheep emptying their bowels.

He sipped his tea to hide his smile.

"Don't I get a say in the matter?" Beatrice cried.

Bugger. What had he just agreed to?

"A say in what?" he asked.

"In who chaperones me in the future! Aunt Euphramia is perfectly capable."

"With all due respect to your aunt, Beatrice dear, she's hardly the most suitable chaperone," Lady Irma said. "She's an invalid, for heaven's sake."

"She's not!" Beatrice cried. "She's perfectly capable of looking after herself."

"If she were capable, she'd be taking tea with us now, instead of resting in her chamber," Irma said.

Beatrice pulled a face. "Stop poking your nose where it's not wanted."

"Beatrice!" Giles cried. "That's most uncivil."

Lady Irma turned her gaze onto him, a resigned expression in her eyes.

"*Now* do you see what I mean, Lord Thorpe? The chit's had no direction in life. Such behavior and disrespect are evidence of a poor upbringing."

"You know nothing of my upbringing!" Beatrice cried. "Aunt Euphramia loves me. As for Mama and Papa…" She broke off, tears glistening in her eyes.

"A lady must not succumb to such outbursts," Irma continued. She set her teacup aside with the measured motion of an elegant lady as if every little gesture was a ritual to be followed. "Your poor aunt deserves our sympathy, but you must acknowledge that she's not been schooling you properly with regard to your behavior."

"There's nothing wrong with my behavior."

"With all due respect…"

Beatrice interrupted with a snort. "*With all due respect*, indeed! Can't you think of anything else to say? Or is that how you begin a speech that's intended to insult?"

"Beatrice…" Giles warned, but Lady Irma placed a hand on his arm.

"No, Giles, darling, if I'm to take charge of Beatrice's training, you must let me deal with her myself."

"My cousin's not some filly needing breaking in," he said.

"I'm afraid that's precisely what she is," she replied. "The blame is not entirely hers, of course, but had she been properly schooled in the correct way to behave, she'd never have let herself be fooled by that little savage."

Little savage. He winced at the words, more so because he'd once uttered them in Irma's presence. It was as if his own anger was being reflected back at him—and he didn't like what he saw.

Savage she might be, but Miss Redford—*Henrietta*—viewed Beatrice with compassion. She saw Beatrice as a friend, not a commodity to be sold off in marriage as quickly as possible.

"Henrietta's not a savage!" Beatrice rose to her feet, hands balled into fists. "I'll defend her, even if Giles won't."

"It matters not," Lady Irma said. "I hear she's been packed off to the countryside. Good riddance is all I can say."

"Giles, how can you sit back and let her say such things?" Beatrice demanded.

He opened his mouth to reply, but Lady Irma tightened her grip on his arm.

"Because he, as I do, understands the danger of being associated with her," Lady Irma said. "My dear child, she abducted you from the safety and security of your home and led everyone to believe that you'd eloped."

Beatrice rolled her eyes. "Does *she* speak for you now, Giles?"

"Yes," Irma said. "I do. You must forget Miss Redford. She was sent away in disgrace. Her poor father will have an impossible task trying to get her off his hands. Your reputation is hanging by a thread, Beatrice—a very thin thread, which will snap at the first sign of improper behavior. We, or rather, *I*, must work quickly to effect its restoration."

"So you can get me off your hands?"

Beatrice stood before Irma, eyes flashing with defiance, like a shield maiden, defending her fortress against marauders. All spirit and courage—qualities he couldn't help but admire—the opposite of Lady Irma.

In short, she looked like Henrietta.

"Miss Redford set out to ruin your reputation, Beatrice, *dear*," Lady Irma said in a tone of condescension.

"Why the devil would she do that?" Beatrice cried.

Lady Irma sighed. "I have no idea. One cannot imagine what their sort think."

"Their sort?"

"The Bourgeoisie. Those who believe themselves to be above that which they are, simply because of the size of their coffers, but who, nevertheless, can never scrub themselves completely clean of the stench of the *shop*."

"How dare you—you *shrew*!" Beatrice cried.

Giles leaped to his feet. "Beatrice, that's enough! I insist you apologize to Lady Irma."

"I'd rather be thrashed!" came the reply. "Shall I tell you the truth about Henrietta?"

"*Henrietta*, indeed!" Lady Irma scoffed. "Such overfamiliarity. No wonder she took liberties with you."

"If it weren't for Henrietta, I wouldn't be here," Beatrice said. "Do you honestly think she'd be foolish enough to whisk me away from home without seeking permission, knowing the risk to my reputation and that everyone who cared about me would be worried?"

"But she said…"

"I know what she said, Giles," Beatrice interrupted. "That was the plan." She folded her arms. "Dear Lord, you're even more of a simpleton than I thought. Why do you think I wrote that first letter? Do you honestly think that was a ruse devised by Henrietta as a jape?"

The first letter…

The one in which Beatrice had confessed to an elopement.

Surely not.

Surely Beatrice hadn't really eloped…

Oh shit.

"Giles!" Lady Irma squeaked and clutched her neckline, her eyes wide with shock.

It appeared that he'd uttered the profanity out loud.

He glanced at Beatrice, and understanding slid into place. How could he have been such a simpleton as to have believed

Beatrice's second letter?

Because you'd wanted to believe it.

Believing the second letter gave rise to the least deplorable outcome—at least for Beatrice.

"Yes," Beatrice said. "You understand now, don't you? You understand your mistake."

"What mistake?" Lady Irma asked.

"It's nothing for you to be concerned about," he said. At all costs, Lady Irma mustn't discover the truth. Even if he married her, he couldn't trust her with the knowledge.

He drew in a sharp breath at the realization.

He couldn't trust her.

In fact, there was only one woman he could trust.

And he'd lost her—by his own hand.

"I think it *is* your concern, Lady Irma," Beatrice said, "so you're aware of the full extent of the challenge you have on your hands."

"Beatrice…" Giles warned, but she was not to be deterred. Showing the same degree of resolution that he'd seen in Henrietta countless times before, she approached Lady Irma and leaned over her. Lady Irma shrank back, her eyes widening in fear.

"I eloped," Beatrice said. "I was infatuated with someone, and he persuaded me into an elopement. Giles would have forced me to marry him, with no thought for whether it would make me happy. Henrietta was the only one who considered *my* happiness. She considered what I *needed,* rather than what propriety demanded."

Lady Irma paled and glanced at Giles.

"I-is this true?"

"Of course it is!" Beatrice said. "Giles doesn't want to believe it, but it's what happened. Henrietta brought me home, then she devised a plan whereby the world would believe that she took me away for a vacation and that she persuaded me to tell Giles I had eloped for a joke."

"If you're playing a joke now, it's not particularly amusing," Lady Irma said. "A lady's sense of humor should be tempered in accordance with propriety and honor."

"Honor!" Beatrice scoffed. "Henrietta has far more honor in the tip of her finger than the both of you combined. I made a silly mistake. I was infatuated with a man and ran off with him. The only person who did anything to save me—not my reputation, but *me*—was Henrietta. Knowing that she would be derided for it, she took the blame because she cared for me. She loved me." She glanced at Giles. "Perhaps she did it for another—who knows? But look how she's been repaid. You've supplanted her with that..." she pointed at Lady Irma, "...that *witch*."

"How dare you—you ungrateful chit!" Lady Irma cried. She drew her hand back to strike Beatrice, but Giles caught her wrist.

"Madam, do *not* lay a finger on my cousin."

"She needs bringing into line."

"What she needs is not your concern," he said. "I think it's time for you to leave."

Irma's eyes widened. "Leave? You mean now, so you can chastise her?"

"I mean permanently," he replied. "I find we're not as well suited as I thought."

He glanced at Beatrice, and her mouth curled into a smile, a genuine smile—something he'd missed, and found he enjoyed seeing again, as if the sun had broken through the mists of winter and melted the ice.

"What are you saying?" Lady Irma asked, her voice tight.

"You know perfectly well what I'm saying," he replied.

"But you're courting me," she said. "We...we were going for a drive tomorrow in your barouche."

"I hadn't invited you."

"Don't you recall my suggesting it?"

"That was you inviting yourself," he said. "A lady should wait to be invited. Isn't that how propriety works? I know how much reliance you place on propriety."

She rose to her feet. "I see I'm not welcome," she said, "but may I point out the folly of rejecting me?"

"By all means," he said, "though I fail to see the end of our courtship as anything other than a blessing."

"You should be more considerate of Beatrice," she replied, a glitter of triumph in her eyes. "A union with me would help to maintain her reputation and ensure that she makes a good, solid match, despite her indiscretions. Whereas the alternative…" she shook her head, her mouth downturned in mock sadness, "…it simply does *not* bear thinking about."

Her expression turned cold—calculating, even. She had no need to voice the threat. Reject her, and she'd spread the word about the elopement, and his cousin would be ruined. He glanced at Beatrice. If Miss Redford could sacrifice herself for the girl, then so could he. He'd marry Lady Irma if he must, even if she made him miserable for the rest of this life.

Beatrice met his gaze, then glanced toward Lady Irma and back. She shook her head and mouthed "no," then she turned on Lady Irma.

"Gossip and be damned," she said. "I believe my cousin made it perfectly clear that you're not welcome here. James, would you be so kind as to escort Lady Irma out and ensure that she's no longer admitted? Make sure the whole household knows this."

The footman glanced at Lady Irma, who glared at him, almost baring her teeth.

"Allow me," Giles said. He placed a hand on Lady Irma's arm, and she snatched it free.

"Don't touch me!" she cried. "I'll see myself out. But you'll regret this, Lord Thorpe. Nobody rejects me without retribution. Your cousin will be the scandal of the Season—your family the laughingstock of London. Everyone was expecting us to marry."

"*I* wasn't."

She drew back her hand and pain exploded on his cheek as she slapped him on the face. Though he'd anticipated the move, he remained still and weathered the blow. Given that he'd broken off their engagement before it had even begun, it was the least he could do.

She swept out of the room, followed by the footman, her sharp voice echoing through the house as she barked out an order to fetch her pelisse. Shortly after, the door slammed.

So much for Mother taking her rest. Lady Irma's shrill tone was enough to waken the dead.

Beatrice pressed her nose against the window.

"Stay back, Beatrice," Giles said. "It's rude to stare."

"I'm just making sure she's really gone," she replied. "Lady Irma's like a bad stain. Impossible to scrub out."

The calm in Beatrice's voice couldn't completely disguise her distress. She glanced at him, apprehension in her expression. "I should go and see if Aunt's awake."

"Are you all right?" he asked.

She nodded. "I am now. I couldn't imagine anything worse than being related to that creature. Had you married her, she'd have achieved her objective of ridding herself of me. I'd have accepted the first man who asked, just to get away from her."

Giles shook his head. "You mistake my meaning. Are you fully recovered from your…elopement?"

She nodded. "Are you angry?"

He sighed. "What would be the purpose in that? What's done is done, and what matters now is that we ensure you're protected in the future."

"You heard Lady Irma," she said.

"What of her?" he replied. "Unless any of the parties directly involved say anything publicly, it'll be mere conjecture." He sat beside her and took her hand. "I doubt Phillip Meredith will say anything." He let out a soft chuckle. "Not after the shiner I planted on his face. He'll know there would be more to come if he blabbed."

"And…Henrietta?"

Oh, Henrietta—what have I done!

"She'll not say anything."

He jumped as she placed her hand on his and stroked the back of it with her thumb. "No, I mean what about *you* and Henrietta? What you did to her…do you have no regrets at all?"

Of course he did. But there was no time for regrets.

"I'm sure she's forgotten all about me," he said.

"I don't think she has," Beatrice replied. "She hasn't mentioned you in her letters—not once—though she's written about everything and everyone else. What other proof is there that you're always on her mind?"

"You've been *writing* to her?"

She nodded.

"Against my express wishes?"

"*I've* not abandoned her, even if you have."

Giles didn't have the heart to admonish his cousin. How many nights had he lain awake, regretting what could not be, and wondering what might befall Henrietta? Had her father punished her? Would Mr. Redford marry his daughter off to the first man who knocked on his door?

Does she hate me?

"Should you care to ask, cousin," Beatrice said, "I could tell you that she's well." She paused, waiting for him to respond, then she sighed. "She's happy—at least that's what she says, now that her future has been set."

Her future…

His gut twisted at Beatrice's words, which could only mean one thing.

Henrietta—*his* Henrietta—was engaged to be married.

He winced at a sharp pain in his palms and looked down to see his hands curled into tight fists where he'd dug his fingernails into the flesh.

"Who's the lucky fellow?" he asked.

Beatrice frowned. Understanding dawned in her expression, and she laughed. "Oh, *cousin*! Don't say you're jealous? Do you regret having let her slip through your fingers? You've nobody to blame but yourself."

"Who is he?" he demanded. "Good grief, it's not the Meredith boy, is it?"

She laughed again. "Of course not."

"Then—who?"

"It's no longer your concern," she said. "I'm sure her father's made the right choice, and she writes to say she's in complete agreement with him."

His heart sank. Had Henrietta transferred her affections so readily onto another?

But, what could he expect?

Beatrice laughed again. "Shall I put an end to your misery?" she asked. "Henrietta has chosen not to marry. She's decided that no husband is a better prospect than the wrong husband. She is learning how to run her father's business—to gain the independence she has always craved and has always deserved."

So, she wasn't wasting her life on a man unworthy of her.

"She's luckier than most," Beatrice continued. "She'll be mistress of her own destiny."

Relief washed over him, and the nausea, which had threatened to consume him at the thought of her in another's arms, receded.

"I should speak to her," he said.

"For what purpose?"

"To apologize and make amends."

"You'll not be welcomed with open arms," she said. "Apologize by all means, but do it for her sake, rather than yours."

"What do you mean by that?" he asked.

"People apologize for one of two reasons. The first, in order to express their regrets."

"And the second?"

"To fuel their self-gratification, because they want something from the other party," she said. "It works in most cases. But, in yours, unless you're going for the first reason, you'll have a wasted journey. If you want something from Henrietta Redford, you're too late."

In all likelihood, Beatrice was right. He was too late. He'd caused irrevocable damage and behaved abominably.

But, even if she ran him through with her sword—to which she was entitled, given his treatment of her—he, at least, had to try.

CHAPTER THIRTY-FOUR

THE BRANCH CREAKED under Henrietta's weight, but it held firm. She leaned forward and looked through the leaves at the lake below. The water glistened and rippled across the surface in the breeze, tiny diamonds dancing in the air.

She drew in a deep breath, relishing the purity of the country air. How she'd disliked London! All those people milling about, ready to disapprove of her doing anything remotely adventurous. Town and Society had stifled her—like the walls of a prison, closing in around her, suffocating…

Much like the prospect of marriage.

A sharp sound echoed across the water—the cry of a moorhen from the opposite side of the lake—and Henrietta wriggled forward to get a better view. A bird emerged from the reeds at the far side and glided along, exploring the water's edge.

She closed her eyes, relishing the rush of the breeze through the leaves and the gentle scent of blossom. No people. No demands.

She had the best of both worlds—the adult world and that of a child. She had the independence to earn a living helping Papa, and the freedom to indulge in the simple pleasures of climbing a tree or swimming in the lake with no recriminations.

How could marriage ever compete with that?

To be beholden to a man, to have pledged to obey him…

To lose her identity so that she would only ever be considered as a wife…

…and a mother.

A slight twinge needled at her heart at the notion of motherhood. When younger, she hadn't particularly wanted children, though she'd assumed that one day they might come along, given that it was every young woman's objective to marry. But now the prospect was denied her, she struggled with the notion of not having a miniature version of herself to grow and thrive in the countryside, and indulge in the simple pleasure of climbing a tree.

Last night, she had dreamed of swimming in the lake with a child of her own—teaching her to swim and to plunge into the water from the edge, mimicking the grebes which dived so elegantly, their sleek bodies cutting through the surface of the water as they hunted for fish.

But, in order to have children, she'd have to give herself to a man.

And, she couldn't contemplate the notion of giving herself to a man she didn't love.

A man other than *him*.

Was it possible to love more than one person in a lifetime? Papa had thought not. After Mama had died, he couldn't bring himself to marry again. He said that he would always consider himself married to Mama, that if a love was complete, pure, and all-consuming, it could only happen once.

And nothing but the most complete, all-consuming love would persuade Henrietta to marry.

She let out a sigh and stretched her legs, pointing her toes. On the ground below lay her boots and stockings. She'd snagged her stockings too many times climbing trees, so the least she could do was keep the mending to a minimum, given that Papa had given her leave to return to her tomboy pursuits when she wasn't helping him with his ledgers or practicing marquetry.

She closed her eyes to dispel the image in her mind—a little girl, hair unkempt, leaping out of the branches of a tree and laughing with joy as she thrust a wooden sword into a hay bale.

What might a daughter of hers have been like? Or a son? Any son of hers would have been a hardworking young man eager to learn, and any daughter would have been a handful who terrorized her brother.

Would they have looked like her? Or, perhaps another…

Henrietta…

She shook her head to dispel the memory of his voice. Would she never be free of the thought of him—even here? While he was, most likely, courting Lady Irma Fairchild or the odious Juliette Howard, why did he have to continue to shatter her peace of mind?

"Henrietta!"

She glanced toward the path at the base of the tree and caught a flash of a black jacket, cream breeches, and highly polished boots.

It was Giles Thorpe.

What the devil was he doing here?

She fought an overwhelming urge to laugh as she recalled the moment she'd seen him from a vantage point up a tree two years ago, just before she'd thrown the water bomb and soaked his pristine jacket.

"Are you there?" he called out.

She held her breath. With luck, he'd pass on by.

"I know you're here, Henrietta."

She remained still. Giles had said that before, too—the day she'd hidden in the tree at Thorpe Hall. It was merely a ruse to flush out his prey.

Well, he wouldn't triumph this time.

The footsteps slowed, and his tall, broad-shouldered form came fully into view. At close quarters, she could see that his jacket was not black, but dark blue, like a deep ocean. His hair had grown—a thick, black mane which curled round his chin— but she couldn't make out his face from her vantage point. He stopped and leaned against the tree trunk, thrusting his hands into his pockets, the polished tips of his boots mere inches from her discarded stockings.

For what seemed like an age, he merely stood there, while she clung to the branch, willing her heart to stop hammering in her chest.

He tipped his head up and his clear blue eyes focused on her.

She drew in a sharp breath. For a moment, they simply stared at each other. The memory of his angry words replayed in her mind, and she dug her fingers into the branch to control her fury.

How dare he disturb her peace! Hadn't he done enough?

"What are you doing?" he asked, softly.

"Sitting on a branch."

A smile twitched on his lips. "Are you…" he hesitated. "Are you well?"

"I am in good health."

"Henrietta, I…"

"It's *Miss Redford*, to you."

"So formal? We're not in Society now."

She sighed. "You're right—Giles."

He smiled, the sunlight illuminating his beautiful eyes. *Dear Lord!* Was she in danger of weakness—even now?

"We're not in Society," she continued. "I have been removed from it, so that I might be prevented from *ruining any more lives.*"

His eyes narrowed as if in pain. "I suppose I asked for that," he said.

"You suppose correctly."

"I wish to speak with you."

She blinked and looked away. If she continued to look at him, her resolve was in danger of crumbling.

"I have no wish to talk to you," she said.

"Why not?"

"First, I doubt *I'd* be doing any of the talking, and second, you said quite enough the last time we spoke. I don't particularly want to hear any more."

"I've come to…" he hesitated, "…to apologize."

"You don't sound so sure."

"Please."

She let out a snort. "Don't tell me you're going to resort to *begging.*"

"Heavens above!" he cried. "Just come down. I can't talk to you while you're halfway up that bloody tree."

How dare he order her about! She'd been having such a pleasant day. Trust him to come and spoil it.

She glanced at the water below and smiled to herself.

If she had no paper to make a missile with, then she must turn herself into the missile.

"Very well," she said. "Come out where I can see you properly."

"Do you need help climbing down?"

"No."

He smiled. "I forgot, you don't like accepting help, do you?" He moved toward the water's edge and waited.

"Are you coming down?"

"As you wish."

She swung a leg over the branch, then let herself fall, curled her body into a ball, and wrapped her arms round her legs.

She hit the water head first, and her chest tightened at the cold. But, to her delight, a deep cry of shock rang out. When she surfaced, she saw him standing by the water's edge, a dark stain covering his breeches and the lower half of his jacket.

Not so pristine, now.

"Why the devil did you do that?" he cried. "I came all the way from London to apologize!"

"I applaud your efforts, but you've had a wasted journey."

"Won't you even listen to what I have to say?"

"I already told you," she said. "I don't want to hear more."

"Well, I'm going to say it anyway, whether you wish to hear it or not."

She kicked out with her legs and floated away.

"Henrietta!" he cried.

"Go away!" She turned her back on him and swam toward

the center of the lake, slicing through the water with her arms, as Papa had taught her.

"I'm sorry!" he roared.

A moorhen burst out from the reeds, squawking in alarm, its wings flapping in an attempt to gain height, while its feet scrabbled along the water. It bumbled along the surface for a few yards, landed in the water again with a splash, and disappeared among the reeds further along the bank.

Her arms began to ache, and she slowed the pace, turned to face him, treading water. Her skirts tangled with her legs, and she kicked out to free them.

"I behaved abominably!" he cried.

"I'll not disagree with you!"

"I should have known that you'd never put Beatrice in danger," he continued. "Quite the opposite, you saved her. Can I ever repay you? Can you ever forgive me?"

"Why would I do that?"

"Because I love you!" he cried, his voice echoing across the water.

"You…" She panted and drew in a deep breath, struggling against the weight of her clothes. "You d-don't know what love is."

"Yes, I do!"

She kicked out with her legs, and something caught her ankle—weeds, in the center of the lake.

"Henrietta!" his voice grew insistent—panicked, even—and she kicked out with her legs again, but her feet had become entangled in the weeds. She drew in a deep breath, then slipped under the water, reaching down with her hands, tugging at the weeds. But she couldn't free herself.

Panic swelled within her—a black tide in her mind.

Stay calm!

She reached up with her arms and broke the water's surface. Then she drew in a lungful of air and dived down once more.

Muffled cries came from above—her name, repeated over

and over. Closing her mind against her surroundings, she focused on the task in hand and fumbled at the weeds—which had knotted around her ankle like ropes.

The water around her began to swirl as if she were caught in a vortex, bubbles surrounding her. A deep ache swelled in her chest. Her leg muscles ached in protest as she tried to kick free again, and the cold of the water began to seep into her bones, immobilizing her. She opened her eyes and reached out toward the light from the world above, but though she willed her arms to move, her body refused to obey. The light from above flickered as if it mocked her, and a dark ache swelled inside her mind, roaring in her head, pulling her toward the blackness…

A pair of hands grasped her wrists and pulled her upward. At first, the ropes binding her ankles resisted, then they released her, and she rose through the water and broke through the surface. She opened her mouth to draw air into her aching lungs, and tried to reach out, but she couldn't lift her arms. All she could focus on was the cold—the intense cold—seeping into her.

She looked up into a pair of eyes the color of a warm, summer sky, filled with tenderness. Her heart ached to see it. Then she heard a voice.

"Be still, my little hellion. You're safe with me, my love."

The voice was filled with such warmth, that it reached out to her soul, willing it to trust him.

And she did. She relaxed as a pair of strong arms held her close, and submitted to him in the knowledge that she was safe.

You're safe with me, my love.

Where had she heard those words before?

When she'd fallen out of the tree—when a mysterious savior had rescued her and carried her to Dr. West's home.

By the time she recovered her senses, they'd reached the water's edge. He lifted her into his arms and carried her out of the lake. He placed her on the ground.

She blinked and stared up at him. His shirt and breeches clung to his body, emphasizing the contours of his muscular frame, and she felt herself blushing. His jacket, which he must have removed before diving in, lay at the foot of the tree, and he walked toward it, his boots squelching with every step, and picked it up.

He kneeled beside her and draped the jacket over her shoulders. She tried to push him away, with no success.

"Y-you'll ruin it," she said. "I'm soaked."

"Do you think I care for a jacket compared to the woman I love?"

She tried to look away, but he took her face in his hands.

"No, Henrietta," he said. "Look at me. Let me tell you how sorry I am—sorry for misjudging you, for jumping to conclusions." He shook his head, and his voice cracked. "What a fool I've been!" he cried. "I would do anything to atone for what I said—and did—to you."

He took her hand and held it to his lips. Then he blinked, and a tear splashed onto his cheek.

"Henrietta, I know I deserve nothing from you, but I have to ask. Even if I have no hope of ever succeeding, at least I can say that I asked."

He brushed his lips against her hand, closed his eyes, inhaled, and let out a deep sigh.

"I thought I'd lost you," he said. "I've never been so frightened, when I saw you struggling in the water—except, perhaps once."

"When would *you* ever be frightened?" she asked.

"When you fell out of that tree," he said. "I think it was then that I realized I loved you."

"So, it *was* you," she said. "You saved me then, as you saved me now."

"No, my love," he said. "You've saved *me*." He shook his head, as if in disbelief. "When I think of what you've done for my family—my mother, Beatrice, and I. You saved us all, and, in doing so, you lost everything."

"I've lost nothing that I valued," she said.

He placed her hand on his chest, and his heart beat faintly against her fingers. "Have you not?" he whispered. "I fear that I have lost everything I valued. Mother misses you, Beatrice is distraught. And, as for myself—I cannot comprehend my desolation at having lost you. Tell me, must I give up all hope of redemption in your eyes? Is there nothing I can say to convince you that I'm sorry—that I love you beyond all comprehension?"

He caressed her skin with his thumb.

"Am I too late for redemption?" he asked. "I have no right to ask you to make me the happiest man that ever lived, but I ask it anyway. Would you do me the honor of becoming my wife?"

"Giles, I…"

"Hush," he whispered. "If you are to reject me, may I ask that you wait a few heartbeats so that I might indulge in hope a little while longer? If hope is all that I have, then I wish to treasure it while it lasts, as I will treasure the memory of it for the rest of my life."

Her blood warmed at the sincerity in his eyes, and she looked away, her cheeks warming.

"A pretty speech for a man of such a staid character," she said.

"I can never be staid with regard to you, dearest Henrietta," he said. "You have always stirred such feelings in me—a passion I struggled to conquer, but the violence with which it engulfs me is something I gladly submit to." He lifted her hand to his lips and kissed it again. "I love you, Henrietta. I kneel before you now, humbled by your superiority of character, courage, and honor, hoping that I might be given the opportunity to prove that I might be worthy of you."

She met his gaze, and his soul stared back at her—exposed, vulnerable, asking only one thing…

To be given the opportunity to love her.

And to be loved in return.

And she did love him. Whatever he had said, or done, the love which had ingrained itself into her soul, could not easily be extinguished.

Hope flared in his eyes—hope mixed with apprehension.

She placed her hand over his, sealing her fate.

"Yes," she whispered. "I will marry you…" she smiled, and the hope in his eyes morphed into joy, "…if only to plague you for the rest of your life."

"It's no more than I deserve," he said. "Oh, Henrietta! I'm the most fortunate of creatures!"

"As am I."

He drew near and placed his mouth against hers.

"My love," he said, his breath warm against her skin. "May I kiss you?"

He caressed her lips, his tongue probing, teasing until she yielded and parted her lips. Then he kissed her, claiming every inch of her.

He slipped his hand beneath her neckline, and her skin tightened at the wicked sensations rippling through her body. His warm fingers caressed the skin of her breasts, and she sighed as he traced soft circles around her breast, spiraling inward. Then he flicked her nipple, and she let out a cry, as a delicious warmth pulsed between her thighs.

He kissed her again. "Your body is cold," he said.

"You must warm it."

He met her gaze, a soft inquiry in his eyes. "You cannot…" He shook his head. "You cannot mean…"

"Can I not?" Henrietta asked. Taking his hand, she lay back on the ground and pulled him toward her. "What better way to show your love?"

"But…"

"My reputation is already ruined," she said, "and I understand that ruination is the result of having indulged in pleasure. May I not, therefore, enjoy the pleasure, now I've suffered the ruination?"

"What—here?" he asked. "Outside?"

"Is it too adventurous for you?"

A flash of hunger glimmered in his eyes, and his nostrils

flared. He leaned forward and placed a kiss on her cheek, and followed a path along her neckline with his lips, until he reached her earlobe, which he grazed with his teeth. "I find I relish the prospect of adventure," he said, his voice a hoarse whisper.

"There's hope for you yet," she teased.

He let out a chuckle. "I see I'll have a challenge on my hands," he said. "But that's what I love about you. You make me want to defy convention, to seek out new opportunities, new *pleasures*." A fizz of need rushed through her at his words, and she shifted her thighs to ease the ache—that same delicious ache that had begun that night on the terrace when he'd shown her pleasure. Would he take his own pleasure this time?

A warm hand touched her thigh, and she whimpered at the feel of his fingers on her skin.

"Do you like that?"

She nodded.

"Do you wish me to move my hand?" he asked. "Higher, perhaps?"

"Please…"

His hand moved, gentle fingers teasing, caressing. The cold, which had struck her before, had now all but disappeared—replaced by a delicious heat radiating throughout her body, centering in the secret place of pleasure between her thighs.

The tips of his fingers reached their destination, and a pulse of pleasure ignited in her center as he ran a fingertip along her flesh.

"Oh, Henrietta…" he whispered, raw need in his voice. "Oh, my love! You are ready for me. You want me as much as I want you."

He lifted her skirts, and she shivered at the brief sensation of cold before he lay on top of her.

Then she felt him—hard and hot—against her flesh, waiting to be invited.

"My love," he whispered. "Are you sure?"

She nodded. "I have never been more so."

He remained still until need drove her forward, then she

yielded to the instinctive, primal need of her body, and arched her back, lifting her hips in offering.

He thrust forward, and she let out a cry at the sharp sting. He grew still and clung to her, while she felt her body stretch to accommodate him.

"Be still, my love," he whispered. "The worst is over."

"The—the worst?"

"From now on, there is only pleasure."

He shifted inside her, and she let out a whimper at the flame which ignited deep within. She had expected it to feel the same as when he'd touched her at the ball—but this time, it was deeper, stronger, with the promise of something more.

"Are you ready, my love?" he whispered.

She nodded. Then he kissed her, devouring every inch of her mouth. She yielded, curling her own tongue round his, as he moved his body, withdrawing from her, plunging in again and again, to a slow, steady rhythm.

The pleasure began to build, rippling through her body. She shifted her legs, then cried out as a flame ignited deep within her. Each time he plunged back inside her again, the flame grew, until it threatened to engulf her.

The flame burst, and her body shattered into a million pieces, splintering through the sky until she screamed with the force of it.

"Giles! Oh—Giles!"

She looked up to see him above her, his eyes closed, face contorted as if in pain, the tendons in his neck protruding as he lifted his head to the heavens.

He cried her name, and with one final thrust, collapsed forward onto her.

She wrapped her arms round him and held him close, relishing the warmth of him inside her—the feeling that they had become one, their bodies fused into a single creature. He continued to move, weak thrusts, as aftershocks of her climax rippled through her body, until, at last, he grew still, his chest rising and falling against hers.

At length, he lifted his head. Moisture glistened in his eyes, then he blinked and a tear splashed onto her cheek.

"Oh, my love," he said. "You've made me the happiest of men. I came here today in the hope of earning your forgiveness, but I have gained the most precious gift of all—your heart."

She smiled up at him. "I suppose I can be content with that, given that I have the heart of the man *I* love best."

He sat up, buttoning his breeches, then helped her up.

"I fear we've ruined your jacket," she said.

"I told you I care nothing for a jacket compared to you." He grinned. "Besides, my valet is the one who'll have to deal with it, not me."

"You're incorrigible!" She gave him a playful slap on the arm.

"Can you blame me," he teased, "given that I am under the influence of a little hellion?"

He rose to his feet and pulled her up beside him. "I think, perhaps, it's time I took you home and spoke to your father."

She glanced at her skirts, and his breeches, smeared with mud. "We can't be seen like this!" she cried. "At least, *you* can't."

He shook his head. "My dear Henrietta," he said, capturing her mouth in a swift kiss. "Do you not realize that I care nothing for my appearance? The muddier the better—for it declares to the world that I belong utterly and completely to the tomboy of the *ton*."

EPILOGUE

Surrey, October 1814

"Y OU MAY KISS the bride."

Clutching her posy, Henrietta turned to face her husband.

My husband…

He stood beside her, resplendent in a dark green jacket, cream silk waistcoat, and soft, cream breeches that clung to his thighs, leaving little to the imagination. She inhaled the woody, spicy aroma of him—the masculine scent which always seemed to intensify when they made love.

A wicked glint shone in his eyes. Then, glancing at the parson, he lifted her hand to his lips and kissed her fingertips.

The parson nodded approvingly at the chaste gesture, and Henrietta suppressed a giggle. The poor, pious man had no idea that Giles had kissed her fingers in exactly the same manner during a session of premarital lovemaking on the Aubusson rug in the morning room of Thorpe Hall. The skin of her back was still tender from the exercise, the delicious friction having heightened the pleasure.

She fluttered her eyelashes in a gesture of innocence, and his lips curled into a smile.

"Lady Thorpe," he said, holding out his arm. "Shall we?"

She took his arm and retraced her steps along the aisle. But, this time with her husband, rather than Papa, who stood next to

Giles's mother, grinning with pride.

As they emerged through the church doors into the bright October morning, the bells began to ring, deep notes echoing across the land, heralding their marriage. Beyond the lych-gate, a small crowd of tenants had gathered, and they cheered as the couple stepped out into the sunshine and approached the waiting carriage.

The wedding guests followed them outside, and Papa approached Henrietta, arms outstretched. He embraced her and kissed her forehead, then offered his hand to Giles.

"Take care of my daughter," he said.

"I wouldn't dare do otherwise," Giles replied with a smile. "Besides, I think she's the one who'll be taking care of me."

Giles's mother approached, her eyes wet with tears. "My dear," she said. "You have no idea how happy I am to see Giles making a sensible decision at last."

"Euphramia…" Henrietta began, but Lady Thorpe interrupted.

"Ah, no, my dear, it's *Mama*, now."

The three bridesmaids approached them, wearing matching gowns of pale blue silk. Lavinia rushed toward Henrietta and took her hand, giving Giles a sidelong glance.

"I suppose if you must succumb to the marriage state, you've at least picked a man who's a little less reprehensible than most."

Giles chuckled. "I'll take that as a compliment."

"I was complimenting my friend, not you."

Giles lifted his hand in a gesture of surrender. "I must speak to the parson." He detached himself from their party and returned to the church where the vicar stood, talking to Dr. and Mrs. West.

"Lavinia!" Henrietta exclaimed. "That was most uncivil."

"But, you must admit it was true," Lavinia replied. "What do you say, Ellie?"

Eleanor gave a shy smile. Henrietta had thought Eleanor might stay at home, but with Lavinia and Beatrice in attendance, she had conquered her fear of attention and accepted the invitation to be a bridesmaid.

Henrietta took Eleanor's hand. "I'm glad you came," she said. "I know it must have been difficult for you."

"Nothing would have prevented me," Eleanor said. "You're my friend. So few people understand me. I appreciate each and every one of you."

"We can be misfits together," Henrietta said. "Married or not, I have no reputation to speak of."

Beatrice colored and looked away, and Henrietta immediately regretted her words. The poor girl had suffered in the weeks since she'd confessed her elopement to Giles in front of Lady Irma. The gossipmongers of London had indulged themselves at her expense, and though Giles had swiftly removed her to the country, it had only fueled the gossip.

Eleanor had told Henrietta that her sister Juliette had remarked on the likelihood of Beatrice retiring to the country on account of *a little embarrassment*. As far as Henrietta knew, the rumor had not reached Beatrice's ears. Lavinia had told her of another rumor circulating around London, a rumor related to why Miss Juliette Howard was sporting a bruise on her left cheek—which, perhaps, explained why Eleanor wore gloves today, to conceal her knuckles.

Lavinia slipped her arm through Beatrice's. "We're all misfits," she said, "and we should be proud of it, for who wants to be a soulless little mannequin like that Fairchild creature?"

Beatrice wrinkled her nose. "Not I."

"Then, we're happy as we are," Lavinia continued. "The misfits of the *ton*. And nobody should underestimate the power of friendship. Insult one, and you insult all."

She turned to Henrietta. "You have nothing to fear, Hen," she said. "Ellie and I will look after Beatrice while you're away. A month visiting the Lakes—how I envy you!"

Henrietta embraced her friends.

"I'll miss you," Beatrice said.

"And I you."

"Forgive me for breaking up the party," a male voice said, "but I believe it's time I claimed my wife."

Giles appeared at Henrietta's elbow and lowered his voice to whisper in her ear.

"Beatrice will be all right," he said. "It's now time to place yourself first." He took her hand. "Come, Lady Thorpe, the Lakes await your pleasure."

He lowered his voice as he uttered the last word, and a secret thrill coursed through her. Then, to the cheering of the onlookers, he helped her into the carriage and climbed in after her.

The carriage set off with a lurch, and Henrietta leaned out of the window, waving at the well-wishers. Before the church was out of sight, her husband pulled her into his arms, shut the window, and drew down the blind.

"What are you doing?" she asked. "It's a beautiful day."

"Aye, it is," he whispered, his tone hoarse.

"Why close the blind?"

"Because," he said, hunger in his eyes, "I have no wish for an audience for what I have in mind."

"Here, in the *carriage*?" she gasped in mock horror.

"We have at least four hours before we reach the inn."

"Then we'd better get started."

He gave her a devilish grin and ran the tip of his finger along her neckline before slipping it inside.

"With pleasure."

Acknowledgments

Thank you, as usual, to my critique group, the adorable Beta Buddies, for your support and encouragement, with an extra-huge thank you to Liz for such a fabulously encouraging critique. Thanks to Neil for your tips on fencing, and to Sarah, as always, for your continued help and moral support.

About the Author

Emily Royal grew up in Sussex, England, and has devoured romantic novels for as long as she can remember. A mathematician at heart, Emily has worked in financial services for over twenty years. She indulged in her love of writing after she moved to Scotland, where she lives with her husband, teenage daughters and menagerie of rescue pets including Twinkle, an attention-seeking boa constrictor.

She has a passion for both reading and writing romance with a weakness for Regency rakes, Highland heroes, and Medieval knights. Persuasion is one of her all-time favorite novels which she reads several times each year and she is fortunate enough to live within sight of a Medieval palace.

When not writing, Emily enjoys playing the piano, hiking, and painting landscapes, particularly the Highlands. One of her ambitions is to paint, as well as climb, every mountain in Scotland.

Follow Emily Royal:
Website: www.emroyal.com
Facebook: facebook.com/eroyalauthor
Twitter: twitter.com/eroyalauthor
Newsletter signup: mailchi.mp/e5806720bfe0/emilyroyalauthor
Goodreads:
goodreads.com/author/show/14834886.Emily_Royal